Welcome

New London — where
the really good
stuff happens

Giles
2023

Dupes...

DISHONESTY IS THE RAW
MATERIAL NOT OF QUACKS
ONLY, BUT ALSO IN THE
GREAT PART OF DUPES.

*Thomas Carlyle:  1833.*

# ACKNOWLEDGMENT:

I would like to thank all those people I have met in my life who have betrayed my trust, or shown me how to lie and cheat with a smile, without you none of this would have been possible.

# CHAPTER ONE

THE LONGER I'VE THOUGHT ABOUT the whole affair, the more convinced I am that Charles Buchanan was simply playing a game.

Most mornings, before driving across London to his studio, he gathered together his post and tried to predict the contents of each letter before opening it. Sometimes if he was stuck, he would hold an envelope up to the light in an effort to avoid admitting defeat; the idea that this was cheating did not occur to him.

He stood and contemplated a pile of correspondence in his hands. The only item not in an envelope was a post-card from one of the Greek Islands; after glancing over four or five lines of paper-denting handwriting describing the *'great'* pool, and the *'great'* beach, and the *'great'* bars, he gave up reading and let his eyes slide down to the bottom where, as he expected, an ornate *'Sophie'* nestled in a cluster of kisses. Sophie was a bank teller he had dated briefly before deciding she was yet another piece of living proof that God didn't exist - no truly omnipotent Deity could have created a body so free of flaws, and then paired it with a brain seemingly incapable of absorbing anything but gossip and skin-care tips. By the time he had begun to concentrate on the next envelope, he had even forgotten whether she was visiting Mykonos or Crete.

Moving on, he then correctly predicted the following items: a letter from a local estate agent asking him if he wanted to sell his house; the final demand for the service charge on his flat - he couldn't stall them much longer on that one; his Visa bill - in spite of his erratic payments, they were offering to increase his credit limit from five thousand pounds to seven, and he made a mental note to take up the offer; two copies of the same travel brochure with his name and address mis-spelled in alternative ways; an invitation to a Private View at Waddingtons Gallery - the first of this month's crop; another bloody letter from another bloody estate agent.

It all fell apart when he reached a handwritten letter from London W.1.: a handwritten letter in a security envelope that resisted his best efforts to see through it.

*A handwritten letter from London W.1.?*

It looked like a man's handwriting too, he thought. Puzzled, he put it temporarily in his jacket pocket and resumed his guessing game: a small package emblazoned with the words 'Congratulations on your New Baby' that seemed to contain a disposable nappy and that had obviously come to the wrong Charles Buchanan - he shuddered at the prospect of fatherhood and all that it represented; two parking tickets; another private view invitation.

After each guess, Buchanan ripped open the envelope and grinned with satisfaction at being proved right, until he was left with only the handwritten letter from central London. He was immensely irritated at not being able to divine its contents and maintain today's 100% success rate. Finally, with an inward grunt of annoyance, and after another unsuccessful attempt to see through the envelope, he ripped it open. The contents did nothing to cheer him up.

It was a bill for professional services from Robin Malcolm, Psychotherapist. Well, bugger him, thought Buchanan, he won't even make it into the hat for consideration until he starts sending his bills by recorded delivery and threatening legal action - especially now that he was wise to the man's little trick of handwriting the envelope. Thirty quid for half an hour's chat with a middle-aged wine-bar socialist. He'd only gone in the first place because someone had told him that the man bought art; things had not worked out as Buchanan had planned. Far from selling anything to the psychotherapist, Buchanan had been lulled by the man's sympathetic, paternal tone into saying far more than was wise. It was going to be a frosty day in Hades before he sent a charlatan like Malcolm thirty quid.

With the comfort that this thought gave him, he tossed the entire day's post into his tiny private elevator and shut the door on it. Clearing it up would give Mrs. Higgins something to do: in between the long-distance telephone calls she made in his absence. If he could have raised the energy to be tidy he would have sacked his 'daily' long ago, but he couldn't, and she had become indispensable. He took a look at himself in the hall mirror and straightened his jacket.

The mirror was about six feet by four, speckled with foxing and surrounded by an ornate, carved frame. At some point in its history it had been a very beautiful object, but now the decorative carving was damaged in several places and the plaster molding showed through the gilt. Apart from a narrow, and rather nasty, reproduction mahogany table, the mirror was the only piece of furniture in the hallway that Buchanan shared with the other occupants of the house, and it dominated one wall of it.

He had the top floor apartment (it had been rather grandly referred to as a Penthouse in the sales literature) of a recently converted house in Notting Hill Gate. Like the mirror the building had had its glory days. Although the developers had spent large amounts of money splitting it into flats, they had balked at spending the last few thousands that would have made all the difference. The cornice-work in the hall clearly showed where walls had been moved and rebuilt in new locations; no effort had been made to re-instate it. The tiny elevator that served only the 'Penthouse' had necessitated a smaller staircase to the other flats, and this had completely altered the proportions of the lobby. To anyone familiar with the glorious spaciousness of the entrance-way in its prime, the new layout was a disaster, but it was freshly painted and carpeted wall to wall, and Buchanan could live with it.

The figure reflected in the mirror presented exactly the image Buchanan wished to project. His hand-made two-piece suit from an up-market East End tailor was sufficiently loosely cut to be stylish, but not so baggy as to be overtly fashionable. The button-down collar white shirt with its narrow blue stripes was almost imperceptibly worn around the collar and cuffs. It was from a shop in Paris and one of his favorites. It looked and felt stylishly comfortable. He viewed it almost as a lucky talisman.

His eyes shone from behind the narrow gold frames of the glasses he wore only for effect. He liked the extra line of defense and in conversation often stood deliberately facing the light, so that his eyes were obscured by reflections. His whole face presented an image of honesty and candor; it had an aristocratic blush on the cheeks and a thinness to the nose which taken together gave him an air of raffish nobility. His haircut and posture completed the picture of somebody who could easily pass for a slightly consumptive Italian Count - conventional amongst the fashionable, and yet elegantly dapper in the higher echelons of society. He was well pleased with the success of his image and nurtured the appearance of weakness because it often gave him an edge. Even though he was just on the wrong side of thirty-five, many women found his 'little boy lost' look attractive. And occasionally men were fooled into thinking he could be bullied.

With a last check through his pockets for his wallet, keys, fountain pen and glasses' case he stepped out of the front door and down the stairs into the street. It was a bright autumnal day. It took him back nearly twenty years, evoking memories of the rare happy days he spent at school: the few occasions when soccer wasn't a struggle in ankle-deep mud, and exams were a long way off.

He felt good. He felt lucky.

On days like this he felt unstoppable.

His car looked good too. It was a 1960's Mark II Jaguar. British Racing Green. It was in the same condition as when it left the factory, or maybe better. At Buchanan's suggestion, his mechanic had fitted a newer Jaguar engine and gearbox, which raised the top speed by several miles an hour. The body panels had been totally replaced by unused ones bought from a bankrupt coachworks company, and the new paintwork had been baked on. It was possible that to a purist it would no longer be of much value, but to Buchanan this was absurd. The car looked and drove better, so they could stick all their theories on authenticity.

He walked leisurely around the car, running his hand every now and then over the paintwork, looking for damage. This neighborhood looked elegant enough with its wide tree-lined streets, but at night the low-lifes appeared from all around. Several of the B.M.W.'s and Mercedes' had collected key scrapes along their highly polished paintwork, but for some reason his Jaguar was surviving.

He was just turning the key in the car door, when his attention was drawn by a noise in the street. A large old Rover was approaching. The windows were open and Reggae was pumping out. The black driver slowed to crawling pace and shouted over the top of the music as he passed,

"Nice wheels, man. H-E-A-V-Y wheels!"

Buchanan ignored him and climbed in, slamming the door on the retreating Reggae.

He had two major items on his agenda for the day: first, he had received a worryingly oblique request to pay a visit to Babbington's (a gallery in Cork Street that he frequently did business with); and, second, he faced a drive down to see Megan Copeland-Watts in her big lonely house in Oxfordshire. On a cold rainy day he would have been a worried man. But today he was sure everything was going to work out. As he pulled away from the curb, he caught himself humming the refrain that had been pounding from the passing black man's car:

> *"People don't worry*
> *About a thing,*
> *'Cos every little thing's*
> *Gonna be alright ....."*

He drove a couple of hundred yards to a late-night delicatessen he frequented and stopped outside. He was out of tobacco, and the deli was one of the few places that stocked the Three Castles hand-rolling brand that he preferred. He was pleased that the attractive young girl on the cash register smiled at him as he went inside; she obviously remembered him from his previous visits.

There was something about her that reminded Buchanan of an image from a piece of art that was somewhere in his mental catalog. Her hair made him think of Elizabeth Siddall in one of the Pre-Raphaelite paintings, but her face was different from Siddall's. This young girl had none of the hard angular jaw and cheekbones that Rossetti had captured so exquisitely; her face was softer, rounder and much more feminine. He couldn't

[ 12 ]

quite put his finger on it, but she bore a distinct resemblance to the subject of another painting. It would come back to him later, he reassured himself.

"Hello there. How's your luck?" she asked.

"I can't complain, not on a day like today." He grinned at her.

"Ounce of your usual?"

"Yes, please." He fumbled for, and eventually found, his monogrammed, Dunhill tobacco pouch and took out the empty packet from inside. He looked vaguely around for somewhere to throw it. She obligingly held out her hand,

"Here, I've got a bin," she said. "Nice pouch."

"Thank you. It was a present."

"Girlfriend or wife?" asked the young girl inquisitively.

He found the young punkette's directness refreshing and quite forgave her the intrusion into his private life.

"**Ex**-girlfriend," he corrected. "I believe it cost her nearly a hundred pounds."

"How much?" said the girl incredulously.

"Your reaction was pretty much the same as mine when she told me," chuckled Buchanan.

"You're having me on, aren't you? A hundred quid for a tobacco pouch? Can I have a look at it?"

Buchanan handed her the tobacco pouch and watched as she turned it over in her hands. "Don't rub it too much; it has unique qualities."

"Huh?" she said looking at him nervously.

He leant across the counter and whispered conspiratorially, "I'm told it's made from an elephant's foreskin - and the last time someone rubbed it like that..." He paused and looked over his shoulder, as if to check that no-one was listening. "...It got so big it turned into a suitcase."

She tried not to laugh, and Buchanan wished he didn't have so much to do today; the girl was attractive and it would be fun to flirt with her for a while. With a bit of work, he thought, he might even be able to persuade her to model for him. Judging by the blanched skin of her hands she was a true redhead - there was a Munch drawing that came into his head.

She ran her finger across the letters embossed in gold on the black leather, "Charles Buchanan?"

He nodded.

She handed back the pouch. "Well, Mister Charles Buchanan with the hundred pound pouch, how come you roll your own? You could afford to smoke tailor-mades."

"Only now and then. And, unlike regular cigarettes, this tobacco hasn't had potassium nitrate added to it. Here." He offered her a fifty pound note, taking care to show the others in his billfold. She laboriously counted back the change.

"...Thirty, forty, fifty. Anytime you fancy a wild night out, you know where to find me. You obviously need a woman to help you spend some of that money."

"I can do that quite fast enough on my own, but I'd love to take you for a drink sometime. Look, much as I want to continue this conversation, I have to go and earn a living. I'll hold you to your invitation."

"Yeah, sure...and if you do it standing up, you don't get pregnant."

It was his turn to chuckle. On his way back to the car he turned and mimed raising a glass to his lips. At the same time, he furrowed his eyebrows questioningly. His question was obvious.

She smiled and nodded; so was her answer.

Buchanan glowed with sexual anticipation as he drove into the West-End, but if he had known how much of his appeal to the young girl was due to the image of wealthiness he presented, then he might have been less content. For, at the moment at least, the image was primarily an illusion.

Knowing how difficult it was to park outside the gallery, he left the car in the multi-storey car park off Saville Row and walked the couple of hundred yards to Babbingtons. It was worth paying the money to avoid the risk of damage, or a wheelclamp. With so much to be accomplished today, he didn't need to make trouble for himself.

Babbingtons was a small commercial gallery halfway along Cork Street. It was owned jointly by Cordelia and Jeremy Babbington: the middle-aged children of the late Henry Babbington, the founder. Both were unmarried, though for different reasons. Cordelia had prolonged her promiscuous adolescence through her twenties and thirties and into her forties. She hadn't made many friends along the way, but in the process she had acquired enough material to blackmail many of her married male customers - if she so desired - or needed. Unfortunately, these days her reputation preceded her, and as a result her chances of finding a husband had become progressively more remote.

By way of a contrast, her younger brother, Jeremy, was faithfully monogamous...and homosexual. His sexual disposition was of no concern to Buchanan at all; it was akin to being left-handed - something he wasn't, but something he accepted unquestioningly in another person. What irritated Buchanan were mannerisms and affectations of any description, and Jeremy Babbington was almost a caricature of everything camp. Jeremy and Paulo, his Anglo-Italian lover, ran the gallery on a day to day basis, but Cordelia was in overall control.

Buchanan was surprised to see a new receptionist behind the front desk.

"Hello there. You're new," he said to the seated young woman.

"Yes sir. I started this week," she said. And in response to his smile she added, "My name's Terry - Theresa Maguire. Can I help you at all?"

"Is Mr Jeremy or Miss Cordelia in?"

"Mr Jeremy is in the back office; I'm not sure about Miss Cordelia. Do you have an appointment?"

"No, but Jeremy asked me to call in. Could you tell him that Charles Buchanan of Romulus Fine Art is here."

She got up and Buchanan began to survey the pictures on the walls. Out of the corner of his eye he watched appreciatively as she traversed the room to the back office. Her high heels produced an almost caricatured swing in her hips as she walked slowly and deliberately: placing one foot directly in front of the other. He felt his mind returning to the girl in the delicatessen, and it was with some difficulty that he forced himself to concentrate on a particularly dull Constructivist painting in front of him.

The receptionist knocked on the door at the rear of the gallery, and while she waited for a reply, Buchanan drifted to a spot from where he could observe what went on in the office, and yet remain out of sight. He heard a voice bark from the other side of the closed door, "Yes?"

As the receptionist opened the door, Buchanan saw Jeremy Babbington look up in irritation from a begonia that he was apparently repotting on his desk.

"Yes, Theresa?"

"There's a man outside, Mr Jeremy. He says you're expecting him."

"Well, darling, are you going to keep me in suspense all day, or are we going to play charades to divine his name?"

"Pardon?"

"Who is it, sweetie?"

"Oh. He's called Charles Buchanan, from Romulus Fine Art."

Savagely Jeremy Babbington plunged his trowel into the opened bag of potting compost and wiped his hands on a paper towel.

"Oh, yes. Mr Cock-on-castors Buchanan: The world's greatest lover. I want to see him all right. He didn't mention anything about going into liquidation again, did he?"

"Pardon? I'm sorry, I don't understand?"

"Mr Buchanan has an irritating habit of going broke when it

suits him. He's risen from the ashes more times than the proverbial phoenix. At the last count he had shortchanged us by over ten thousand pounds, spread over three companies and five years. If Paulo and I had our way we wouldn't even let him over the threshold."

"Do you want me to send him away?"

"Unfortunately not, my sweet. Mr Buchanan's other irritating habit is fornicating with my sister; she will not hear a word against him. To give him some credit he is also a regular, if not totally reliable, customer. He brings us a lot of business. Just make sure he pays cash for anything he wants to take out of the gallery until I tell you otherwise. Anything, do you understand? Can you send him in?"

During this last tirade, Buchanan drifted casually back - grinning - to the other end of the room. And when the secretary returned to the main showroom, he was sitting in an armchair near her desk. He was leafing through the exhibition catalogue.

"Mr Jeremy will see you now, Mr Buchanan. Will you come through?"

Buchanan rose to his feet. He waved the catalogue and said, "I've taken a catalogue, Terry."

"Excuse me, but they're twelve pounds each."

"And very good value too."

"But I was told to charge everyone," said the girl desperately.

"Stick it on my account, there's a good girl. I'm short of cash and seem to have forgotten my check book."

Buchanan patted his pockets in an exaggerated mime of a search as he disappeared into the office. The receptionist sighed miserably and sat down at her desk.

Buchanan was sure he had been welcomed less enthusiastically at some time in his life, but he couldn't actually remember when.

Jeremy Babbington's thin lips pulled back almost into his mouth as he waved his visitor to a chair and continued preening the leaves of his begonia. Every inch of window-sill was filled with specimens of rare and exotic flowering plants, and the large desk was almost buried under a comprehensive collection of gardening paraphernalia. With infinite care the gallery owner replaced the freshly potted plant in its allotted space, and settled into his chair facing Buchanan across the desk. The air almost crackled with undisguised hostility. Buchanan reached into his pocket and pulled out his tobacco pouch.

After waiting until Buchanan was about to put the freshly rolled cigarette to his lips Babbington snapped,

"Please don't smoke, the plants hate it."

"Truthfully so do I, but I like something to do with my hands. I don't suppose your little pals have that problem do they?"

"My plants? No. They toil not, neither do they spin. Their beauty is purrrfect." He rolled his R's exagerratedly. "And, as William Shakespeare said, 'There is no point in gilding the lily.'" He looked lovingly at his indoor garden.

"It wasn't William Shakespeare, Jeremy...although I guess it could have been Eric."

"Eric Shakespeare?" said Babbington incredulously, before sighing deeply. "Buchanan, I assume your crass ignorance is feigned to cause me irritation. You have heard of the Bard of Avon, I take it?"

"Actually, I don't think it was Eric, but it might have been Brian," mused Buchanan out loud."

"Huh?" Babbington looked confused.

"Anyway, Jeremy, the point is, if you've really called me all the way in here just to spout 16th-century literature at me, you might at least get it right."

"What?"

"Actually, I don't know who said 'Gild the lily,' but it wasn't Shakespeare; he said, 'Gild refined gold.' In King John. I forget which act. You might check it out," said Buchanan mischievously, enjoying the involuntary twitch in the corner of Babbington's mouth.

"Buchanan, I am not playing games. I am talking about a possible forgery," these words were again delivered to the plants in the window boxes, "And it involves you."

Luckily for Buchanan, Jeremy Babbington did not see the effect his words had on his visitor; his body jolted as if connected to a live wire. However, within less than a second Buchanan had regained enough composure to ask,

"What do you mean?"

"I mean, cherub, that one of your precious clients may be trying to rip us off. And although my sister seems to give you carte blanche to do it, I refuse to extend the privilege to all your chums and concubines."

With an almost perceptible sigh of relief, Buchanan busied himself with putting away his tobacco pouch as Babbington continued speaking.

"Some years ago you introduced a young man to us; a young man about town who wished to own a Picasso. I seem to remember you collected one from us yourself and delivered it to him. He was here last week."

"Oh? Was it Justin Van Helde? I haven't seen him for ages. How was he?" Buchanan stalled. He was certain he was going to need all his sharpness in the next few minutes.

"He was broke. It seems his Pater had finally refused to pay off his debts and the young waster wanted to know if we would buy back a Picasso. I, of course, said we would, and we settled on a fair price for it."

"So...where's the problem?"

"The problem is Paolo."

"He hasn't run off with Justin, has he? I never knew he was that way. Well, well, well."

"No, he has not! HE noticed the difference. Come with me down to the storeroom." Jeremy Babbington scuttled around the desk to the door. Without waiting to see if Buchanan was following him he set off across the showroom to the cellar door.

Buchanan racked his brains in an effort to remember exactly which pictures he had sold Justin Van Helde. There had been several lithographs, and at least one drawing. Buchanan swore a silent curse at Van Helde and his cocaine habit. The young European aristocrat spent money like water; he had been a pushover for Buchanan's polished sales patter. But, in common with most 'wasters' (as Babbington had so quaintly called him), there were occasions when his penchant for cocaine, and his free spending, exceeded the generous allowance which his doting parents provided. Hopefully it was one of the lithographs and not the drawing that he had returned to the gallery. Buchanan feigned nonchalance as Jeremy Babbington leafed through a plan chest.

Finally, with a little squeak of triumph, Babbington stood up, a sheet of paper in his hands. He turned it over and flourished it in front of Buchanan.

"Look. Paolo says the ink is a different color black to the others."

"Hmmm...How much did you pay him for it?" asked Buchanan innocently.

"Two hundred pounds less the V.A.T."

"How much?"

"...Two hundred pounds less the V.A.T."

"HOW MUCH?"

"...Er...Two hundred pounds," said Babbington, his confidence evaporating.

"Two hundred pounds? Are you serious? For God's Sake, Jeremy, you really elevate meanness to a high art. You're a tight-fisted, disaster-loving, little housekeeper! You know he paid me more than that for it five years ago! The idiot has probably had it hanging in front of a window and the bloody thing has faded. Do you honestly think that Van Helde would go to the trouble of faking a print for TWO HUNDRED POUNDS?"

Jeremy Babbington sputtered, "But Paolo said..."

"But Paolo said..." mimicked Buchanan acidly. "You amaze me Jeremy. You really amaze me. I have a living to earn: time is money. I can't believe you dragged me all the way here to confront me with a faded Picasso print. I'll show you how important your 'discovery' is." With these words, he pulled out his billfold and peeled off four fifty pound notes, which he stuffed into Jeremy Babbington's top pocket. Then he snatched the print out of the stunned man's hands and began ripping it into tiny pieces. He rounded off his performance by gathering up the torn fragments of paper and stuffing them in his pockets. "As confetti this is expensive, so I will keep it in case I get married. As a major art fraud it is PATHETIC. Is there anything else you want to discuss with me?"

Babbington shook his head miserably. He seemed to have inwardly collapsed under the onslaught of Buchanan's torrent of carefully constructed rage. He turned to busy himself with the plan chest as Buchanan climbed the stairs.

Theresa watched Buchanan emerge alone and smiling from the store-room.

"Oh...Mr. Buchanan?"

"Yes?"

"Miss Cordelia rang while you were in the store-room; she asked me to find out where she can get hold of you this afternoon."

Buchanan pulled out his diary and wrote a telephone number on a blank page before ripping it out and dropping it on the girl's desk.

"These first numbers are the code?" she asked.

"Yes, it's an Oxfordshire number. Tell her I'll be there, and then I'll be at home."

Jeremy Babbington appeared red-eyed at the top of the cellar stairs and tried to slip unnoticed across the gallery to his office.

The receptionist took one look at him and then whispered at

Buchanan, "Is everything all right?"

"Sweet as the proverbial nut. Although I think Mr. Jeremy might disagree. Be nice to him; he's had a trying morning."

The air of self confidence that Buchanan displayed as he left the Gallery was largely a brave pretense. Jeremy Babbington had rubbed a very sensitive spot with his mention of a forgery. Especially as he had linked Buchanan to it. Buchanan tried to use the walk to the car as a cathartic exercise. By degrees he slowly calmed his jangling nerves. He shifted his hands through the shredded paper in his pockets and enjoyed the sensation. It felt like a concrete proof of his ability to think on his feet.

In fact his grand gesture had not been nearly as dramatic as Jeremy Babbington had perceived it to be. For, as Buchanan had pointed out to him, it just wasn't economically viable to forge one relatively cheap Picasso lithograph. But, if one made as many as fifty copies...and knew enough status seeking people who would pay a couple of hundred pounds for the privilege of having a "genuine" signed Picasso print on their walls.... Well, then it became very profitable indeed. And even though he still had nearly a dozen on top of his wardrobe at home, they had been a highly successful introduction to the forger's trade for Charles Buchanan.

In the car-park, he took the Babbington's catalogue from his inside jacket pocket and threw it on the passenger's side of his car before hanging his jacket on the hook behind the driver's seat. He wanted to look presentable when he arrived at Megan Copeland-Watts' house in Oxfordshire, and it was a long drive. So much could depend on their first few moments together. Buchanan ran his hand over his chin thoughtfully: watching himself in the rear-view mirror. He reached into the glove compartment and pulled out the electric razor he kept for occasions like this - when he needed to be at his most charming. He buzzed it over his chin a few times. "I hope you appreciate the trouble I'm taking on your behalf Megan," he thought as he replaced his razor and started the car. "I'm counting on you to make me a happy man."

# CHAPTER TWO

MEGAN COPELAND-WATTS CRANED her neck to see past the cab-driver's head. The gap in the trees which marked the entrance to the grounds of her house was sufficiently well hidden to be missed. She didn't drive and was frequently caught out by the speed with which her driveway came into view and was passed. Usually she gave instructions: go past the crossroads and then turn right at the third oak after the dead elm tree. However, she was fairly certain that this particular driver wouldn't be able to find an oak tree without stopping the car and getting out to scour the ground for acorns. So she simply warned him to slow down half a mile away, and pointed out the gravel driveway as they crawled towards it.

The old brick house came into view as the cab rounded the vast Lebanon cedar tree that shaded what had once been the croquet lawn. As always, Megan was pleased by how 'right' it looked. She could imagine living nowhere else, even though the house was far too big for her needs. Designed and built at the peak of the Georgian period, it was a classic of its kind. There was a simplicity and completeness about the symmetry and clean lines of the house that somehow eluded present-day copies of the double-fronted style. She had often wondered how it was that modern architects given the same components could manage to produce such ugliness.

On the ground floor there were three openings in the brickwork: one housing the gun-stock-stiled front door, and, on either side of that, two large floor-to-ceiling windows - twelve-paned sliding sashes - with old, flawed glass that gave a very gentle distortion to the view. Upstairs were three more windows, directly above the ground floor openings. These were marginally less tall, but exactly the same width. Above them, the brick cornice-work rose until it was sufficiently high to obscure any sight of the slate roof from the drive. Despite the squareness of the building, any tendency to boxiness was softened by a massive Virginia Creeper that swarmed across the entire front, brilliant red in the autumn light.

There were three south-facing windows on the first floor overlooking the front gardens: the one on the left was Megan's bedroom, the one in the middle the bathroom, and the other the guest bedroom. At the back of the house were two more rooms with the staircase rising between them. The one on the same side as Megan's room was the nursery, which had never seen children, but which was where her late husband had spent the last twenty years of his life as an invalid. The one on the other side of the stairs was the room she had converted into a studio where she could paint.

On the ground floor, leading from the front door was a central hallway which opened on the east side to the drawing room at the front, and the library at the rear; and on the west side to the dining room, and the kitchen. Tacked on to the rear of the house were a narrow laundry/utility room, a toilet and a huge conservatory.

The conservatory had been built in the early days of her husband's illness - as a place of refuge for him when it was too cold for his wheelchair to be left in the garden; it had been a spectacular white elephant. Very rapidly Peter Copeland-Watts had made clear how much he hated the manhandling which attended his removal from his bedroom to the rest of the house, and he had elected to stay in his room. Meanwhile the north-facing conservatory had killed the plants that the gardener placed in it almost as quickly as he could raise them from seed. After a couple of years it had become a store for wheelbarrows, rakes and lawnmowers.

Megan directed the cab around the far side of the house to the yard at the back of the building and got out. The driver watched as she struggled with her bags of shopping and made no move to offer any assistance. His rudeness resulted in a tip of exactly ten percent, to the penny, but he was blissfully unaware of her calculated snub. Courtesy and service she rewarded with generosity; this was her attempt to bring back former times - and people that regularly worked for her exploited this habit of hers ruthlessly. She knew this, but she was happy to pay for the privilege of being properly treated.

With her hands full of carrier bags, she used her elbow to open the door from the utility room into the kitchen. The scene which greeted her generated a surge of annoyance.

Mrs Williams, her elderly, ruddy-faced, cook/house-keeper was stirring a saucepan on the Aga. The thick smell of Irish mutton stew filled the room, and probably most of the house. Making as much noise as she could, Megan dumped her bags on the scrubbed pine top of the kitchen table.

"Mrs Williams, I told you I didn't need you today," said Megan evenly.

The woman continued stirring the contents of the saucepan and without even turning her head, replied in her faded Welsh accent,

"That's all right, my lovely. I wasn't busy, so I thought I'd just come by and make you a nice, nourishing stew. You sit yourself down, and I'll make you a nice cup of tea."

"I don't want a cup of tea, and I have just been into Oxford to buy lunch and dinner, so I won't be needing the stew. You may go now. I'll do the cooking today."

Sensing a confrontation, the cook put down the wooden spoon and turned to face Megan, wiping her hands on her apron as she did so.

"I'm sure whatever you've bought will keep. This just needs to simmer for another couple of hours, and it'll be lovely."

"Mrs Williams, I do not want your stew. I don't want to be abrupt, but I clearly told you that I would prepare the food today."

"What's wrong with my mutton stew then? God knows, it was good enough for Major Watts all those years."

"It may have escaped your attention that Major Copeland-Watts was a hopeless geriatric, suffering from senile dementia for the last twenty years of his life, but if he hadn't been, he probably would have told you exactly what he thought of your cooking." Megan instantly regretted using her late husband as a vehicle for her own unnecessarily strong, but accurate, attack on Mrs William's culinary capabilities, but it was out of the barn now. There was no getting it back.

The cook's chubby hands scrabbled at the strings of her apron. "Right, that's it then. I didn't come in on my day off to listen to you speak ill of the Major; God rest his soul. And definitely not to have my cooking insulted."

In a reflex response Megan began to apologize, "Mrs Williams, I'm sorry. I'm sorry. But I have a guest, and I wanted to do something special. That's all."

For a second Mrs William's curiosity as to the identity of the visitor got the better of her anger.

"And just who is this person that's too good for my stew? And what do you propose to cook instead?"

In a last ditch effort to placate her cook, Megan found herself explaining, "It's Mr Buchanan, the picture dealer from London. We're having scrambled eggs with smoked salmon for lunch, and I've got a couple of grouse for dinner."

"Smoked salmon and grouse?" echoed Mrs Williams incredulously, "For Mr Flash-Harry with the Flash-Harry car? The one what was here last month? I never thought I'd see the day. He's turned your head. For goodness sake, you could almost be his mother. He's more than ten years younger than you. The Major would turn in his grave if he could see you now." She finally got the strings on her apron undone and pulled it over her head with a flourish. "I did for the Major for over thirty years, Mrs Watts, and he never treated me like this. Not ever. As God is my witness, I hope you enjoy that stew, because it's the last one of mine you're going to get. You can have my notice. And a piece of advice too, though goodness knows you don't deserve it: that man's up to no good. He comes by here with his fancy car, and his clever talk, and he's got you jumping. You mark my words. It just isn't natural, an older woman, and a younger man....not to mention a spiv like that. You can send my money over; I'll not come back for it. Not ever!"

Megan watched as Mrs Williams banged her way out of the utility room and across the back yard. She had not wanted to upset her, but these violent flare-ups occurred every couple of years, and the pattern was usually the same. Megan would wittingly or unwittingly insult the old woman's cooking and she - perhaps with the unhappy knowledge that most of her meals tasted the same - would storm out. Eventually the isolation of Megan's country life would start to wear on her and she would even begin to miss the scolding and chiding. So she would send a peace offering over to the cottage where the old woman lived: a bunch of flowers, or a parcel of fruit. It would usually entice her back, muttering and complaining, and for a few weeks the menu would improve.

All Megan had wanted was to have the day by herself with Charles. She certainly could have done without the reminder of the disparity in their ages. Mrs William's words echoed in her head - "Not natural....an older woman..." She felt her own doubts and fears rising again. She was older, but Charles had never mentioned her age. Yes, she was older. It was a heavy knowledge that sat at the forefront of her mind whenever she let herself think about her recently acquired young lover.

Oh, damn the bloody woman! Was it so much to ask for: a quiet day without any disapproving clucking?

With a little of the gloss gone from her excitement, she sorted out a bag from the pile on the kitchen table, carried it upstairs, and set it down on her bed alongside the clothes she had laid out earlier in the day. She pulled from the bag a small tissue-wrapped parcel: it contained some silk and lace underwear from one of Oxford's most exclusive stores. The items of lingerie had cost £175 - a sizable chunk of her month's allowance from her late husband's estate. The attractive young sales assistant had talked...and smiled...and talked some more...and smiled...and before Megan really knew what was going on she found herself trying the fragile garments on; and the instant she did she had closed her mind to the expense. They looked elegantly erotic, and she felt fabulous. Everything about today had been carefully chosen. She wanted to look as good as was possible for Charles when he arrived.

She started running a bath, undressed, and examined her body critically in the bathroom mirror. At least I'm not fat, was her first thought. Neither am I sexlessly thin, was her second. All her life she had been slim, and from her boarding-school days on, her breasts had been the envy of her classmates and the object of many covert glances from men who thought she wasn't looking. It was true that nowadays they seemed to be ever so slightly under-inflated, but they didn't actually sag and...as she turned and checked their shape in profile...she knew that they still looked good. There was no escaping the truth though, now that she was in her late forties, it was her legs and belly that were her best features - the crisp muscle tone was a reflection of her love of walking and reluctance to learn to drive.

The hairdresser she had visited on her trip into Oxford had dyed her hair a shade of ash blonde that gave it a shine and uniformity but that also acknowledged her age. Her face she would camouflage with make-up. By hiding the wrinkles which were just beginning to form on her neck she felt she could pass for someone a decade younger. And that would narrow the age gap between her and Buchanan to just a couple of years. She added a generous measure of the perfumed astringent that made her skin feel tight and fresh, and lowered herself into the steaming bath-water.

*

Whilst she was soaking, Buchanan was sitting in a pub on the Oxford by-pass. As he listened to the incessant electronic peeping and hooting of the slot machines which crowded the walls, he forced himself to eat a revolting beef pie which the barman had microwaved to unnatural hotness...and thought of Megan. Megan. Was there any part of him that wanted to see her? Or was it only the letters. The letters she'd mentioned so casually. There was no doubt he wanted the letters, so he would have to go through with the visit, and all that it entailed. He hauled himself to his feet and made his way to the exit.

Hanging just inside the lobby of the pub were four balloons that caught Buchanan's attention, relics of some long ago celebration. They were covered with dust, and the once-taut rubber was now wrinkled. Buchanan knew it was unfair, but his mind spun to an image of the corner of Megan's eye and the powder on her cheek. Her cheek and the balloon; in a drawing he would use the same marks to define both images.

As he crashed through the doors and into the fresh air, Buchanan suddenly found himself imagining Graham Sutherland spreading his hands weakly and trying to explain to a raging Winston Churchill, "...I'm sorry....I can only paint you as I SEE you....'

*

Megan dressed, lit a fire in the drawing room and began organizing the kitchen. After several attempts, she finally persuaded the last grains of pearl barley to disappear round the bend of the toilet where she had flushed the Irish stew. The lingering smell of boiled mutton she dispelled with four or five blasts of air-freshener. Her last chore was to prepare the potatoes and top and tail the mange-tout peas that were to garnish the grouse. By the time she heard the sound of a car on the gravel drive, everything was laid out ready on the kitchen table, and she was on her second glass of dry sherry in the drawing room.

From the window she watched as Buchanan climbed out of the car, straightened his clothes and slipped on his jacket. This simple set of actions caused a mixture of emotions to tumble in her brain. After she had spent so many lonely and frustrating years caring for her invalid husband, Charles had uncovered feelings she had long ago pushed into the unused box-rooms of her mind. In the intervening weeks since they spent the night together, she had replayed every detail of the time they had shared. The warm satisfaction she had felt from their lovemaking - what was it, five weeks ago now? - had ended with a brief sequence of events that the last few seconds had just revived: Buchanan had climbed out of her bed, dressed, and then straightened his clothes and pulled on his jacket.

His departure had filled her with sadness - she fully expected it to be the end of their brief affair. Yet, here he was again, fastening his jacket buttons - just like she remembered - and emerging from his car with a book in his hands. If there was even a chance of more, she was going to fight for it.

He turned to face the house, noticed her at the window, smiled and waved. She skitted to the front door and threw it open,

"Hello, Charles. How are you?"

"Hello, lover. I'm fine. Here, I bought you a present from Babbington's new show." He offered her the catalogue.

"Thank you. Come in. I've lit a fire in the drawing room. I hope you don't mind - I know it's really too warm outside for a fire, but it makes the room look so cozy." She took the book, ushered him to a sofa in front of the fire and poured him a drink. As he sipped at the chilled glass of Chablis she settled herself next to him, pulling her feet up under herself like a young girl.

"Why the secrecy on the telephone? What brings you back down to see me after so long?" she asked.

"The paintings I bought from you."

"Did you pay me too much for them?"

Buchanan laughed, "No, on the contrary, I think I may not have paid you enough. They're with Oscar Morganstein being restored at the moment. I understand they may prove to be a bit of a surprise."

"How exciting for you. Look, it really doesn't matter about the money. But I think it is lovely, and so typical of you, to come all the way out here to tell me about it." Megan knew she was whittering like an adolescent but still couldn't stop, "...I never liked them that much. They were more Peter's taste than mine. If you can show a profit on selling them I want you to keep it. After all you've spent so much on me already: there were the theater tickets, the meal at *Read's* which must have cost a fortune, and that signed Picasso lithograph you gave me. I don't want to hear another word about money. Do you promise?"

"If you insist," answered Buchanan calmly, trying to keep the emotion out of his voice. At that moment he felt like jumping into the air with excitement. He had predicted her response almost to the word. Although he had been in the house less than five minutes, he was well on his way to making the trip he had dreaded worthwhile. She had voluntarily given up any future claim to the paintings. He still wanted the letters, but they could wait for an hour or two. He leaned forward and kissed her on the forehead. "Thank you."

She reached her arm around him and pulled his mouth down to hers. Buchanan was again surprised by the way she kissed, as he had been the first time. It was like a schoolgirl; her tongue fluttering and probing in his mouth. When she guided one of his hands to her breast he knew that if he really wanted the letters, one way or another, he was going to have to pay for them. And so, conscious of how important the next few hours could be, he tried his best to return her passion and enthusiasm.

After what seemed like an age she pulled away from him, flushed and breathless. He felt the faintest chill of foreboding.

"Oh Charles, I can't tell you how happy I am to see you." She wiped her knuckle at precisely the junction of eye and cheek that Buchanan had visualized in the pub, and erased a teartrack from her face powder. "I've prepared lunch and got some Champagne in the icebox specially for you."

An hour later Buchanan pushed away his plate, finished his fourth glass of Dom Perignon, and was relieved to feel an alcohol-induced glow spreading through him. He was in no doubt what she had in mind for the afternoon and he hoped the champagne would help him to relax.

He knew he should never have taken her to bed in the first place, way back at the beginning - that was the bottom line. But he had been curious, and what was done, was done. There was no changing that. He thought about trying to explain to her why he'd done it, but decided against it.

Megan would hardly be very flattered to know that from the moment he had discovered sex Buchanan had tried fucking lying down, standing up, from the side, from the rear, with sixteen year-old's, with colored women, with Orientals and - looking at the woman across the table from him - even with widows in their late-forties; hoping to find somewhere, someone with whom it would make sense. Without success.

*

He woke with a headache. The late evening sun was shining into the bedroom and fell directly on the pillow. With a groan he lifted his head and looked about him. Megan was sitting, smiling and contented, on the end of the bed; a tray loaded with cakes, cups and a steaming teapot in front of her. She was dressed again and looked a different woman from the one he had grappled with over the previous hours. She had obviously been sitting watching him for some time. He sank back onto the pillow.

"What's the time?" He asked, his tongue fat and dried in his mouth.

"Quarter to seven. I let you sleep; you looked all in." She moved the tray to the bedside table and came to sit beside him. "I made us some tea."

"I had no idea it was so late. I have to get going." He started to get out of bed.

Megan put a restraining hand on his chest. "Whatever you've got to do will wait while you drink your tea, won't it?"

"I guess so," said Buchanan taking the cup from her and sipping at it. His temples throbbed and he felt slightly nauseous. Megan snuggled against him as her hand moved gently down his body stroking and teasing at the skin of his belly and below. Against his will he felt himself hardening at her touch. Already today she had proved herself more demanding than he had reckoned possible. As her mouth began to follow her hand downwards, he knew he would have to stop her before his reflex enjoyment of the act took over. With a sigh he lifted her head and kissed her softly.

"No more. I've got to be back in London by eight."

"Oh surely not. I feel I could keep going all night."

"I have to go," said Buchanan firmly.

"Isn't there anything you want? Anything at all?" There was a pause and she chuckled, shocked to hear herself taking the lead.

Through the pain of his daytime hangover Buchanan suddenly remembered the purpose of his visit.

"Now that you mention it, there is. Do you remember those letters from Germany you told me about when you sold me the paintings? The ones where your husband talked about buying them for you?"

"Yes."

"Could I see them?"

"Now?"

"Yes. Yes please."

"Oh...I'll see if I can find them."

"Do that."

With a look of disappointment Megan went out of the room.

He wondered how to play the next few minutes. She obviously wanted to continue their sexual calisthenics but, well, surely he'd repaid the debt? All he wanted now was to get his hands on the letters and go. She returned with a bundle of letters tied with a ribbon, to find him putting on his shirt.

"Why are you getting dressed? It's my turn to give you pleasure. I want to so much. You don't understand what you've done for me. I'd forgotten so much...it's been so long. All those years on my own in bed forcing myself not to think about it. I don't mean to be demanding, but..." Her face began to crease.

"Hey. Hold on. I think I do understand...a little," said Buchanan slipping his arm around her waist and guiding her to the bed where he sat down with her. She looked on the point of breaking down. He kissed her and ran his hand softly though her hair. "Whoa! Come on, cheer up. We'll have other days. It's not the end of the world. Show me the letters."

She looked gratefully at him.

"Will we?"

"What?"

"Have other days?"

"Of course."

"Do you promise?"

"I do," said Buchanan ambiguously, wondering what he would say if she said 'Say it properly, say you promise that...' Thankfully she seemed satisfied and began leafing slowly through her old correspondence. After a couple of minutes she stopped and offered him an envelope,

"This is one."

"May I look?" asked Buchanan trying to control his impatience.

She held it out of his reach. "Kiss me first. Kiss me and promise you'll see me again."

"I already did," he said, taking the letter from her.

She looked doubtfully at him as he turned the envelope over in his hands. It was official forces issue and clearly postmarked. On the back the Major had written the acronym usually favored by the other ranks, H.O.L.L.A.N.D. - Hope Our Love Lives And Never Dies. It was evident that the middle-aged Major had been crazy about his teenage bride. Buchanan speed-read his way down the first page. It was a typical love-letter from the early, golden days of a relationship, full of 'I miss you's' and 'I can hardly wait to see you again's'. Midway down the second page Buchanan saw what he had been dreaming of,

> ...I think the landlady in the boarding house we have requisitioned will agree to sell me two paintings I have taken a shine to. They are simple views of the countryside here around Munich, roughly painted but pleasing all the same. I think you will like them, and they will look very well on the wall of the drawing room....

In his excitement Buchanan almost snatched from her hands the second letter she was holding. He read the opening paragraph with mounting agitation,

> ...Darling, do you remember the paintings I told you about last week? I finally persuaded the old kraut battle-axe to part with them. I'm sure I paid over the odds, but I wanted to bring you back something special and all the other chaps are buying beermugs. I got one of the Yanks to swap me some dollars and that did the trick. She took frightful umbrage when I made her sign a receipt - I've heard that some of the locals shout 'looter' as soon as they've spent the

*money. I hope you like them ...*

Buchanan began putting the letters in his jacket pocket. Megan reached out and caught his hand,

"Charles, what are you doing?"

"I need them."

"But..."

She was interrupted by the telephone ringing. She moved to where the old-fashioned, black bakelite telephone sat on a table beside the fireplace and answered it.

"Hello, Megan Copeland-Watts."

There was a pause while she listened, then she handed the receiver to Buchanan. "It's for you, it's Babbington's gallery."

"Hello, Charles Buchanan speaking."

"Hello, Charles, Cordelia here. Thank goodness I've finally tracked you down.....Hold on. I get the feeling you've just been fucking. I can smell it even down the bloody phone."

"Oh really, that's great news," said Charles as neutrally as he could, "Hang on a moment...." He put his hand over the receiver. "I'm sorry Megan it's business. I won't be a moment."

Megan nodded, picked up the empty tea tray and politely backed out of the room, shutting the door behind her.

"....Cordelia you are so gross," hissed Buchanan, opening the door a crack and listening to Megan going downstairs to the kitchen. When he heard crockery being clattered about in the sink, he closed the door and walked back to sit on the unmade bed. To his discomfort there WAS a heavy smell of sex in the air. "Cordelia, you still there?...."

Downstairs in the kitchen Megan took a brief break from rinsing suds from the Royal Copenhagen - just long enough to dry her hands and...ever-so-quietly...lift the receiver on the telephone hanging on the kitchen wall.

She knew it was something she should not have done. Yet, for some reason, even though she had a cold dread knowledge that she wasn't going to like what she heard, she found herself listening in on Charles's conversation

What caused her so much distress was not the fact that Charles finally gave way to the woman's insistent questioning and replayed the details of their lovemaking - all of them. No, she was inexplicably rather proud to hear all that, especially as he confessed to having enjoyed himself. What destroyed her...what filled her with distress and anger...was when he said,

"..Actually, Cordelia, the honest truth is she's a far better fuck than you ever were: she enjoys it. You know, with you it was, somehow, always business. The difference is that you're a friend, and a friend can be any age. But I have just got out of bed with a woman who is CONSIDERABLY older than me. I mean, it's all very well now, but in five years time she'll look like she needs ironing when she takes her clothes off. She is old, O-L-D. Anyway, look I'd better get off the phone and get home. It's no use pestering me; I'll tell you all about the paintings later. I've got work to do...."

Charles noticed the change in Megan the instant he came downstairs and walked smiling into the kitchen. She wouldn't look at him, and, instead of trying to keep him in the house, it was as if she just wanted him to go. Puzzled by the change in her behavior, but too excited by his own good fortune over the letters to pursue it, he allowed her to hustle him out to his car.

Megan was filled with an immense weariness. She didn't even try to kiss him good-bye; she just slumped in the doorway and watched as Buchanan climbed into his car and roared away up the drive. The spinning wheels sent a shower of gravel into the air. For several minutes she stood clutching at the door frame. Through the trees, from the copse on the top of Disston hill, she could hear a nightingale calling to its mate. She wondered if other lonely women of her age felt this way: condemned like the Greek Sibyl who asked for eternal life but forgot to ask for eternal youth - condemned to live for ever, old, alone and merely longing to die.

Of all the reasons he could have picked to deny her, he chose the one she dreaded most...the one she was powerless to change. Without even knowing what he had done, he had hit her on her rawest nerve.

And yet, if she hadn't listened in on his conversation she would never have known. It was the part which her own duplicity played in her misery that slowly, bizarrely began to catalyze her distress into anger. A rising wave of anger began rolling and building: a rising wave of anger against the unfairness of wanting what you couldn't have, against the unfairness of getting older, against the unfairness of being alone.

A rising wave which she suddenly wished, above anything else, to bring crashing down on Charles Buchanan.

In the speeding car, oblivious to the unhappiness he had caused, Buchanan was laughing and pounding the steering wheel in delight. The letters were beside him on the passenger's seat. The final piece of an immensely complex jig-saw had just slotted neatly into place.

# CHAPTER THREE

ALL THE WAY BACK through the narrow country lanes towards Oxford, Buchanan kept glancing down at the letters alongside him and laughing out loud. The headache which had gripped him earlier faded as quickly as his memories of the afternoon with Megan. With his mission accomplished, he was enjoying himself, and he knew his car operated at its best when it was being driven hard. He pressed his right foot a little closer to the floor and leaned into the corners as they approached. It was a heavy vehicle, but it still responded quickly to the slightest touch on the accelerator or steering wheel. In front of Buchanan the dials on the walnut dashboard shone dimly in the light of the old-fashioned incandescent bulbs that illuminated them. He loved the gentle glow which was superseded on modern cars by the impersonal, high-tech glare of liquid crystal displays. At times like this, his car felt like an extension of his body.

He turned the stereo player on and slipped in a cassette of classical music. Although the label showed it to be Pachebel's 'Canon in D', to Buchanan it was simply the music that accompanied the wool advertisements on the television. He grinned. The man in the music shop had looked sneeringly at him when he had referred to it as such. So Buchanan had deliberately rubbed in his hatred of intellectual snobbery by not asking him for Ravel's 'Bolero', but 'the music from that film with Dudley Moore and the American bird with fabulous tits'. To his delight the be-spectacled aesthete had recognized the reference and produced the right cassette. As the opening notes of the 'Canon' swelled through the sound system, he turned the volume as high as was comfortable and opened the window.

By the time the car had nosed its way through the heavier traffic around Oxford and out onto the motorway towards London, his earlier elation had subsided to a warm glow of satisfaction. The letters beside him were a crucial part of the evidence - some genuine and some not - in an argument he had carefully constructed over a long period of time. The argument concerned whether two paintings he was about to release on to the private art market were genuine or faked. Not, he would add privately, that it made any difference.

Since his early attempts at hoodwinking the cognoscenti of the art world, Buchanan had thought a great deal about the whole concept of faking a work of Art. And as he sat cocooned in the Jaguar, cruising effortlessly at eighty miles an hour towards London along the A 40, he speculated about his chosen occupation. To him there was a kind of paradox about the nature of the deception involved: The decision as to whether a work of art was genuine or not rested with the experts; yet if the so-called 'experts' could not prove by a detailed examination of the work whether or not it was by the hand of the alleged Artist - then who was to be the final judge? With a little bit of manual dexterity, sufficient practice in the techniques of painting, and the correct usage of the tricks of the forger's trade, more or less anyone could produce the finished product. After all, he had passed off several pictures and he knew he was no modern-day Vermeer. If the budding forger limited his field of operation to the twentieth century, then some of the technical tools, like carbon dating and paint chemistry, were removed from the expert's armory. The weapons left to disprove validity were whittled down to style and provenance. In the battle for acceptance, the forger's task became that much easier.

Why weren't his paintings as good as those of the artists whose style he assumed? Why? All the experts agreed they were genuine works. And yet, thought Buchanan, if I was to walk into a gallery and prove that I had painted one of those pictures, its monetary value would come crashing down. So where did the value come from? Why was it that a given painting could be revered and admired for years prior to the discovery that it was a fake, and then, overnight, it could become little more than a curiosity? - as had happened to poor Tom Keating and his beautiful Samuel Palmers. The experts talked glibly about vision and ideas, about originality and unique mental processes. To Buchanan it was all nonsense. There had been times when his versions of work by accepted modern 'greats' had hung alongside genuine works in private commercial galleries, and even on a couple of occasions in major National collections. Experts and innocents alike had filed past them talking in hushed tones about 'unmistakable works of a genius' and 'inner truth'. No-one had ever voiced a doubt as to their authenticity - so where did the value come from?

He suddenly became aware of flashing headlights in his rear view mirror. He gently increased the pressure on the accelerator and surged away from a new B.M.W.; smiling to himself as he remembered his early days as an apprentice faker.

He had taken a work from Babbington's, ostensibly to sell to a client. It was a Victorian 'genre' painting in oils. A crowded street scene with a moral message, titled something like 'The Liar Exposed'. Within a week he had convinced himself where his future lay: he bought an old and badly damaged painting of little value from the same period, softened the paintwork gently with solvents, scraped it away to leave the canvas clean, restretched it on an old frame that he had carefully recut to the right size, and then onto this canvas he faithfully copied the original genre painting. Or almost faithfully copied it. In fact he had altered one of the faces in the background so that it was a miniature self-portrait. To ensure accuracy in the paint he had mixed the colors from formulae used and recommended by the Royal Academy at the time: grinding the pigments himself by hand in a pestle and mortar. The drying and craquelure he had simulated with a couple of minutes careful use of a hair-dryer, and by standing the freshly-painted canvas in front of his gas oven. As a final touch, he had toned down the pigments with a finishing technique he had developed himself, so that the painting could be restored in a similar manner to the original. With a fair degree of nervousness, he had returned his version to Babbington's and declared that his clients did not wish to continue with the purchase because they were convinced it was a forgery. Babbington's, who had paid over a thousand pounds for the original at an auction, had taken the disputed painting to an expert for his opinion. He had examined, cleaned, restored and returned it - pronouncing it genuine, and valuing it at over three thousand pounds. He, Charlie Buchanan, had discovered his metier and developed a vehement distrust of experts, whatever their field, in the process. The original now hung in his studio.

The other thing he had learned as a result of this exercise was the importance of a picture's provenance. Provenance: the simple book-keeping which showed where a painting had come from. It was no use forging a Vermeer if there was no record of where it had spent the last three hundred years. With the 'Liar Exposed' Babbington's had been able to plot the owners of the painting from its first public showing to the present day. He was fairly certain that, given the right paperwork, an expert could be persuaded to accept the most atypical painting as part of an artist's oeuvre. It was for this reason that getting the letters from Megan had been so important. If a fake was backed by a verifiable history - the letters beside him on the seat were perfect examples - that stretched back to the artist's lifetime and locale, then it was more than halfway to being accepted as a rediscovered treasure. It was Buchanan's intention to be credited with the discovery, and the financial rewards, of finding, not one lost twentieth-century masterpiece, but two.

The end of the cassette refocussed his attention on his driving. He was already back on the outskirts of London, approaching Hangar Lane Tube and the final run in to Marylebone Road. The elevated section of the A 40 that swirled from White City into Paddington never failed to give him a boost. In sunlight it reminded him of the approach to an American city: New York, or Boston. At night he enjoyed the high speed entrance deep into the heavily built-up heart of the capital. From the end of the motorway to his front door was less than five minutes. It had been a demanding day, and he was looking forward to a celebratory drink. He touched the brakes gently, slipped the engine out of fourth gear, blipped the throttle slightly to raise the revs, and slammed it into third without touching the clutch.

Perfection!

At times like this he could accomplish these gear changes without a clash or grind from the gearbox. He hit the exit ramp at sixty instead of the recommended thirty, and the tires screamed in protest as they reached the limit of adhesion. A broad adrenaline-induced grin spread across his face as he slowed the car to take the roundabout ahead of him.

It wasn't long before he stepped out of his lift and into the open-plan living and dining space of his flat. The time switches on the lighting and heating had cut in earlier and the room was warm and inviting. It was sixty feet long, a vast space by London standards, and ran the width of two houses. Four tall

French windows opened off one long side of the room onto a tiny balcony overlooking the street. The floor, which was covered with a top quality vinyl tile almost indistinguishable from the marble it aimed to reproduce, was on three levels. A semi-circular pit ten feet across had been cut out to form a comfortable sitting area at one end of the room. At the other end a simple galley type kitchen, also finished in Carrera marble, was raised on a platform reached by a couple of gently-curved steps. Strategically placed around the room were several items of reproduction Bauhaus furniture whose clean lines Buchanan admired so much, and three original Wurlitzer juke boxes, complete with concealed, powerful modern amplifiers.

The two bedrooms and bathroom were behind the lift, and compared to the rest of the flat were decidedly small. He had acknowledged this by having them decorated in warm earth colors that made them womb-like and inviting. The walls in the bedrooms were hung with Bokhara rugs, in the rest of the flat with posters of art exhibitions from around the world. There were also a few Picasso etchings and litho's, all genuine, scattered amongst the posters. If any of Buchanan's business contacts happened to visit him in the flat they would not be surprised at the quantity and quality of his art collection. It looked modest.

Buchanan poured himself a generous tumbler of Carlos V fine Spanish brandy and settled himself down in the sheepskin rugs that covered the sunken seating area. After a couple of mouthfuls, he leaned over and switched his telephone answering machine from record to play. It buzzed and whirred for a while and then began replaying the messages,

"...Hello, Buchanan. Oscar Morganstein here. If you get back before lunch could you call me at the office. Thank you...

The picture restorer was obviously keen to tell him how the final stages of the restoration were progressing. He allowed the tape to continue running.

...Buchanan. It's one p.m. and Morganstein again. I'll be out of the office for a couple of hours but call me as soon as you get in...

As Buchanan had suspected, Morganstein was bursting to break the news of his 'discovery' to him. He wondered how rapidly the old man's excitement would leak out into the rest of the Art World. He thought it unlikely that he would be able to keep the secret for very long, even though he was one of the most reliable restorers in the trade. His thoughts were interrupted by a breathless young woman's voice from the answer-phone,

...Charles. It's me, Sally. You'll never believe it - I got the job! They want me to go out to the West Indies next month to settle in the new rep. Isn't it brilliant? I NEVER thought I stood a chance. Sheila from accounts was up for it as well, and you know what a brown-nose she is. Anyway, I'm really excited. I know you're going to be late home tonight, so I'm going to go out for a drink with Pete and Chris from work. Tomorrow night old Harper HIMSELF is going to take me out for dinner to celebrate. ME having dinner with the boss! So I won't see you then, either. I'm sorry about that, Buggsy. Why don't you pop in to the office and see me if you've got time tomorrow? Please, please do. Lots of love and kisses and stuff. Oh, by the way I got the job even though Sheila from accounts...Did I tell you this already? I hate these machines. Be good and please come in and see me...

He switched the machine to pause for a few moments as he tried to think of a way to get his apartment keys back from the young girl who worked in the Travel Agents - and also how to convince her that she was not likely to be the future Mrs Buchanan, as she seemed to think. Eight months ago the gamble had seemed worth taking: he had convinced himself that he hadn't found the woman who haunted his sub-conscious because he was looking in the wrong places. One night stands and casual affairs...his cockeyed reason had proposed...were all very well, but...at the time it seemed worth the try...so he had handed over a set of keys and made a few rash promises.

They had little in common - apart from her face, which was as close as he had ever seen in the waking world to his dream woman. If he had the stomach for the job he would simply tell her he was sorry, but he'd fucked up - it was all a mistake - it was all off...sure she would be upset for a day or two, but in the long run she'd understand. However, for some reason, the decision he had taken was to try and let her down slowly, try and make her think that she was ditching him - only it didn't seem to be working. He now realized that he couldn't repress his irritation at her demands on him and his time much longer. He was pleased that she wasn't going to be bothering him over the next couple of days when he had so much to do. With a mixture of relief and irritation he continued playing the tape.

...Buchanan it's Morganstein. I've got to leave the office now, it's just gone six thirty. If you're home before about ten tonight give me a ring at home on 555-8061. The paintings are finished, and I really think you should know what we've uncovered. If we move fast I might be able to interest an American friend of mine who happens to be over here on business. If you are late back, come over for a spot of lunch about one. I'll speak to you tomorrow...

Well, it seemed that Morganstein had cracked and spread the word sooner rather than later. Buchanan smiled as he thought of his secret being earnestly shared with first one person then another. When he recognized the next voice on the tape he cheered up even more - it was Cordelia Babbington, obviously just before she reached him at Megan's.

...Lover boy it's your favorite bit of class action here. You really must be more careful about the way you torment my poor brother Jeremy. He and that dreadful boyfriend of his have been quite inconsolable since your visit this morning. I wish I had been there to see your performance. It sounded most dramatic. On another subject, I hear through the grapevine that you've had a bit of luck. I positively insist that you come over to the gallery tomorrow and tell me all about it. Don't you dare let me down. I shall expect you at four. After all the work I've done for you I will take a very dim view if you don't show. Bye!..."

With the satisfaction that she too seemed to have heard about the paintings, Buchanan switched off the machine, refilled his brandy glass and elected to have an early night. Poor old Morganstein had been having kittens at not being able to speak to him. Well, let the old buzzard dream. It wouldn't do him any harm to wait a while, would it? Even though it was only just ten o'clock, he decided to let him stew until tomorrow before putting him out of his misery. It would be very interesting to hear the 'official' verdict on Megan's paintings.

He got into bed, relishing the touch of the crisp, cool linen sheets Mrs Higgins had put on that morning, and thought, without a moment of guilt, of Megan Copeland-Watts moving maniacally above him like a jockey on a thoroughbred - he spared himself the guilt because, even in his dreamland replay, the damn woman was beaming like the cat with the cream.

# CHAPTER FOUR

BUCHANAN WAITED UNTIL THE MORNING rush hour had cleared a little before driving from his flat to the Liverpool Road in Islington. The Marylebone Road and Pentonville Road were almost impassable earlier than ten o'clock, and there was no easier route through the morning London traffic. His studio in the mews behind the main street was a legacy from the time when he had rented a small bedsitter in a house in Lonsdale Square. With the success of his business he had bought the studio and made the move to Notting Hill. Even though Islington was now as gentrified as any inner London borough, it still conjured images of the underworld in Buchanan's mind. In a night-time fog the looming gothic facades of Lonsdale Square resembled a film-set for a Dickens novel. It was an ambiance that suited his work but not his lifestyle.

The studio itself was wedged between garages where mechanics sometimes worked through the night, and rag trade sweatshops. The oil-smeared men never asked about Buchanan's use of the space, in the same spirit as he never questioned the midnight resprays of expensive cars. The black-clad women in the garment factories were almost exclusively culled from the Greek immigrant population of Camden Town, and very few of them spoke enough English to ask questions more complicated than, Nice raining we have, no? In addition to all this, Wesley the black proprietor of the 'Empire Coachworks and Mechanics' next door to the studio, had fallen in love at first sight with Buchanan's Jaguar. He worked on it with a care and devotion that money could not have bought. There had been a few nudges and winks in the mews when Buchanan's burglar alarm had first been installed, but apart from that he came and went unnoticed. It suited him perfectly.

He opened the garage doors on the ground floor, drove the Jaguar in, closed the doors behind him and turned the key in the alarm. This was his sanctuary and his workplace. No-one had been inside in the ten years since he first started working there. On the rare occasions when he had not been able to forestall people meeting him at the mews, he had met his visitors outside and diplomatically escorted them away. There were perhaps a dozen people that could connect him with the building. Most recently, Sally, his current lover, had been hugely indignant at being denied entry. Knowing his involvement in the art world, and having a Hollywood inspired vision of anything called a studio or an artist, she had imagined naked women posing decadently in the intervals between passionate periods of lovemaking. To Wesley's delight there had been a loud and uncivilized shouting match in the street which had ended only when Buchanan threatened to drive away and leave her there. Sally had surveyed the grinning, grease-stained, faces of the mechanics exchanging ribald remarks at her expense in the twilight and climbed meekly into Buchanan's car.

Inside the building, a narrow, worn, wooden ladder led from one side of the garage up to the workroom. The first-floor space was completely functional: Dexion shelving racks filled with paints in carefully dated jars stood around two walls; at one end of the room plan-chests were stacked four feet high across the entire width; a rack of canvasses filled the space above them; and against the tiny, barred window stood a desk, a bookcase and a filing cabinet. In daytime the room was lit by a line of north-facing skylights, their panes filled with obscured glass. Buchanan could work here unobserved and undisturbed. The privacy and secrecy was vital. It would take a knowledgeable visitor only seconds to grasp that this was no ordinary artist's studio. It was Buchanan's opinion that there was no way of concealing the work of forgery, unless it was rendered completely invisible. And, he had concluded, the only way to do that was to deny people access.

For that reason he was unconcerned about the paraphernalia scattered about the room. There were half-finished copies and paintings done in the manner of well-known masters propped against the paint racks and standing on easels. A Grant projector, which he used to enlarge drawings and sketches, stood beside the desk, next to an area of white painted wall that served as a screen for showing slides. Dated pieces of stripped, but unreworked, canvas were rolled and stored in boxes. Pinned to the wall over the desk were dozens of Polaroid photographs showing stage-by-stage the progress of each of the major fakes that Buchanan had produced. In the white space at the bottom of each picture was the date when it was taken. Beneath the Polaroids of the finished works were the prices that they had fetched and the names of the buyers. This private 'gallery' was the only way that Buchanan could express his satisfaction with himself.

Today he was here to collect documentation and not art. Laid out on the desk were several letters, receipts and pieces of newspaper. He gathered them together and put them carefully into a marbled, cardboard file, labeled *MEGAN COPELAND-WATTS*, ready to take with him to his meeting with Morganstein. Before setting out on this trip he spent several minutes looking at the Polaroids of the transformation that Megan's paintings had undergone.

From the first picture to the last it was impossible to discern a change. He could have returned them to her and she would not have known the difference. Of all the challenges that he had set himself this one was the biggest and potentially the most profitable. Within the space of a few weeks he would earn enough to pay off the outstanding debt on his flat. The most beautiful thing about his plan was the degree to which it was foolproof, at no stage could any manipulation of the paintings be laid at his door. For the first time in his career as a forger, he had no nerves about the approaching meeting with the experts. There was just a curiosity as to how much money he was going to make. He picked up his folder and descended the stairs to the car.

Morganstein's restoration workshops were crammed into a basement off the bottom end of the Edgeware Road. Buchanan announced himself into the entryphone and pushed open the door as the buzzer sounded. Before he had closed it behind him, the portly, diminutive figure of the middle-European émigré was in front of him in the hall, his hand outstretched in greeting,

"Charles, my friend, it's so good to see you. Come in to the office." He led the way into a sparsely-furnished cubicle that really merited the title of office only because it was here that the telephone sat on a desk covered with paperwork that never seemed to change. Shooing away a grossly overweight cat from one of the two chairs, Morganstein motioned for Buchanan to sit down.

"I got your messages, but it was too late to call you when I got home last night," apologized Buchanan.

"It's not a problem. I wanted to show you what I had found for you. Would you like to see the paintings?" His excitement was concealed with difficulty and Buchanan noted with amusement that he was trying to take some of the credit for the discovery.

"Of course. Where are they? Shall I come into the workroom?"

"No. Stay where you are, I will fetch them."

A couple of minutes later Morganstein returned holding a canvas in each hand. They were about eighty centimeters wide and fifty high. With reverential care he propped them on a lipped shelf that ran along the wall behind the desk. It was built precisely to display finished works, and it was lit by two spotlights shining from the ceiling. He stepped back beside the seated figure and threw the switch to illuminate them.

"There. What do you think?"

Buchanan came slowly to his feet, leaning forward with his hands on the desk to get a closer look.

The two paintings were of the same subject, a naked young woman reclining on an unmade bed. The hollows and hillocks of her body were drawn with staccato brushstrokes that made her look unnaturally thin. A single flowing line described the form and position of her limbs with an accuracy and economy that was breathtaking. Vivid highlights of color shone through around her spread thighs and the almost adolescent buds of her breasts. With just two or three flourishes of the brush the artist had conveyed precisely an expression of total calm and relaxation on her face.

Although he had painted them himself, it was as if he was seeing them for the first time, and Buchanan paused for several moments, taking in the newly-cleaned paintings. The old man had certainly done his job well; the colors were as fresh and clear as the day they were painted. "It's astonishing. They're so beautiful. These are the work of a master. For a few seconds I thought they might almost be by Schiele."

"No," said Morganstein with such finality that for a second Buchanan's heart missed a beat. "This is no **might be**....I am convinced that these are indeed the work of Egon Schiele. Apart from the fact that they bear his initials here, you only have to look at the handling of the paint - the rhythm of the brushwork. These things cannot be reproduced. You can feel the tortured genius of a man ahead of his time. To my mind these are from the first golden days that Schiele spent at

[ 55 ]

Neulengbach. I'm certain that they are some of the first paintings he did of Valerie Neuzil - his beloved Walli. I'm convinced the pose is adapted from the nude studies he did of his sister Gertie. You see, Charles, until this point, Schiele had been without a professional model, and he was desperately short of materials. With his move from Krumau to Neulengbach, and the arrival of Valerie, he was able to explore the aspects of sex that he had avoided when painting his little sister.

"There was an earlier painting of Gertie lying down with her arms crossed in exactly this gesture - which has since disappeared - but for which the studies remain. Do you notice how Schiele has opened the legs and painted the sex? This was not something he could have done before. Not with his sister. I think these are simply smaller versions, studies we must assume, for the painting that is now in the collection of the Staadtsgalerie in Munchen." In his excitement he slipped easily into the German pronunciation. "Let me tell you how we found them."

Buchanan sank back into his chair muttering, "They are so beautiful...so intense..."

"Yes, and somebody else must have thought so too."

"What do you mean?"

"The paintings you brought to us; you were convinced they were valuable. I could not understand how it was so. They were clumsy. My cat paints better. But, as I told you on the telephone, when I examined them closely I became aware they were nothing more than a disguise. I explained to you that they were worthless, but that there might be a painting underneath, and I solved the mystery. I unlocked the safe. Someone had taken these beautiful works and deliberately covered them up."

"But why?" asked Buchanan innocently, knowing that this was exactly what he had done. After he had stripped off Megan's paintings, he had created the fake Shiele's, and then painted the original landscapes back over them. If Morganstein hadn't uncovered them, he would have taken them to someone else, or suggested an X ray.

"My friend, you work with paintings, you know where these paintings come from. It is simply a matter of putting together your knowledge of these areas. In Germany in the time before the second World War Hitler was trying to exterminate many things beside the Jews. He was burning books, and the canvasses of the so-called decadent artists. You have possibly heard of the *Entartete Kunst* exhibition at the Archäologishes Institut in Munich? Well, although his work was not in this terrible - this wonderful - exhibition, Egon Schiele was nevertheless one of the decadents."

"I know all this, but I still don't see the connection," said Buchanan.

"Someone must have known that the paintings that they loved were at risk. The overpainting was done with much skill. The originals were first varnished and then covered with a ground color. But not just any ground color." Morganstein wagged his finger at Buchanan. "If I may be technical for a moment; you must remember that paint is not just 'paint'. Oil paint is three things in balance, in harmony. There is the pigment - the color, the solvent or dryer - turpentine, or nowadays white spirit, and the retarder or binder - an oil to make the paint workable. Varnish sometimes has a different solvent. Instead of turpentine it is methyl alcohol; called methylated spirits here in England. Do you follow me?"

"Yes. I think so."

"The varnish of the Schiele's and the ground color of the second paintings were carefully chosen so that the two would not mix. It was possible to carefully remove the top picture and then to see this beauty underneath."

"Do you mean to say that this top painting, that I thought from my paperwork must be valuable, was nothing but junk?" bluffed Buchanan.

"In some ways, yes. But in others it had value almost

beyond price. Without it these paintings might have been burned, or disappeared into the South American bolt-hole of some Nazi."

"I think I understand what you're saying. It would explain why the landlady had the paintings."

"Did you bring with you the letters you told me about when you brought me the paintings?"

Buchanan smiled broadly at Morganstein. "Yes. Here they are. Your German might make more sense of them than mine. I was able to understand just enough to want to see the paintings in the flesh." Buchanan opened the cardboard folder. "Most of this paperwork came from a small writing cabinet I bought in a junk shop in Bavaria when I was there last year. I was visiting the Munich Beer Festival and after a couple of days I had had enough of drinking and drunks. So I took some time to travel round the area looking for paintings. In a small town north of the city I came across a second-hand dealer. His specialty was clearing houses when relatives had taken what they wanted after a death in the family. Most of the stuff in his shop was rubbish, but a box of papers interested me."

So far Buchanan was telling the truth; it was only later that the plan had formed in his mind.

Morganstein was listening intently, nodding as the young man spoke.

"On the top of the bundle was something that caught my eye: It was a receipt for the sale of two paintings to an English army officer. Out of simple curiosity, I bought the box of papers. Here is the bill for it. The man in the shop should remember all this because I pointed out to him the reference to Major Copeland-Watts, and he joked about the British Army getting everywhere."

As Buchanan gathered himself to launch from reality to fantasy, he rummaged in the file and found the receipt from the second-hand shop, and the piece of paper bearing Major Copeland-Watts' name and unit number. He handed them to

Morganstein, who inspected them carefully before laying them out on the desk in front of him.

"When I got back to my hotel room, I went through all the papers. It was obviously the contents of the desk from a small boarding house. There was a register of guests, an account book, and a lot of other things I couldn't understand. In the accounts book I found this letter. Perhaps you could read it to me in full. I know what I think it says." He handed it to Morganstein and the old man began to translate out loud,

" Liebe Frau Mueller - Dear Mrs Mueller. I am sorry to be behind with my rent. I am still waiting to be paid for my last month's work. Tomorrow I have to report to the S.S. headquarters. As you know they have been rounding up all the Jews and sending us away to workcamps. I fear I may be gone for quite some time. I would like you to look after these two paintings for me. They are very precious and I hope you will take them as security on my debt to you. When I come back I will bring the money. PLEASE - ON NO ACCOUNT SELL THEM; it is unlikely anyone will pay you what they are worth. They were a gift from the Artist when I worked at Klammer's Gallery in Munich. He is dead now, and they mean a lot to me. Yours etc. Erich Schumacher." Morganstein placed the letter down in front of him with the others and rubbed at his eyes with the back of his knuckles. "Did you make the same sense of it as this?" he asked.

Buchanan nodded his agreement.

"What did you do next?"

"I was intrigued by Schumacher's comment about their value, and decided to see if I could trace them in England. The British army has many faults, but they keep very good records. After a search I tracked down the Major's widow - he had died some years earlier. With a little persuasion she agreed to sell them to me. I brought them to you, and the rest we both know. Just yesterday she also gave me these letters from her husband which mention his purchase. They are personal, and so I've marked the passages which are relevant." Apart from his reference to Schumacher's letter, and the description of the love-letters as a gift, this part of the story was also true.

Morganstein read them and turned to look again at the paintings. After a couple of minutes he picked one of the pictures up and ran his hands lovingly over the paintwork.

"So what we have is more than just a piece of art. We have a piece of history. Herr Schumacher must have been working at Klammer's when Schiele had his show there in 1911. For some reason Schiele made him a gift of the pictures. With the rise of the Third Reich, and the start of the persecutions, he became nervous for them and covered them with the overpainting. We must assume that he was sent to Dachau and suffered the same fate as millions of others. After the war, when he did not return to pay off his debt, the landlady was only too happy to sell them for what she could get. If it hadn't been for the Major, your curiosity, and my restoration, they might have stayed lost for ever."

Buchanan nodded his head gravely in agreement with Morganstein.

"I can't begin to tell you how happy this has made me, Mr Morganstein, I have always had a dream that something like this would happen to me. That I might discover a lost Rembrandt in an attic, or something like that. Now that it has happened I scarcely know what to say."

"I understand exactly what you mean. I too have had this dream. This last week my soul has been dancing." He smiled at Buchanan before adding, "What do you intend to do now?"

"What do you mean?"

"Do you have any idea how much these paintings are worth?"

"Well, I know a little bit about European painting, but my forte is the Victorian era, as you know. I should imagine they are worth several thousands."

"More, much more. If a buyer can be convinced that they are

genuine, I would expect the pair of them to fetch as much as fifty-thousand pounds."

Alarm bells began sounding in Buchanan's brain. A buyer convinced of their authenticity should be paying at least double that figure. He wondered what Morganstein was leading up to. He decided to play along for a while,

"I had no idea! I can scarcely believe it. I only gave five-hundred pounds for them from the widow. Even after I have paid you for the work, it is more than I have ever made before. What do you think the chances are of persuading the Art World of their authenticity?"

"My friend, I would not dream of taking money from you for the privilege of uncovering these discoveries."

The gentle ringing of the alarm bells became a deafening roar: Buchanan knew that Morganstein never did anything for free. He was renowned in the trade for his tightness with money. His clients received bills that itemized even the nails used to fasten canvasses to stretchers. It seemed there was to be a sting in the tail of this meeting. He listened intently as the old man continued.

"As to proving whether or not they are genuine, it is difficult to say. But, I have a friend, a collector from America who is by chance over here on business. I think he might be willing to run that risk for the opportunity of buying them now." "How does he know about them?" asked Buchanan.

"He was here only yesterday, and he happened to catch a glimpse of them when he was in the work-room. He wants to know if you will consider an offer."

"I don't know," hesitated Buchanan, "This has all come as a bit of a shock."

"I understand. Would you be willing to at least talk with him?"

"I have a meeting later today. I don't have much time."

"If you wish we can join him for lunch. He is dining over the road at 'Diana's.'"

Buchanan was curious to hear what the prospective buyer had to offer, and relieved to discover the reason for the low valuation put on the paintings by Morganstein. He was presumably getting a percentage from the collector. Buchanan said, "Seeing as we were going to have lunch together anyway, why don't we join him? After all, I can at least talk to him."

"Excellent. Shall we go?"

"If you don't mind I'd like to take the pictures and put them in my car. Even if I decide to sell, I would like to feel that I owned them for a few moments!"

The old man laughed and helped Buchanan wrap them in a protective layer of bubble-wrap. Together they gathered up the documentation and returned it to the file, before placing everything in the boot of the Jaguar and crossing the road to the restaurant.

# CHAPTER FIVE

'DIANA'S HAD BEEN A DOWN-AT-HEEL PUB only a couple of years ago, but now it had been moved upmarket by the brewery that owned it. The mahogany-stained plywood paneling that covered the walls bristled with reproduction Victoriana and cases of butterflies. What the bar and restaurant lacked in genuine atmosphere and variety of choice, they made up for in speed of service and cost.

Seated alone at a table for four in the back dining-room was a man in his early forties who was obviously an American: he sported a definitive crew-cut, and he was dressed in the light gray flannel trousers and blue blazer that were almost a uniform for transatlantic businessmen. As he saw Morganstein approaching, the man uncoiled from his chair: the straighter he stood, the more obviously powerful he became. He was about six feet four, and, although he probably didn't weigh more than about a hundred and eighty pounds, it looked as if he was built entirely out of the densest materials. When he was fully upright, he moved aside the heavy cast-iron chair and took a couple of steps forward. He didn't walk all the way to meet Morganstein and Buchanan though; he stopped and waited for them to come to him, as if to let them know who was in charge of the situation.

Morganstein put his arm around Buchanan and pushed him forwards.

"Charles Buchanan," said Morganstein affably.

A hint of an expression appeared on the man's face which, after a moment's hesitation, Buchanan decided could have been a smile.

"This is James Nares," said Morganstein. "His friends call him Jimmy."

Buchanan looked again at the man's implacable face, and found it hard to believe that anyone other than the very, very, rich had ever called him anything other than James - or Mister Nares.

"Good afternoon," said Buchanan coolly.   It seemed pointless trying to be too friendly, not at this stage anyway.

"Good afternoon, Mr Buchanan. I hope you don't mind doing business here in the bar. I just got in from New York this morning.   I don't know how much Mr Morganstein has told you about me..."

"Nothing, really," said Buchanan.

Nares guided the two men back to his table. "Well, although I occasionally do invest in Art, primarily I finance art purchases by other people.  I'm told, by Mr Morganstein here, that you are a good man to know in London at the moment. And I'm not certain in which capacity I am here yet: investor or banker.  So, shall we talk while we eat?  I don't get to London too often, I have some other people to see on this trip, and my time is a scarce commodity."

The waiter took orders for drinks.  Nares ordered a mineral water and Buchanan followed his lead.  Morganstein's nerves seemed to demand something stronger. While they waited for their drinks, Morganstein struggled to make small talk. Every time Charles looked directly across the table at Nares, Nares was looking directly at him.  The American's examination was ruthless and insistent.

Buchanan forced himself to relax; his scheme was foolproof, he told himself. He and Nares locked eyes for a second, and Buchanan suddenly realized he wasn't scared by Nares' involvement; he was excited. Here was a real challenge. If Nares could be taken, anyone could be.

Charles smiled at the American and raised his glass. "A toast...Jimmy?"

Nares turned his glass in his hands and smiled back. "I take it you're not a superstitious man, Mr Buchanan?"

"Why do you ask?"

"They say that you shouldn't toast with water. It's supposed to be unlucky. Personally, I don't believe in luck; I think it's like prayer - a refuge for those that don't prepare adequately. But what about you? To quote from one of my favorite movies, 'Do you feel lucky?'" Nares held up his glass.

Buchanan lifted his glass and touched it against the American's. "Lucky? ...No. Fortunate?...Yes. I think there's a difference between good luck and good fortune, isn't there?"

Nares smiled. "I think so. Shall we drink to fortune, then?"

"To good fortune," said Buchanan.

They touched glasses.

Morganstein raised his glass of wine and touched it against theirs. "To good fortune," chimed in Morganstein belatedly.

Nares took a sip from his Perrier and said, "Speaking of fortune, Mr Buchanan, if everything about this deal is as it's cracked up to be, Mr Morganstein and I could be putting a great deal of money in your direction very shortly. As soon as I heard the details, I dropped everything and did a little research. I don't get personally involved in many transactions, Mr Buchanan, but when I do I like to make sure they're solid. I'm not a man that likes to be surprised."

Buchanan smiled as he noticed Morganstein wincing and trying to catch the American's eye. The deception over the chance viewing in the restorer's studio crumbled away. "Did the quality of the pictures surprise you?" asked Buchanan.

"I barely looked at them, if you must know," said Nares. "I stopped trying to understand quality in Art when I saw that urinal signed *R. MUTT* in a museum. Especially when I discovered how much it was insured for. I leave aesthetics to those that can understand them; I understand money. For me, the excitement and pleasure of Art is in its acquisition. As I see it...do you gamble Mr Buchanan?"

"Only when I can't lose...or when I can afford to lose," said Charles.

The conversation was interrupted by the waiter appearing alongside the table with the menus. Morganstein and Nares took the waiter's advice and had the Dover Sole; Buchanan settled on a rare sirloin steak, which, on the evidence of the one being eaten at a neighboring table, was likely to arrive hanging over the edges of the plate and dripping with garlic butter.

Nares continued talking with the polished ease of a TV evangelist warming to his message, "The way I see it, Mr Buchanan is this: Artistic taste is changeable, it is - if you like - a bluff, but *two percent over prime rate* is like the little pit on the roulette wheel with the double zero - it makes money in the long run. If others..." He looked at Morganstein, "want me to finance their 'investments' I will do so, but if I am going to risk my own money I want to see the wheel first. Do you know what I'm driving at?"

"Yes, of course. How much might you be thinking of investing?" asked Buchanan.

"As I mentioned in the office," interrupted Morganstein desperately, aware that he was in danger of becoming irrelevant to the conversation, "Jimmy and I had talked about fifty thousand pounds."

Nares glared at Morganstein and turned back to face Charles. "Thank you, Oscar. Okay, fifty thousand, let's say that's how much you can see on the table in front of me, but I'm not saying that I'm prepared to use it all to back one hand."

"Two hands...there are two pictures," said Buchanan.

[ 66 ]

"Okay. Fifty thousand. Two hands," conceded Nares.

Buchanan turned the numbers over, "Fifty thousand...Fifty thousand...I'm not sure. I know that a painting of Schiele's called *'Liebespaar'* went for nearly two million pounds the other year."

Although Buchanan knew he was revealing a depth of knowledge about the value of Schiele's work that he had previously denied, he had decided to call the American's bluff - a little. Nares probably knew all this, he had after all mentioned doing some research, but Buchanan wanted to remind the gambler in Nares to be fully aware of the size of the pot: the man should begin to see how much his potential profit could be.

"Obviously," he continued, "I know my paintings are not worth nearly that much, but it shows which way the market is moving. And I think it might be rather nice to hang on to them and see them as an investment. I'm still not at all sure that I want to sell them."

"This all assumes that they are genuine," interrupted Morganstein.

"Of course," replied Buchanan evenly, "But, somehow, I don't think Mr Nares would be offering me fifty thousand pounds if he didn't think they were. Would you...Jimmy?"

"No," said Nares. For a fraction of a second he looked - almost worried - then he turned and said, "Would you, Oscar?"

"Err, no," said Morganstein. "Look, what I want to know is how much Charles would want to sell them for? After all, he is right; Schiele's work is increasing in value all the time. On the other hand, these works are small; they are studies not finished works; and their provenance is good, but not faultless. Tell us, how much do you think Charles?"

"I had been thinking of something along the lines of....Ah! The food. Thank you, waiter. The two Dover Soles are for my friends here, and the rare steak is mine."

Nares had been listening in resignation to Morganstein

trying to hurry the negotiations. Now, as the waiter busied himself with the vegetables, Nares relaxed, and focused on the food.

But, the instant the waiter had gone, Morganstein picked up where he had left off, "So, how much are you looking for, Charles?"

Buchanan placed an extravagantly large piece of meat into his mouth, and he chewed it with slow deliberation as Morganstein waited for his answer. Finally, he patted at his chin with his napkin, and sucked at his teeth appreciatively, before answering,

"I don't know - say seventy-five thousand pounds?" He quickly lowered his head for another mouthful of steak, and watched out of the corner of his vision as Nares gave a practically imperceptible nod.

"Well, that *is* an awful lot of money, Charles." Morganstein paused to cut himself a piece of his fish which he balanced on the end of his fork, "But I think, in the circumstances, I can just about afford that much for two such beautiful paintings." With a smile he pushed the lump of white flesh into his mouth.

"One beautiful painting," said Buchanan quietly, "I meant seventy-five thousand pounds each."

"EACH!" spluttered Morganstein, showering the tablecloth with half chewed sole. Slowly his face contorted and turned bright red. He gesticulated frantically at his throat. "BONE!" he gasped, eyes wide with panic.

Buchanan unhurriedly broke off a large chunk of bread roll and motioned for him to eat it. He watched as the man crammed it into his mouth and then slowly began to subside to normality.

Morganstein finally managed to wheeze, "Charles, no more jokes. Please?"

"I wasn't joking. I was being serious."

Nares reimposed himself on the situation. "Look, take your time, Mr Buchanan. A good deal is never hurried. I don't want

[ 68 ]

anyone saying I browbeat you."

*

Forty minutes later, Nares motioned to the waiter for the bill. He produced his charge card and the man took it away to the till.

"Now, can we talk realistically about these paintings, Mr Buchanan?" Nares asked. "Have you settled on a more reasonable figure?"

Charles looked at Morganstein and back at Nares; he suddenly realized that despite the American's powerful pose, he had the strongest hand. It was all he could do not to laugh. He turned to look directly at Nares. "To be honest, I haven't given it too much thought. I was enjoying the food too much. But, in principal, I have no objection to you buying the paintings. I like your attitude, Mr Nares. You seem to be a man who would *really understand and appreciate* their true value. I just need a little more time. I think if I slept on it I might know better how I feel. Is that all right with you?"

"It seems to me," said Morganstein icily, "That you are not taking the offer in the spirit in which it was meant. If you walk away from us now then the matter is closed. You have only to take a second opinion to destroy the basis on which Jimmy decided the value of his bid. If the second opinion is favorable, then you will refuse us, because we both know the paintings will be worth around one hundred and fifty thousand pounds for the pair. If the verdict is bad, you will accept our money and swindle Mr Nares with two pictures of questionable value. I think I do not tread on anyone's toes if I say that I am prepared to put in some more money of my own and increase our offer to a final one hundred thousand pounds - cash. You may take it or leave it."

Buchanan was staggered by this last speech - and by the fact that Nares seemingly concurred: the American objected to nothing Morganstein had said. And now Buchanan realized that Morganstein was prepared to put up more of his own

[ 69 ]

money...well, the restorer must have no doubt in his mind at all about the paintings. And his opinion was one of the most highly respected in London. For a second Charles wavered on the brink of saying yes, before deciding he had nothing to lose by giving them one last chance to put more money on the table.

"I'm sorry, but I want to have these paintings on my wall for at least one night. I hope you understand. If you wish to call me tomorrow I will be pleased to reconsider."

"There will be no phone call tomorrow, Charles, not on this matter," said Morganstein with finality, "I will repeat one last time our offer of one hundred thousand pounds, cash. Mr Nares has a bank draft in his pocket for fifty thousand, we can walk from here to my bank where they will prepare you another - this is a measure of how serious we are. If you chose to turn us down then that is your affair. But remember we are prepared to assume all the risk on these paintings - right now...."

"What we are offering you is more than it might appear, Charles. We are offering you a very large amount of money for a chance just to play your hand. You have NOTHING to lose," said Nares. "But, quite frankly, I don't care how you decide; I've been around this business long enough to know that there will always be another deal. You, however, are the one who is rejecting our offer. For you, this might not be true."

"Yes, Charles. Don't be too hasty to say no; at some later time you might regret your impetuousness. What do you say? Do we have a deal?"

Charles thought for a second and said, "No, Mr Morganstein, we do not. And I'll tell you why: you're making a big thing about taking the risk they might be forgeries; that doesn't concern me. If you like the paintings so much, then buy them. It's different for Mr Nares; he's told us that he is an investor, and not an Art lover, but for you there is more, isn't there? It is, after all, the paintings you like, isn't it? Does the paint somehow magically change if they're not genuine? I don't think it does. Like you, I'm certain they are work of Schiele. But let us say for the moment that they are not - are they any less beautiful? I think not...as to the price to put on beauty...Well, I don't think the value should be in the name of the painter. I think it should be in the paintings themselves."

He offered his hand to each man in turn, unable to resist the chance of a final snipe at them both, "Thank you for the meal...Jimmy. And thank you for the wonderful restoration job Mr Morganstein. I never expected to have it done for nothing. You know where to reach me."

The old man's cheeks blew in and out as he swallowed the pain that his earlier offer now caused him.

Buchanan turned and walked out of the restaurant to his car; astonished at how easily he had refused so much money. And wondering if he would regret his decision.

# CHAPTER SIX

CORDELIA BABBINGTON WAS NOT EXPECTING HIM until four o'clock, so Buchanan used the intervening couple of hours to take the faked Schiele's back to his studio. Better there than in the boot of the Jaguar. Especially now that they had received Morganstein's approval. Previously his plan had been to sell them on the private market, but with his confidence soaring after the meeting with Nares, he contemplated sending them to auction. He knew that would create problems: they would be subjected to the severest scrutiny by both the auction house and the buyers, and it wasn't unknown in the art world for a maliciously spread rumor to decimate the price of a work: even a genuine one. There was a huge element of risk in putting the pictures in the public eye, however good they were.

The more he thought about it, the more it seemed that Morganstein's offer was the one to chase up. Setting up another private sale of this size could take months. People that were prepared to spend a hundred thousand pounds on a pair of paintings were not exactly thick on the ground and he didn't have the resources to wait indefinitely. So, even though the offer of a hundred thousand was less than they could fetch in an ideal world, it was a lot more than they might end up being worth at auction in the real world. Content with the memory of Morganstein's appraisal, he spread all the papers he had forged or collected in front of him.

From his filing cabinet he pulled out his first drafts of Schumacher's letter to the landlady and congratulated himself on the handwriting he had finally chosen for the imaginary Jew. The language of the note displayed a mixture of haste and care, which was mirrored in the lettering. He was well pleased with the success of his scheme so far, and he was looking forward to sharing the news of his 'fortunate find' with Cordelia. The discovery would be further proof in her eyes of his talent for inspired guessing. He sat and smoked one of his hand-rolled cigarettes whilst he enjoyed the glow of satisfaction in his scheme. Finally, after sorting through the file which contained his original layout of the entire plan once more, he checked the time on the wall clock and set off for Cork Street.

On his way he called in at his bank and wrote a check for another two hundred pounds from his current account; yesterday's incident with Jeremy had almost cleaned him out of ready cash. Miraculously, even though it was Friday afternoon, the bank was almost empty and he had a choice of tellers. He avoided Sophie, the young clerk whose post card he had read so inattentively the day before; he had no desire to get involved in a Greek island's travelogue. Instead he handed over his check to a weasel-faced youth at the window next to hers. As another customer presented himself in front of her, Sophie noticed Buchanan and asked,

"Hello, Charlie. Did you get my post-card?"

He assured her that he did and thanked her for it as the teller in front of him disappeared with his check to the Bank's computer terminal. Sophie waved a cheery good-bye and returned her attention to the man waiting at her counter.

Buchanan gave a silent prayer of thanks for her acceptance of his gentle rebuff, and he found himself wondering why some women seemed to be able to accept the end of a relationship and some didn't. His reverie was interrupted by the rat-like teller asking,

"Fifties alright, Mr Buchanan?"

"Sure. I seem to spend it just the same!"

"So it seems. Did you know that you're overdrawn past your credit limit? I had to clear this withdrawal with the manager. Here we are then: fifty, one, one-fifty, two. Have a nice day."

Irritated by both the content of the young man's speech, and his pseudo-American delivery, Buchanan took the money and left. He was still thinking about the precariousness of his financial situation as he climbed back into his car, transferred the cash from his pocket to his billfold, and started the engine.

He left the car in his usual multi-storey garage and walked along Saville Row to Burlington Gardens. On the corner of Cork Street he pulled up short. Gazing into the window of the Darby and Browse gallery were a couple who seemed to have climbed straight off a canvas by Ludwig Kirchner - the man was in his fifties, wore glasses, had a pointed, black goatee beard and sucked wetly on an unlit pipe; she was maybe five years younger, was wearing heels too high for her age, had a fox stole around her neck and wore a hat which sported an array of long, black feathers. For a second Buchanan could feel himself sliding across time and space to Berlin at the beginning of the First World War.

He was rescued when the woman turned to her husband and said in a broad Brooklyn accent,

"F'Chrissakes, Hun, willya get a load of the crap deese guys call Art."

Buchanan smiled at the way she pronounced the last word, it sounded like the bark of a seal. He was still smiling as he swung open the door to Babbington's. Terry was with a customer when he walked in, but she quickly excused herself

[ 75 ]

and came over to speak to him,

"Miss Cordelia said I was to send you straight upstairs to her office, and I wasn't to let you talk to Mr Jeremy or Mr Paolo. I don't think she wants you upsetting them again."

"Did I upset them?" asked Buchanan innocently.

"I should say so. They had a terrible row after you left." She smiled conspiratorially at him, "Mr Jeremy said one day you'd go too far and that he wanted to be there to see it. He doesn't like you much, you know."

"Really? Thanks for the warning."

"I better get back to my customer. I'll see you later, Mr Buchanan."

He went through the side door of the gallery into the hallway and climbed the deep-pile carpeted stairs to Cordelia Babbington's first floor office. Outside the door he paused and listened for a moment. A woman's voice was talking angrily. Cordelia was obviously involved in a shouting match on the telephone. As he listened a smile spread across his face; it sounded like the kind of situation that only Cordelia could become involved in.

"...Please don't threaten me Lord Price, I just get more determined. Your son is quite old enough to be able to make decisions for himself. I enjoy his company and he seems to enjoy mine....Hold on a minute, I don't exactly remember you kicking me out of bed....No, I don't care that he is half my age. If you must know, that is one of his main attractions.... The photograph in the 'Tatler' was none of my doing and I'm certain Frank was fully aware of the cameraman....Yes, of course I'm sorry it made him look debauched. So what? Don't you read the tabloids? Everybody is debauched these days, even royalty. I'm sure it will only help his career - and that includes his accession to the House."

Buchanan knocked gently on the door and pushed it open. Cordelia Babbington motioned for him to come in and continued her conversation into the telephone as he settled himself in the wing armchair in front of her desk.

"You must excuse me, Tony, but I really have to go. I have company....No, I will not stop seeing Frank....Before you hang up I think you should know that this conversation has been stored on our 'Agreement Verifying System'.... Thank you for those kind words. If and when I do go there, I am certain you will already be simmering in a vat of sulfurous brimstone. Good-bye."

She hung up.

"Agreement Verifying System?" queried Buchanan, "What the bloody hell is that?"

She laughed, "It doesn't exist. But it scares the pants off people. They're never sure whether they said anything incriminating or not. I got the idea from one of our clients in the city, apparently recording phone conversations is all the rage these days. How are you Charles? You look ravishing as usual." She raised herself slightly from her chair and leant across the desk, "Do you want to kiss me?"

It was less of a question than an order and Buchanan obediently complied. Cordelia Babbington was almost six feet tall and unhealthily thin. Unlike most women of her stature, she wore high heels and carried herself aggressively upright. Her hair was dyed a shade that was almost ecclesiastical purple and shaped in a severe, geometric cut. She was not a woman who liked to be ignored or argued with. From a safe distance she was referred to by her enemies in the Art World as Cruella De Ville - the name of a villainess in a Walt Disney cartoon. She knew about the nickname of course, and rather liked the allusion.

As a rule she was immaculately dressed in hand-made clothes from Caroline Charles or one of the couturiers in Beauchamp Place. But on the rare occasions when she showed her relaxed self in public she still wore the baggy sweaters and tight trousers of her beatnik youth. Her insatiable craving for social activities that lasted into the small hours of the morning had taken its toll on her looks. Her eyes were surrounded by an impressive variety of wrinkles and because of this she often wore large dark glasses late into the night. On the couple of occasions when she had asked him to act as her escort, Buchanan had enjoyed her company, but he had found sex with her to be closer to having a fight in a bone-yard than anything else.

"I overheard your telephone conversation; I was eavesdropping outside the door," he said candidly.

"Have you no shame?"

"It sounded so interesting I couldn't resist it. Who, if I may ask, is Frank and what have you been doing to him?"

"He's my dream lover: the eldest son of Lord Price of Wenden: my toy-boy - as the gutter press would call him."

"I find it ironic that one of the world's arch cynics has a dream lover. Especially knowing you as well as I do, Ropey."

"Charles, if you're going to use that offensive name you can just piss off now."

Buchanan grinned sheepishly in apology, and she continued,

"Anyway, even you should know that cynics fall in love. Just a couple of months ago you announced to me - in this very office - that you had discovered the woman of your dreams. YOU were even mentioning marriage, for God's sake."

"Ouch," said Buchanan. "That hurt. I don't need you to remind me; she does it quite well enough on her own."

"Ah, ha. I detect a certain change in sentiment. Has your vision of the ideal woman altered?"

"My vision?" He wondered whether there was any point in trying to explain to Cordelia about his vision: about the attraction that Sally had had for him in the first place. Would Cordelia be able to understand that the travel agent bore a passable resemblance to the face which constantly recurred in his nightmares and his dreams? - That sometimes when he was making love and was totally absorbed in what he was doing, he felt the presence of another woman? - That it was always the same face that floated in front of him, moving constantly as he tried to look closely at the features? That, try as he might, he had never been able to capture the likeness in a drawing or a painting.

No; no; no; and no.

To Cordelia it would be incomprehensible that Charles Buchanan, the arch-realist, was tormented by an illusion.

The rational side of his nature rightly told him that she would scoff at such an idea. It was the sort of thing she expected to hear from awful romantic poets and not from the arrogant, self-assured bastard she wanted him to be - a role that in her company he had no trouble playing.

Did he really expect her to believe that for a while it had seemed as if Sally had HER face?

Trying to explain to her exactly what went on in his mind was like describing a painting over the telephone. He gave up thinking about it and attempted to lower the shutters on the whole subject.

"Let's just say by the time I'd taken aim, the target had moved."

"How wonderfully enigmatic you can be, Charles. What have you done with the poor girl? Have you ditched her yet?"

"No. However hard I try to give her the hint she manages to ignore it."

"Hinting? Hinting isn't usually your style. Don't tell me she loves you, and you don't want to hurt her feelings?"

"Her feelings? I can't control her feelings - that's for her to do. Neither do I think she loves me. She's a career virgin, if you know what I mean. She's twenty-seven and been saving her cherry all these years for the man that she marries. According to her own particular brand of logic, as it was me that was first through the chute, I must be Mr Husband. I have other ideas on the subject. However, she's got a twenty-four-carat Irish temper and I've got a sneaking suspicion she's going to be mighty cross when she finally realizes I want her out of my life. So I keep putting it off." He took out his tobacco pouch and asked, "Anyway, how have you been upsetting the nobility?"

"It's a storm in a teacup. Have you seen the latest edition of 'Tatler'?"

"Yes. Why?"

"If you look closely in the background of this picture of Princess Margaret at the Orphans Benefit Fund ball you will see me with my escort," she paused and indicated a picture in a glossy magazine on her desk, "Do you notice anything odd?"

Buchanan studied the picture carefully, "I can't even see you. Oh yes, there you are in the background with that young man. For God's sake, Cordelia, he's got his hand up your skirt. In a photograph with royalty too. Have you no shame!" chided Buchanan.

"Don't be so boring Charles - unless someone points it out to you it does look as if we're dancing. Doesn't it? It was late, it was dark, we were both three-quarters cut - you know the scene. Nobody was looking at us with all that Royalty about, and then off went the flash-gun. Even then I thought we were well out of the shot. Everybody else was concentrating on trying to get in the picture, so they could get a mention in the blurb. The irony is that amongst the names they did print were ours!"

"Miss Cordelia Babbington and the Hon. Frank Price," read Buchanan, "I take it Lord Price is a bit miffed?"

"Absolutely. Apparently he's been getting frightful stick in the House. Some of the peers with longer memories remember when I was humping HIM. His wife didn't take too kindly to it then, and she doesn't much care for being reminded of it now. The old boy wants me out of the family circle."

"And you'll be buggered?"

"Too right. Frank is intelligent...witty...sensitive...and a gifted painter....He is also better hung than a horse. You know, Charles, as far as I can see, all that stuff Masters and Johnson wrote about size making no difference is a load of crap to make men with small willies feel better. Believe me, I know. He will have to be pried out of my grasp. Figuratively speaking of course."

Buchanan smiled and asked, "Does this mean we can expect a show of another 'undiscovered genius' at Babbington's sometime in the not too distant future?"

"Oh no. He's not an artist."

"I thought you said he was a painter. Do you mean he's some kind of aristocratic decorator?"

"No," said Cordelia slyly, "He works for Oscar Morganstein."

"Ah ha! Now I understand how you knew about the paintings."

"What, the Schiele's?" asked Cordelia innocently.

"The Schiele's?"

"That's what I said."

"How much do you know?"

"Only that you bought two paintings off some old biddy in the country on a hunch, and it paid off."

"Is that all?"

"And that Morganstein has a buyer lined up for them if you want to sell."

"Yes, I met him today."

"Him?"

"Yes. Some yank called Jimmy Nares."

"Oh, that corpse! He's not the buyer; he's just bankrolling Morganstein. They're selling them on and splitting the profit. I gather Morganstein has just bought himself a ridiculously over-priced Frankenthaler and couldn't lay his hands on enough cash to buy your paintings on his own."

"What do you mean, they're selling them on?"

"Really, Charles, I'm surprised you don't know. After the 'Vienna' show at the Museum of Modern Art in New York last year, the word went out that some French woman was bonkers about anything from the Vienna School. If we do find anything she can be contacted through Christie's. From what Frank tells me, Morganstein has been in touch with them and she's offered over a hundred thousand pounds for them. Anything she pays him and Nares, over what they pay you, they pocket."

"How much has she offered him?"

"I've no idea. How much do you want? Whatever you get you'll be in profit."

"Morganstein and Nares offered me a hundred thousand for them today. I turned them down."

"A hundred thousand pounds? AND YOU TURNED THEM DOWN?" echoed Cordelia incredulously. "Are you out of your mind?"

"What do you mean? I can go for the full whack from Christie's."

"You can try. But I'm not sure you'll get it. Although Morganstein is convinced they are genuine Shiele's, Frank thinks they might be 1930's forgeries. If you'd taken their money, **they** would have had to provide the proof. The difference is that people trust Nares - he's a name. You're just an upstart.  Suppose Christie's decided they weren't interested...Well, you know what that would do to the value? Why on earth didn't you take their money and run?"

"What does Frank know about it anyway?" asked Buchanan defensively, "From the look of this..." He indicated the picture in the magazine. "The guy's hardly out of short trousers."

"So were you when I first took you under my wing, but it didn't stop me thinking you had ability. And I've been proved right. Even allowing for the fact that you've gone bust three times, the purchases I've made on your hunches have made the gallery more money in four years than my soppy brother has made it in twenty. Hey, I'm a great believer in youth. In the bedroom and outside. Take my word for it Charles, if Frank's got doubts, it's for a very good reason. Call up Morganstein and tell him you'll take his money; tell him you've changed your mind. He's confident and greedy enough to take the chance."

"He told me it was a now or never offer. I know if I call him back he'll think I've had a dodgy second opinion. I'll just have to sweat it out and hope he calls me. I'm sure he will; he's a grasping son of a bitch....Or I guess I can take a chance with Christie's."

"Well, I wish you the best of luck, but I can't believe you were so greedy. I didn't think you'd let the offer go. From what Frank told me they were only going to give you fifty thousand."

"They did, at first. I forced the price up."

"That I can believe. I bet Nares was shocked at being out haggled." Cordelia ran her fingers through her hair and sighed, "Dammit, Charles, I expected you to be celebrating a sale, not penniless and hoping. Oh well, I'm sure you'll come out of it all right in the end. You usually do."

"Of course I will and you'll be the first to hear, I promise." Buchanan said with a confidence he did not feel.

"You do realize that you've completely buggered my evening?"

"How so?"

"I was convinced you'd be celebrating , and I was going to offer my services as your chaperone for the night. I think at the very least, you should offer to take me out. I even told Frank I was busy."

"I'm sorry, Cordelia. I've had a busy couple of days. I'm totally knackered. I'm going to go home and see if Morganstein rings. It's not too late to give your stallion a ring. I don't think I can compete in that department. Thanks for everything."

"Oh all right, if you insist. Cheer up, Charles. It'll work out. Still I'm sorry you don't fancy an evening with me; a good, hard workout in cupid's gym is exactly what you need to stop you fretting."

Buchanan said his good-byes and left her office with her final remark ringing in his ears. Suddenly it seemed like a good idea.

Downstairs in the gallery Terry was packing up her things at her desk. He stopped in front of her, flashed his brightest smile and asked,

"Terry, cheer me up and come for a drink."

"I'm sorry, but not tonight, Mr Buchanan. It's Friday night; it's pissing down with rain, and I just want to get home and put my feet up in front of the telly. Thanks all the same."

She was right about the rain. When he stepped out onto the street he had to push his way through a small knot of people sheltering in the tiny porch from a rainstorm that had all the hallmarks of a tropical monsoon. The glorious weather of the last couple of days had finally broken. He cursed his lack of forethought at not bringing an umbrella, or a coat. The car was parked several hundred yards away. There was nothing to do but run for it. He put his glasses in his top pocket, pulled his jacket tightly around his shoulders and set off.

Before getting into the car he threw his sodden jacket into the boot and dried his hair a little with the travel rug from the back seat. By the time he lowered himself gingerly onto the driver's seat and slammed the door, a sizable puddle had formed on the concrete floor of the car-park. He wasn't cheered up by the knowledge that in weather like this cars seemed to appear from every sidestreet until the roads were so snarled up with traffic that forward movement was little more than a forlorn hope.

Five minutes later, he finally managed to bully his way into the unbroken line of cars in the street, and he began to inch his way homewards.

# CHAPTER SEVEN

THE TEENAGER WAS SLICING SMOKED SALMON at the cold meat counter when Buchanan walked into the delicatessen. The painfully slow journey across town had at least given him a chance to dry out a bit, and he had taken the opportunity to straighten out his hair in the car mirror. He looked crumpled - but presentable. He put three bottles of Champagne in a battered wire basket and wandered around the aisles until she had finished serving.

There was a large anti-pilfering mirror hanging high on the wall of the small store; Buchanan used it to watch the youngster unobserved for several minutes. He thought her attractive, without being pretty; her features were so rounded and soft that they almost seemed to have been drawn on something like a boiled egg. The pallidness of her face was pierced by the brightest blue eyes he had ever seen; they shone and sparkled as she worked. For several seconds after her customer had walked away from the counter she stood gazing distantly into space - towards the mirror.

The reflected scene and the blank expression on her face reminded him of the one captured by Manet in his painting of the serving girl at the bar of the *Folies Bergères*: she also stood unseeing, surrounded by things that were not part of her world. The barmaid in the 19th-century painting poured Champagne that she could not afford; this punkette sliced salmon and served pâté de fois gras. His reverie made him think again of his earlier view of her as the model for Rossetti's "Beata Beatrix." She definitely reminded him of a painting, but he still wasn't sure which one. Holman Hunt? Munch? A Fauve or an Expressionist? - maybe someone from *Der Blaue Reiter* group? or *Die Brücke?* They all painted redheads, but the one Buchanan was thinking of was by...

He gave up trying to solve the riddle and lifted his shopping basket onto the top of the glass counter.

The spell that was holding her attention was broken. Her eyes focused on him and she smiled when she saw who it was. He noticed she was scrubbing at her hands in a tiny stainless steel sink.

"Hello, Charlie. Hold on, I'll be with you in a minute. I've just been cutting fish and it stinks on your hands. I don't mind eating it, but I hate touching it. There," she sniffed at her fingers. "What can I do you for?"

"I was wondering what time you got away from work tonight?"

She looked at the three bottles of Champagne in front of her, "Why? What's on the agenda? T.G.I.F. party?"

"T.G.I.F.?" queried Buchanan.

"Thank God It's Friday," she explained.

"Something like that. I've had one of those days."

"Me too. Still, it's Friday. I always do the early shift on Fridays, so I'll be done pretty soon. If you hang on a bit, I'll let you buy me that drink you promised me. What's the time?"

Buchanan checked his watch, "Five fifty six." He had been stuck in the traffic for nearly an hour.

"Ah, sod it. That's near enough. Old man Patel can cut his own fish for four minutes. Hang on; I'll get my coat." She knocked on the two-way mirror from behind which the proprietor kept an eye on his staff and customers, and pointed to her wrist to indicate the time. A disembodied voice faintly wished her goodnight. She hurried away to the back of the shop. A couple of minutes later she reappeared wearing a battered black leather jacket.

Out of the uniform that she wore for work she looked more at ease, and Buchanan could see the gently curved outline of her body. He settled up at the cash desk for his Champagne, and they stepped outside.

It had finally stopped raining.

"Where shall we go for a drink?" she asked. "I'd better stay near the tube; my party's in Hackney. Where's yours?"

"I'm wasn't exactly going to a party, or intending to go to the pub," confessed Buchanan. "I've had the kind of day where I just want to go home and drink as much of this as I can. If I do it on my own I feel like an alcoholic. Why don't you come to my place and give me a hand drinking the Champagne? I'll get you a taxi to your party later."

"What, you'll get me a cab all the way to Hackney?"

"Sure. Why not?"

"It'll cost you a fortune."

"Okay, let's forget it," Buchanan said suddenly. He took a twenty pound note from the change he was still clutching in one hand and tucked it into her pocket. "My treat. Get the cab anyway. I'm too tired to go sit in a pub. Have a wild night. The older generation is going home to get quietly drunk. Maybe I'll see you another time." With these words he gently touched her cheek with his fingers and turned to walk to his car.

There was no sound of any movement behind him; he realized she was going to pocket his money and go. It was what he expected today.

He opened the passenger door, put the carrier bag with the bottles on the seat, climbed inside, and started the engine.

He was about to let up the clutch, when the passenger door opened.

She leaned in and said, "Hey, don't bugger off without me. I guess I'm with you, boss. But I'm warning you, any Frank Sinatra records, and I'm gone. My musical taste is pretty limited. And don't get any funny ideas; I don't normally do this kind of thing....In fact, I wasn't going to come, but then I figured, 'What the hell. He seems like a nice enough bloke.' And, anyway, I fancy seeing how the other half live."

"Don't get your hopes too high," replied Buchanan, relieved that his bluff had worked. "And don't shake the bottles up when you put them on the floor."

During the short ride to his flat she quizzed him relentlessly about the car. He was so pleased with himself that he cheerfully explained what all the dials indicated and what the knobs operated. In return he found out that she was called Nikki, was seventeen years old and shared a squat off the Ladbroke Grove with two girls who worked for a record company. Despite her constant stream of questions, he was looking forward to spending the evening with her. He was even glad that Terry had turned him down; an affair with her could well have put Cordelia's nose out of joint.

He noticed that Nikki was fairly impressed with the key operated lift that served his flat, even though there was barely room for both of them in it. But when the door opened onto the living room she gasped with pleasure.

"Well, this is about as far as you can get from my Mum and Dad's place on the Harrow Road. You certainly have taste, Charlie, you certainly have taste."

"Take your coat off and have a nose around; I'll open a bottle and get some glasses."

As she slipped out of her leather jacket and handed it to him, he smiled. On her 'T' shirt was emblazoned the slogan -FUCK DANCING, LET'S FUCK-. He untwisted the wire on the Champagne and watched her as she went from one juke-box to the next looking at the records on them. He poured two glasses and carried them and the bottle to the sunken sitting-area at the other end of the room. On his way he checked the answerphone, the message received light was on and the indicator showed that there had been one call in his absence.

*Morganstein?*

His pulse rate surged upwards; his stomach contracted.

He hit the play button on the machine.

It was not the voice of the middle-European émigré on the tape; it was Sally's voice that came out of the speaker.

The adrenaline now jolted his mood of anticipation into one of anger; he hit the stop button and silenced the machine.

If he had listened for just a few seconds he would have heard Sally's brief message: her plans had changed, she was no longer going out for dinner with her Boss, and, as a consequence, she was going to be dropping by his flat later on that evening.

But Buchanan did not want to even think about Sally tonight; as far as he was concerned, she was out for dinner with her boss; the evening stretched pleasantly in front of him. He returned his attention to his young visitor.

"Do these things work?" the punkette asked, pointing at the Wurlitzer in front of her.

"Sure. Just switch them on. You don't need any money. They're fixed to play for free. I think the newest records are on that one over there." He pointed to the machine at the far end of the room.

She went over, turned the machine on and punched busily at the buttons while the neon lights inside spluttered into life. There seemed to be plenty she wanted to hear.

"Do you buy a lot of records?" she asked over her shoulder.

"I don't buy any, but my ex-girlfriend hated the ones that came with the machine. She kept calling me an old fart, and eventually, after one of our not infrequent rows, I let her put on some of her own."

The reminder of another of Sally's intrusions into his life

irritated him again. Sooner or later he was going to have to dump her, before her plans for a wedding became an obsession. It had taken less time than he would have thought possible for the woman he had chased so relentlessly to become a nuisance. It just wasn't enough that her face sparked off some deeply-buried images in his mind.

Nikki came over and sat down near him as music began pounding out of the speakers. She downed her glass of Champagne almost at one swallow and topped it up from the bottle. This time she waved it at him,

"Well...Cheers, Charlie. Here's to you...you old fart." She smiled.

"And to you," he replied, chinking his glass against hers.

She drained her drink again, and Buchanan refilled it once more. He sat back and listened as she burbled on about things he could dimly recall being interested in at her age. Fifteen minutes later her glass was empty again; he refilled it and noticed that the first bottle was nearly empty. She could certainly drink. He poured the last of the Champagne into his own glass, and put the empty bottle on the low table in front of him.

He wondered how to make the first move to get her into his bed. If he wasn't careful, he worried, he might scare her away. She relaxed back on the sofa tapping her fingers to the music still pumping from the juke-box,

"This is the life. Eh Charlie? How d'you make a crust," she waved her arm in the air, "I mean what pays for all this stuff?"

"I'm a picture dealer. I buy and sell paintings."

"Piss off - I'm not the taxman, Charlie. That may be the straight bit, but you don't buy a place like this from the proceeds of the daily grind. I was asking about the iffy bit - not the bread and butter money, the monopoly money. I've been trying to work it out. You don't look like a villain."

"I'm not. I love paintings, and I'm just good at my job."

"Crap."

"Don't be so cocky. It really is as simple as that - I do love paintings, and I am good at what I do."

"So, what do you do exactly?"

"I buy paintings when they're cheap...and sell them when they're expensive. It's just like keeping up with fashion. Occasionally I buy pictures from people who don't realize how valuable they are, and sell them to people that do. It's easy, and it pays."

"How come you're so good at it? Why aren't there loads of people doing it?"

"There are lots of people that would like to do what I do, but I've got an 'edge'."

"What's that?"

"If I went around telling people I wouldn't have it for long, would I?" laughed Buchanan.

The young girl realized she had been caught and laughed too. But she was intrigued and persisted,

"Go on, tell me. I'm hardly the sort to go into competition, am I?"

"Okay. Here it is. In Brighton there's a second-hand book shop that specializes in Art. It has over ten thousand books in stock at any one time: all of them about Art. You go there...."

"Yeah? Then what do I do?"

"...You do what I did."

"Which was?"

"You study all the books, of course. And after a while you acquire an encyclopedic knowledge of the history of Art," said Buchanan with a grin.

She laughed and said, "Oh come on, be serious."

"I've never been more serious in my life," chuckled Buchanan.

"But why? How?"

"That's my 'edge'."

She squirmed in frustration, "What do you mean?"

"My dad owned the shop. I was trapped there for days on

end. Every school holiday and week-end between when I was ten and when I was eighteen, I spent working in that shop."

"Why? Didn't your Dad have anyone else that worked there?"

"Assistants? Oh yes. He had loads of them. They all had three things in common: they were young, attractive, and female. My father spent most of his time in the flat upstairs with them while I watched the shop."

"But what about your mother? Didn't she mind?"

"I don't know; she left when I was ten. I haven't seen or heard from her since. She had a choice I didn't have. So, while my dad fucked art students, I read the stock. There was nothing else to do...apart from watch him at it."

"What do you mean?"

"Sometimes I got bored of my Art education...and so I closed the shop. I just crept upstairs and learned all about sex. I hated the old bastard at the time, but I've never regretted it since. You see my 'edge' is very simple. I'm just better educated than most people."

"That's really sad," she said quietly.

"What is?"

"Everything. Your dad making you work in the shop. Your mum leaving. You hating your dad."

"It had advantages too."

"Like what?"

"Like, I became the school expert on anything to do with sex. While the other first year kids were playing 'I'll show you mine if you show me yours' I was having it away with half the fifth form behind the bike sheds."

She laughed, "You're making all this up!"

"Am I?"

"You are, aren't you?"

"I guess you'll have to make up your own mind as to whether any of it's true. You admit you don't know much about Art, so I guess that all you can check out is the sex side of the story...."

"Is that a proposition?" she asked warily.

Buchanan shrugged.

She paused and thought for a second. Then she said, "Oh shit! If I'm going to raise my sights at all, I might as well start now. Most of the offers I get are from spotty kids in Lacoste sweaters. With them it's a couple of halves of lager, and back to my place. I don't want to get too used to fucking kids who still have their trousers round their ankles."

She pulled Buchanan down onto the seat next to her.

He trailed the back of a finger down the side of her face, and brushed his lips against hers. Suddenly he caught a faint smell of his own body; he had worked up a bit of a sweat running through the rain to the car. An idea occurred to him and he asked,

"You ever been in a Jacuzzi?"

"No, not me. As Eddie Murphy said, 'The nearest I get is when I fart in the bath.' If you'll pardon my French."

"That's not the same thing at all. Come on." He led her by the hand to the bathroom.

She watched intrigued and slightly nervously, like a swimmer testing the temperature before taking the plunge, as he filled the tub in the corner of the room. The Jacuzzi was a fitment that had failed to impress him when he had bought the flat, and most of the time the huge two-person bath was little more than an annoyance when he wanted to quickly freshen up. Nikki, however, waited excitedly for the water level to rise to the point where the air pump could be turned on. When Buchanan flicked the switch and the water began boiling up in pulsed surges, she smiled with pleasure.

Buchanan watched intently as she began to undress. She kicked off her shoes, and, the instant she lost the extra three or four inches of height, the shape of her entire body changed. She stopped looking like a woman and became almost childlike. The childlike image remained until, still unabashed by his presence, she reached behind her and grasped the hem of her 'T' shirt, pulling it over her head in one movement. Her jeans joined the abandoned 'T' shirt on the floor, and she stood for a second in her underwear staring at Buchanan. He took her stare as his cue to look away, so she could take them off unobserved.

The instant she was nude she climbed quickly into the foaming water, but not before Buchanan had stolen the chance to look closely at her.

She was no more than five feet tall and in her roundness she was like a scaled down version of a Renoir woman.

*Renoir.*

Suddenly it came to him where he had seen her before. She was identical to the model Renoir had used for his exquisite 'Blonde Bather' of 1882. Although the painting was in a private collection, it had been shown at the Hayward exhibition in 1984, and he had been captivated by it.

At some time she had obviously been overweight; there were the silvery stripes of stretch marks around her tops of her legs, but now her figure was exactly to Charles's taste. On her tiny frame her full breasts hung heavily. Her red hair, which he had assumed to be dyed, was obviously natural, for, in common with many redheads, there was an almost total absence of pigment in her skin - her nipples were barely described by the faint patches of pale pink that spread over the swollen ends of her white breasts. The solitary flourish of real color on her body was the twist of her tightly curled pubic hair.

Once in the Jacuzzi she laughed with pleasure as the air bubbled through the water around her.

It was her turn to watch him undress now, and her eyes never left his body.

He put the two glasses of Champagne and the bottle beside the bath, and unfastened his shirt. Her steady gaze became slightly unnerving as he took off his trousers and socks and stood in his underpants. She was still smiling, and he became very aware of the ridiculous way his boxer shorts were stretched out in front of him like a tent. As he finally took them off, he wondered whether it was only the unremitting stare of an adolescent girl that had reduced him to a degree of self-consciousness he thought he had passed for ever.

*Or was it, perhaps, something to do with Frank Price's doubts about the paintings?*

In the bath he regained control. He began gently soaping her breasts, and her eyes closed with pleasure at his caresses. All thoughts about anything other than this young girl disappeared from his mind: Morganstein, the Schiele's, everything else became unimportant. She slid her arms around his neck and moved closer to him.

It was half past seven in the evening.

*

At about ten p.m. Charles was dimly aware of the sound of a car door slamming in the street outside his flat. On another evening at the same time, he might well have wandered over to the French windows and gazed idly down into the street. Tonight, he was far too preoccupied to do anything. He ignored it.

*

However, if he had not been too busy to get up and look, he would have seen that the car door which had slammed belonged to a taxi...and that Sally Longstaff was now standing alongside it, looking for something in her purse.

*

A moment or two later, Charles was also dimly aware of his front door bell ringing; he ignored that too.

*

Downstairs, Sally Longstaff didn't press the bell again; she waited a few moments, then she took her set of keys and opened the street-level door.

*

In the lobby she stopped in front of the mirror and redid her make-up. These days he seemed to make less of an issue about the fact that her face was 'perfect.' And the way things had been going lately between them, she was beginning to miss the attention, so she paused a moment, wiped the excess lipstick from her mouth with a tissue, and carefully reapplied the mascara to her eyelashes. Satisfied at last, she opened the lift doors and turned the key in the lock. It began moving gently upwards.

She could hear the music before the lift had even stopped, and that surprised her: Charles never played the Wurlitzers. When the door slid open, she looked about the room in surprise. The music was blaring, and there was an empty champagne bottle on the floor next to the bunch of keys he carried everywhere with him. Puzzled, she walked over to the Juke-box and turned the volume down a bit. As she did so she heard the noises coming from the bedroom.

It sounded like a woman in pain or...It couldn't be what she thought it was.

Could it?

In a mounting rush of panic, she ran to the bedroom door.

# CHAPTER EIGHT

BUCHANAN WAS FLYING. Earlier he and the young girl had moved from the bathroom to the bedroom, toweling each other dry on the way as they stayed locked together. She was willing and responsive. Yesterday with Megan he had been uninvolved in what he was doing: playing a part in a play. Now, eyes closed tightly, he was moving and reacting instinctively. Lost in the warm softness of the pale-skinned body, he was spinning through space.

And the haunting woman was beckoning to him.

*If he could just drift a little bit closer, he would be able to see her face clearly.*

From a vast distance he could hear a voice that somehow coincided with the face in his dreams. He arched his back higher, pushing his pelvis against the girl on top of him, and the voice got louder and louder until it seemed to be in the room with him. Slowly he began to make sense of what she was saying, but the words were wrong. They were angry and discordant, not excited and happy.

For several seconds Sally stood in the doorway, seemingly unable to take in the scene that confronted her. Charles was lying on his back with his eyes closed and his mouth contorted in ecstasy as a young girl squatted astride his thighs. With every movement the girl made she uttered the wordless cries of pleasure that had drawn Sally irresistibly to the bedroom. A surge of anger, and hate, and despair began rising from deep inside her as she struggled to form words. At first her mouth opened and closed silently and then finally she began to make herself heard,  "No....No.....No...No...NO.. NO. NO!"

The red-haired girl heard her first, and her eyes flickered open. She seemed unable to control the movement of her hips which continued rhythmically raising and lowering her body. Her mouth was twisted in a weird grimace, and to Sally it seemed almost as if she was laughing at her.

Sally said, "You bastard, Charles! You fucking bastard!" She repeated it over and over again in a kind of chant, while her eyes followed a slow-moving trickle of sweat that ran down between the girl's breasts as he worked them in his hands, Then her tone changed and she yelled, "YOU BASTARD! YOU BASTARD! YOU BASTARD!"

Buchanan opened his eyes and raised his head from the pillow to face the doorway where Sally stood. For several seconds he gazed in confusion. He tried to understand where his hallucination ended and reality began. When his mind cleared and his eyes focused, he slumped back on the bed and said quietly,

"This is my house. Now please get out of here."

Sally flinched as if slapped. Dazed, she spun backwards out of the doorway and into the living-room.

An all-consuming desire to smash Charles Buchanan - his house - his whole fucking life - filled her mind. She picked up the empty champagne bottle from the floor and swung it against the glass front of the still-playing juke-box; it shattered like a car windscreen. The tiny cubes of glass cascaded over the spinning record and lifted the needle out of the grooves. The heavy based bottle stayed intact in her hand as she stood for a second, drained by the first wave of her onslaught.

In the bedroom Buchanan was debating whether to get up -

trying to work out what Sally had smashed. The girl in his bed seemed unworried by the whole affair. The sound of breaking glass seemed to have stopped - and he really didn't want to get involved in a shouting match or a full-blown fight.

He elected to stay where he was.

He shouted, "Get out of here, woman!" Then he began moving again in time with Nikki's motion.

Sally heard the animal cries beginning again, and with a howl of anguish she adjusted her grip on the Champagne bottle and hurled it at the French windows. It hit full-square in the middle of the pane and continued unslowed over the balcony and into the street, where she heard it smash a few seconds later. With tears filling her eyes she turned to run to the lift. After a couple of steps she tripped over something and fell headlong. It was his bunch of keys. She dragged herself back to her feet and hurled them through the hole the bottle had made in the window. As she collapsed into the lift she pounded the steel walls with her fists. There was no sorrow in the tears that filled her eyes - only anger and humiliation. She would make him pay for tonight. Somehow he was going to live to regret it.

In the bedroom the young girl heard the sound of the lift doors closing and slowed her motion.

"Anyone you know?" she asked casually.

"Not any more."

"Boy, was she ever pissed off! You better watch out, she's liable to turn you and your pecker into nothing more than pen-pals."

Downstairs in the lobby, Sally surveyed the wreckage of her face. Black trails ran from her eyes down her cheeks, her lipstick was smeared across her mouth. She spat on a tissue from her handbag and viciously wiped the make-up away. He had let her build a fantasy. When they first met she hadn't even liked him. But slowly he had chipped away at her resistance by sending her flowers and buying her candlelit meals.

Since puberty she had been saving herself, guarding her

virginity for her husband in an old-fashioned notion that that was the way it should be. When Charles had finally realized that there was no other way to persuade her to share his bed, he had promised to be that man.

She had felt so proud that after waiting so long, fearing that she might be passed by, left on the shelf, she had at last confounded the people who mocked her.

And for what?

To be faced with that ghastly sight.

Well, if he thought she would just walk away he was wrong.

Outside the road was covered with fragments of glass that sparkled in the glow of the streetlights. Her attention was caught by his keys in the middle of the debris. An idea flashed across her mind - she would steal his fucking keys! No. It wasn't enough. She wanted to cause him pain, not annoyance. It would be a start, though; she picked them up and looked around for somewhere to throw them. Her eyes settled on his Jaguar.

His Jaguar! What if he were to lose that?

The third key that she tried turned easily in the door of the Jaguar. Sally gave a furtive glance up to the lighted windows of the flat - there was no sign of any movement. She climbed in, adjusted the seat, and settled herself behind the wheel. Charles had consistently refused her requests to be allowed to drive, and even the starter motor beginning to turn gave her a rush of pleasure.

After a couple of mis-fires the twelve-cylinder engine lumbered into life. She selected first gear and let out the clutch. Nervously she moved away from the kerb towards the main road. By the time she reached Westbourne Park Road she was beginning to feel more comfortable at the controls. It wasn't until an oncoming car repeatedly flashed its main beam at her that she realized she had no idea which switch amongst the array in front of her controlled the Jaguar's lights. She pulled over to the side of the road and eventually found it. Full of renewed confidence she checked the mirror and set off again.

With no clear objective in mind, she simply stayed on a straight course until forced to turn. She had taken the car in the heat of her anger, but now she realized that she had no idea what to do next. There was no point in driving aimlessly around the city. What she wanted was for Charles to find the Jaguar wrecked; his precious car ripped apart by vandals.

But how was she to do it? If the Police became involved she wouldn't be able to make the journey to Antigua that her company had promised her. And that trip now offered her only chance to get away from him. Somehow she had to do it without leaving a trace. Even if it took her all night she was determined to think of a way.

Guided by a homing instinct, Sally drove on to the Marylebone Road heading towards Camden Town where she lived. She had been taken this way many times when Charles had dropped her off home on his way to the studio.

The studio! Another of his precious treasures.

She glanced down at the bunch of keys in the ignition. The curiously-shaped key to the burglar alarm was clearly visible. Now was her chance to find out what guilty secret he guarded so jealously inside the mews building. A voice inside her whispered, You bastard Buchanan! I'm going to make you squirm.

It was still only nine o'clock when she allowed the car to roll quietly to a standstill outside the deserted garage where the black mechanic worked. After opening the Studio doors and turning the alarm off, she moved the car inside and shut the doors behind her. No-one had observed her arrival. Inside, with the doors locked, she would be free to wreak havoc at will. She could almost taste the pleasure it was going to give her.

In darkness she felt her way up the narrow wooden staircase and at the top fumbled for the light switch. The sight that greeted her filled her with disappointment. The glaring flood lamps lit a tidy and business-like room. She was expecting to see perverted images on the walls and easels, or a bed for him to use to satisfy his sexual appetite. There was nothing unusual.

From across the room she suddenly noticed the distinctive shape of the Polaroid photographs on the wall over the desk. She remembered it from a time when he had brought the camera into the bedroom and, over her protests, taken pictures of her as they made love. He did have a guilty secret after all. She walked over to look at them more closely.

Again she was disappointed when she got near enough to see them. They were only photographs of paintings. The writing underneath meant nothing to her. She was about to walk away from the desk when two large flat packages on it caught her attention. They were wrapped in protective plastic but through it an image could be clearly seen. They were of a naked woman with her legs spread. She recognized it from the photographs on the walls. Viciously Sally ripped at the almost transparent covering until they were revealed in detail.

They were disgusting. He had made no attempt to show any beauty at all. The hard lines and bright flashes of color between the woman's legs made them almost pornographic. Also on the desk were several sheets of paper covered in writing, some of it in German - which made no sense to her. However, one piece did catch her attention. It was a name and address pinned to two photographs of the paintings. With her anger mounting again she read it,

Megan Copeland Watts, The former Rectory, Omblesthorpe,
Nr .Chipping Norton Oxon.tel: O555 8081

The whore! thought Sally, How could she parade herself like that? The rich bitch, didn't she think about the person she might be hurting? You couldn't pose like that without having slept with the man that did them. It showed in the paintings; they reeked of sex. All the pent up emotion of the evening flooded out as she picked up the receiver and dialed the number. After a while it was answered and a woman said,

"8081 - Megan Copeland-Watts speaking."

Sally was stunned for a moment. She had expected a younger voice. This woman sounded almost middle-aged. The words she had been preparing to scream dried on her tongue.

The silence was broken by the woman asking hopefully,

"Charles? Is that you? Charles?"

So it was true! The paintings must be of her. Sally launched herself into a torrent of abuse,

"You slut! You filthy bitch! YOU FUCKING COW!"

"Who is this? I'll call the Police," replied the shocked voice at the other end of the line.

"Don't threaten me. I've seen the pictures; I know about you. He thought if he kept them hidden I wouldn't find out. You fucking tramp. How could you pose for pictures like that?"

"I don't know who you are, but you must want to speak to somebody else. I have no idea what you're talking about. I have never posed for a painting in my life."

"Don't lie to me; he's written down your name and address."

"Look, who is this? And who is HE?"

"Charles Buchanan of course. And I'm his fiancé. At least I was until I caught him fucking another one of his tramps this evening."

Megan Copeland-Watts still didn't understand why she had been selected to be the subject of the abusive phone call, but she was beginning to want to find out. "What paintings are you talking about?" she asked.

"The ones he's got hidden in his studio. Don't keep pretending you know nothing about them. Your name was with them on his desk."

"I know nothing about posing, but I sold Mr Buchanan two paintings recently."

An icy chill spread over Sally. In her fury she hadn't even considered that possibility.

She stuttered, "You...did...what?"

"I sold Mr Buchanan two paintings."

"Oh, my God. Listen...I'm so sorry....I'm so sorry....I had no idea."

"It's quite all right. You sound terribly upset. Do you want to talk about it?" Megan was keen that this woman shouldn't hang up. She wanted to hear about Charles, and she was intrigued about the paintings.

Sally collapsed. Her anger had gone and all that remained was a strange hollow feeling. After a while she managed to pull herself together enough to speak, "I'm sorry, I'm really sorry."

"It's okay," said Megan sympathetically, "Tell me about it. You'll feel better when you've got it off your chest. And it'll be easier telling someone you don't even know."

The unseen woman sounded gentle, and Sally let it tumble out "I had to work late. You see I was the only one that could operate the telex machine. I was supposed to be going out for dinner with my boss - I just got promoted - but then they decided that they needed me to go to Antigua...I work in a Travel Agent's. You see, one of our representatives on the island broke her leg water-skiing, and we've got clients arriving next week. So they needed me to leave in a hurry. I was excited. I just wanted to tell Charles...."

Megan listened as Sally told her the story. Apart from providing answers as they were necessary to keep the account moving, she remained silent. The incident with the young girl came as no surprise to Megan. Already she knew that expecting to keep Charles Buchanan to yourself was a forlorn hope.

Quietly she listened as Sally described her desire to burn all memory of him: to destroy him and the things he cherished. Every word generated harmonies in her own mind. She wanted to share in this destruction. The paintings obviously formed part of a plan that was important to him. If she could get hold of them she would know what it was. And what to do.

As Sally reached the point in her story where she arrived at the studio and made the phone call Megan asked her,

"What are you going to do now?"

"I don't know. I don't know. What shall I do?"

"Maybe we should do something together."

"What do you mean?" asked Sally in amazement.

"I think those paintings in front of you are the same ones that he tricked from me."

"Tricked?"

"Yes. We had a deal: he promised to give me something I wanted very badly. But he was lying. I'm sure that if you were to take the paintings it would cause him a lot of distress."

"What did he promise to give you?"

"It's not important now. I just don't want him to keep them. I'd give anything to have them back."

"What about all this paperwork that's with them, the letters, the photographs and stuff? Are they yours too?"

The memory of Charles's final insulting request for her love-letters turned the knife in the wound of his departure. Megan could almost see the triumph in his eyes as she said sadly, "Yes. Those are mine too."

The prospect of hitting back at Buchanan made up Sally's mind. She asked,

"If I take them for you will it really hurt him?"

"I'm certain of it."

"I'll do it if you can make it up to London before the week-end is over. I'm going away on Monday. When he discovers them missing, he's bound to think it's me. I'd rather not have them with me too long. But I don't mind taking them home with me tonight."

Megan didn't even have to think about it. She said, "I can collect them from you early tomorrow morning. Will that be all right?"

"If you come about ten my mum will be doing the shopping. I don't want her to know what's happened yet. I'll tell you how to get to my house."

As Megan noted down the address, a thought occurred to

her. "Could you get his keys back to him without him knowing they were ever gone?" she asked.

"Possibly, why?"

"If they're missing he's bound to think it's you. Especially after your performance at his flat. On the other hand, if he still has them he won't know how the paintings were stolen. He might not even discover it until after you've left for Antigua."

"What about his car?" asked Sally.

"Same thing. If I was you I'd take it back. That way he can't connect you with anything. There's no reason on earth for you to take the paintings, and no way I could. Both of us will be in the clear. He'll be doubly annoyed at not being able to work out how they went."

"Yes, I see what you're saying. Okay, I'll drop the paintings off at home and then take the car back to Notting Hill. He'll probably be too busy with that bloody girl to notice me leaving the keys. It'll serve him right."

"I'll be up on the first train in the morning: I'll try and get there for ten. And Sally?"

"Yes?"

"I'm sorry it had to happen this way, but thank you."

"I hate him. If this hurts that bastard it's a pleasure. A real pleasure. I'll see you tomorrow. Good-bye Mrs Copeland-Watts, and thank YOU."

Sally hung up and rewrapped the paintings in the polythene sheeting. From on top of the rubbish bin she took a black plastic sack and filled it with all the papers and photographs from the desk, for good measure she added the ones from the wall as well. She took a cloth and wiped clean everything she had touched in the studio. If Charles did contact the Police they would have nothing on her. With the paintings and the sack safely in the boot, she drove the car out, reset the alarm and locked up the studio. The missing paintings were the solitary sign that anyone had been inside.

Friday was the night her mother went out for a drink with

the 'girls' from work, and Sally was glad that she didn't have to explain what she was doing with Charles's car as she dumped the stuff from the boot in her bedroom. There was no way she would be able to tell her mother about the grisly sight that had confronted her at his flat. She would start spouting, 'I told you so's' and 'isn't that just like a man for you's' at her. Sally could do without her words of wisdom tonight.

At the beginning of the Hampstead Road leading towards the Capital Radio building the Jaguar began to cough and splutter. The engine died and the car coasted to a halt. The only thing she could think of was that it had run out petrol. Luckily she was only about a hundred yards from a filling station.

She climbed out of the car and was about to set off walking when a Police car came around the corner, slowed and then stopped about fifty yards in front of the Jaguar. As it began reversing towards her she could feel her pulse accelerate. The car stopped tight up against the front of the Jaguar and a policeman climbed out. He put on his hat and walked slowly to where she was standing.

"What's up?" he asked affably, "Need any help?"

"I think it's just run out of petrol," she replied nervously.

"Got an emergency tank?"

"Emergency tank?" she echoed, "What do you mean."

"You know, a spare can in the boot."

"No. I don't know. You see it's my boyfriend's car. I'm just borrowing it."

"Trusting sort of bloke isn't he? Letting you loose with a motor like this? Believe you me, if I had one as clean as this my missus wouldn't get her hands on it. Here let me have a look in the back for you."

Before she could stop him he had taken the keys out of her hands and opened the boot. He rummaged about under the paintings until, with a shout of success, he emerged with a red metal can in his hands. He emptied the contents into the Jaguar's fuel tank and then sat for a couple of minutes pumping at the throttle while Sally looked on miserably. Finally he turned the key in the ignition. After a couple of false starts the engine roared into life.

"There you go. Nothing to it," he climbed out of the car, walked around it admiringly and patted the rear near-side wing of the car, "I'd fill up pretty soon if I were you. There wasn't much in the can. Drive safely, that's a lovely motor you're borrowing." He touched his cap in salute and climbed back into his car.

Sally's feeling of relief was spoiled by the Policeman's reminder of the quality of the car. Although the Copeland-Watts woman was getting her paintings back, she wasn't getting her chance to hurt Buchanan. Worse still she was going to have to put more bloody petrol in it. She drove the few yards to the garage and parked by the pump furthest from the kiosk.

She climbed out and went to the pump. Written on it in large red letters was the warning,

> "This dispenser contains
> diesel fuel oil. Do not use
> unless it is suitable for your
> vehicle. Incorrect usage can
> result in serious damage to
> your engine."

With a grim smile Sally opened the boot to obscure what she was doing from the attendant. She took the filler cap off the empty can and put a couple of pounds-worth of diesel in. Then she closed the boot, moved the car to the next pump and put a few liters of petrol in the car's tank. She walked over to the pay-desk. A young Greek was deep in conversation with his girlfriend in the booth.

He scarcely looked at her as he asked, "Two pounds of diesel and one of four star?"

"Yes. You see I had to fill up a can for the lawn mower," answered Sally unnecessarily.

"Listen Creamcheese. I don't care if you piss it all over the floor. Just so long as you pay for it." He laughed at his joke and looked at the girl beside him to check it had not gone unnoticed. She smiled dutifully.

Sally paid him and went back to the car. A few seconds later the Jaguar purred off the forecourt towards Notting Hill.

The space where the car had been parked was still empty when she arrived at the top of the road. She cut the engine and allowed the heavy vehicle to coast down the hill in silence. It wasn't a very good parking job, but it would have to do. There was no way she was going to restart the engine just to straighten it up.

In the quiet of the downstairs lobby to the flats she could clearly hear the pounding of her heart in her chest, and she was sure everyone else in the house could too. Buchanan's flat was also served by the staircase, but it was a route he never used. Sally knew the lift motor could be clearly heard from the bedroom so she inched her way up the stairs.

Outside the door she paused. She waited until she was certain there were no noises from the flat. After a couple of minutes, she turned the key in the lock and opened the door a crack. The room was exactly as she had left it. She crept into the room, placed the keys on the fake marble tiled floor and returned the way she had come.

The flat stayed silent.

# CHAPTER NINE

WITH THE MEMORY OF THE LATE NIGHT TELEPHONE CALL from Sally careering around her head, Megan slept badly for the second night running. The previous day, her devastation at Charles's unpleasant departure had kept her miserably in her bed, but now she was relieved to hear the early-morning bird-song and be able to give up the struggle to sleep. Her depression had been replaced by a feeling of optimism. All night she had been plotting ways to use the paintings to strike back at him.

She was curious to hear how her paintings had been confused with the nude studies his fiancée had described on the phone, and the journey to London was just what she needed to stop her brooding about her own situation. The young woman she had spoken to on the telephone the night before had obviously suffered far more from Buchanan's callousness than she had. It was going to be interesting to meet the woman he had apparently offered to marry.

From the mahogany wardrobe in her bedroom she very carefully chose the clothes she was going to wear. The image she was going to project today was going to be totally different from the one she had chosen for Charles. Sally would meet a woman who presented no threat - the navy Guernsey sweater and pleated Jaeger skirt made Megan look like Buchanan's mother, not his lover. The last thing she wanted to do was to plant seeds of suspicion in the mind of the girl who had presented herself as an unexpected ally in her search for revenge. For the same reasons she applied the minimum of make-up, and scraped her hair back into a stark ponytail: she would not have looked out of place on the committee of the local Women's Institute.

In the kitchen, the untouched, cooked and shriveled carcasses of the grouse still sat in the roasting pan - a reminder of her last meeting with Charles. After gazing at them while she drank her morning coffee and ate a piece of whole-meal toast, she dumped them unceremoniously into the bin.

With them out of the way, she felt the decks were cleared for action. She could begin her battle to extract some satisfaction, even if there was no comfort to be had, from her encounter with Charles Buchanan. If and when he came to her to inquire about the paintings, he would find a very different woman from the one he had left behind. Now she was filled with a desire to regain her pride and tattered self-esteem. His charm and polish would run from her resolve like rain from a roof.

At nine thirty, when her train arrived at Paddington, the station was already ringing to the roars of football supporters waiting for a train to Cardiff. There was a constant stream of aggressive-looking young men emerging from the Tube, so Megan joined the queue for a taxi. When her turn came, she gave Sally's address to the cab-driver and settled back in the black leather seat.

The house that corresponded to the address she had written down was in fact a two-storey maisonette above the offices of a small shopfitting firm. The building had obviously been built in the post-war years of austerity. Faced with machine-made Fletton bricks and small metal framed windows, it had little to commend it architecturally. Heavy goods vehicles and busses thundered by constantly within twenty yards of where she stood waiting for a response to her knock on the front door.

The unremarkable young woman who answered the door did little to solve a riddle that was bothering Megan: what had attracted Buchanan to this woman? Why had he made such an effort to woo this particular girl?

In the dark hallway Megan caught a flash of light from Sally's eyes, but nothing else made her memorable in any obvious way. Even after such a brief meeting Megan could tell Sally's hold was not due to great beauty or wealth. And from what Sally had told her about the reluctant surrender of her virginity it had not been sex. Puzzled she followed her up the brightly patterned carpet on the staircase.

The inside of the flat reminded Megan of the set for a television situation comedy or soap opera. She was ashamed to admit that she had never known real people actually lived like this. The tiny living room where Sally offered her a seat was crammed with furniture. A floral fringed sofa and matching armchairs, brown stained sideboard with brassy knobs, and melamine dining suite took up so much of the room that moving around it was accomplished only with caution. What little of the floor could be seen was covered with the same orange and green swirled carpet as the stairs.

For a second or two, Megan sat perched on the edge of one of the armchairs while Sally made coffee in the kitchen, but as she waited she could feel herself relaxing: she settled back into the cushions and let a feeling of warmth spread through her. The room was not as she would have had it, but that seemed unimportant. It was definitely home. All around the room on every flat surface sat framed photographs of gawky children and serious looking adults. There were holiday snaps of a young couple and a girl with pig-tails - windswept on a deserted beach. Generations of the family were remembered every day. Nothing in the room was chosen because it was tasteful: everything contributed to cheering up an otherwise bleak environment.

Sally reappeared with two brown earthenware mugs of steaming hot coffee. A brief, awkward, silence was broken by Sally asking politely,

"You found us alright then?"

"Yes. I just gave your address to the taxi driver."

"It's a bit different from your house I expect."

"Just a little...but it's lovely....there's a lot more traffic outside," said Megan after a pause when she searched for something to say which would not sound snobbish.

"You get used to the noise. I hardly notice it. Sometimes when I go away on holiday, I miss it."

"I suppose you would. Did you get the car back okay last night?"

"Yes," replied Sally without further comment. She wanted to keep her act of sabotage as a personal triumph. "I left the keys where I found them."

"And he didn't notice you?"

"I think he was too busy," said Sally heavily.

"I'm so sorry for you. It must have been a terrible shock. How long had you been engaged?"

"He never bought me a ring or anything. It wasn't really official. But I told him the first man I slept with was going to be my husband. He told me 'in that case we'd better get married.' I believed him. You see until last night I never had any reason not to. He had always been the perfect gentleman before."

The reminder of Charles's easy promises prodded the sore he had rubbed on Megan's emotions. She chewed at the inside of her lip as Sally continued.

"I hardly noticed him when he first came into the office, but everyone else commented on the way he looked at me."

"What do you mean?"

"They said he seemed to know me already, but I'd never clapped eyes on him in my life. And now I wish I never had."

"Was that how you first met him? He just walked into the place where you worked?"

"Yes. He came to book a flight: to Germany, I think. After that he just kept coming back. He'd send me flowers and take me out for dinner: nothing was too much trouble. He said I reminded him of his dream woman. That pissed me off to start with. I mean it's not good to be told that you're just like somebody else at the best of times, and when it's your first lover it's even worse. I didn't much care for just reminding him of someone else and I told him so. So then he reckoned that it wasn't a real person - just some kind of fantasy he had. I think that's half his trouble; he can't tell the difference between fantasy and reality.

"Even that job of his wasn't like real work. I mean he didn't have to get up every morning and be somewhere at a certain time, did he? He just swanned around buying stuff here and selling it there. If we'd got married I'd have changed all that. Nothing comes that easily, does it? You've got to work at it, haven't you?"

Megan, who had never been out to work apart from the few days she spent as a teenage volunteer making tea for the troops - when she met Peter Copeland-Watts - nodded blankly in agreement. Then she felt inexplicably guilty about the deceit, and she owned up,

"Actually, my parents never let me go out to work when I was young, and then I got married. But I'm sure you're right."

"You haven't missed much. Most of the time it's just dead boring. We needed the money, so Mum got me a job at the office where she worked."

"What does she do?"

"She's a cleaner."

"What about your Father?"

"Dad's dead."

"Oh I'm so sorry."

"Don't worry. Mum used to say that dropping dead was

just about the best day's work he ever did." Sally laughed bitterly, "Still, that's enough gossip about me. Do you want to see your paintings?"

"Yes, please."

Sally negotiated her way past the sofa and picked up a sack from under the table. She set it down in front of Megan and slid out the two packages.

When Megan uncovered them it was all she could do to stifle a gasp of amazement. Even as a part-time painter she recognized Schiele and his work. She ran her hand reverentially over the paintwork.

From a great distance she heard Sally saying,

"I can understand why you wanted to sell them. They're not exactly the sort of thing you'd want on your living-room wall are they?"

"No, maybe not. But they're very precious all the same. Did you say there was some paperwork as well?"

"I shoved everything in the bag."

Megan wanted to have a few moments on her own, so she drained the last lukewarm dregs from her cup and asked,

"Is there any more coffee? That was just what I needed."

"Sure, I'll make us some more, it won't take a second," replied Sally, picking up the cup and disappearing with it through the door to the kitchen.

The instant she was out of the room Megan burrowed in the sack. The transformation that had taken place in the paintings was explained to her within minutes of opening a cardboard file marked with her name. Inside it were a dozen photographs of the stages involved in the process of changing the scruffy impressionistic landscapes to the glowing figure studies. Also in the file were her love-letters and Oscar Morganstein's report on the work he had done during the restoration. She had just finished reading it when Sally came back into the room.

"I hope I picked up everything. Does it look as if it's all there?"

"Oh yes," said Megan brightly, "It's all here. Did you have a look through all this?"

"I had a quick gander at it last night, but I couldn't make head or tail of it. There's a whole load of stuff written in German, and then the photographs didn't seem to make sense. It looked to me like there were four paintings, not just two. But then I never could understand modern Art. I still don't see how a load of old bricks could be worth thousands of pounds. And I really tried to understand it when there was all the fuss in the papers. Sill, I like the paintings Charles usually sells, the ones of real people. But those ones are a bit rude for me."

While she was speaking Megan pushed everything back into the sack. Now she knew Buchanan's secret she wanted to spread everything out on the floor and go through it properly.

There was no point in involving Sally, was there? Besides, she was leaving for the West Indies on Monday, and that would be the end of her involvement with Buchanan, wouldn't it? All in all, surely it would be kinder to let her forget about the whole thing?

Megan drained the cup and stood up.

"I'd better be going. Thank you for the paintings. I can't tell you how pleased I am to have them back."

"Will he miss them?"

"Don't worry about that. He'll miss them more than you ever dreamed."

"I'm glad. I just want to get away now and forget about him. I've got the rest of my life to think about. I think that Mr Charles Bloody Buchanan has done enough damage already. I don't suppose we'll meet again, will we?"

"Nothing is impossible. Maybe we will. Have a good time in the West Indies. When do you leave?"

"Monday night at ten. Here, I'll give you a hand down the stairs with it all."

She helped Megan negotiate her way round the furniture, and in the doorway the two women hugged each other before saying their good-byes.

Megan carried the precious sack out into the street and surveyed the passing rush of traffic for a black cab. When one finally stopped, the flat-capped driver leaned over and said through the open window,

"All right darling? Wotcha doing? Running away from your old man? I'll bet you're still spending his money, though. Here, d'you want any help with that bag?"

"No, thank you. I can manage." While she settled herself, the driver turned and slid open the glass partition that separated him from his passengers.

"Where to, love?" he asked.

"Would you go to Oxford?"

"Oxford Street or Oxford?"

"Just outside Oxford actually. It's a village called Omblesthorpe."

"Christ! Look, I'll go there, sweetheart, but it'll cost you. It could be as much as thirty or forty quid. You'd be better off if I took you to Paddington. The quick train's only one stop."

"I've had a bit of luck. I don't want you to take me if you don't want to. But if you do there's a twenty pound tip in it for you. Do you want me to pay you before we go?"

"Keep your money in your bin, love. I trust you. You don't exactly look the type to go running about ripping people off. As it happens, I quite fancy a run into the sticks. It's better than fighting your way through this bloody lot all day. Now settle back and enjoy the ride."

# CHAPTER TEN

IN BUCHANAN'S DREAM THE TELEPHONE SEEMED to have been ringing for days, and he was desperately searching through the streets of London for the source of the noise to answer it. Somehow he was sure that it was Morganstein calling him to represent his offer for the Schiele's. He had to pick up the receiver before Frank Price - who was trying to get there first and tell Morganstein they were fakes. Buchanan leaned his head out of the window of the Jaguar (which was now swooping low over the Westway like a helicopter). With a sudden flash of insight he knew where the phone was hidden: it was in Oxfordshire at Megan Copeland-Watts' house. He banked the Jaguar away from the city and flew it at full speed out across the suburbs. With his head out of the window the bell could be clearly heard getting louder and louder. When her Georgian house came into view, he saw Megan through her bedroom window trying to stifle the noise by hiding the receiver under the pillows on her bed. He skidded the Jaguar to a halt on the driveway, jumped out and smashed the drawing room window to get into the house. As he climbed through the broken glass he saw Frank Price running at colossal speed across the lawns. He knew it was Frank Price, even though he had never met the man, because the speed of his running was due to the extra propulsion generated by a huge penis that was acting like a third leg.

With every step Buchanan took towards the stairs, the air around him seemed to be getting thicker until, as he crossed the bedroom, it was the consistency of molasses and every movement was an effort. With a silent shout of triumph he pushed Megan away and reached under the pillow.

THERE WAS NOTHING THERE....

The frantic search under the pillow slowly ceased to be part of his dream and became part of waking reality. Buchanan was reassuring himself that the telephone was, of course, in the living room when he realized that the ringing bell was refusing to stop with the end of his dream.

*Morganstein!*

Instantly, he snapped into a state of full alertness and jumped out of bed. Without stopping to gather a dressing gown or trousers, he ran out of the bedroom. He careered towards the phone and halfway across the room he felt a searing pain in his right foot. Cursing he hopped the last few meters. He actually had his hand on the receiver when it clicked into silence.

He roared at the empty room and collapsed into the seating area to inspect his foot. A razor-sharp shard of glass about an inch and a half long stuck out from his instep near his heel. Gingerly he pulled at it. The instant he did, a little geyser of blood welled up from the wound, ran down his heel and dripped onto the floor. He looked around for something to staunch the flow. It was at this point he noticed the reason for the glass on the floor and remembered the previous evening.

Around the still spinning deck of the juke box was heaped all that remained of its toughened glass cover. As he surveyed the wreckage he became aware of the chill wind that was blowing through the room and looked around for the open window. Shivering with a mixture of cold and anger he finally realized that one of the French windows had no glass left in it.

Under his breath he muttered, "Bloody Hell! What a shambles."

The flow of blood from his foot showed no signs of slowing, and a puddle was forming on the floor. Pressing his thumb over the wound, he began hopping his way back across the room. He was almost at the bathroom door when the phone began ringing again. He spun round and, ignoring the discomfort, ran around the carpet of broken glass to the phone - leaving behind him a clear trail of bloody footprints.

He snatched the receiver from the cradle and said anxiously, "Morganstein?"

"So you still haven't heard from him?" answered Cordelia Babbington. "Where the devil have you been? I rang a couple of minutes ago and let the phone ring and ring."

"I was asleep. Is this important Cordelia? I'm bleeding like a stuck pig and I'm stark naked. Can I call you back?"

"Asleep? Bleeding? Naked? God, you're a dark horse, Charles. Is it a private party? I know it's just gone noon, but it might be fun."

"Cordelia, I'm not in the mood. What do you want?"

"No? Oh well, listen, I just rang to find out if you wanted to come with Frank and me to a drinks party tonight at Max and Irene Carver's?"

"Carver? Carver? You mean the wood butcher? Are you serious? You know perfectly well that I hate the man. At this precise moment in time it sounds like my idea of hell, but thank you for asking. If my dentist can't fit me in for some late-night root-canal work I'll let you know."

"Max Carver is not a wood butcher, Charles. He is a fine sculptor."

"In my book anybody that can spend ten years hacking and bashing at lumps of driftwood and then have the nerve to call them by the title...What does he call them all?...Oh yes, 'Surreal

Amorphous Objet Numero-whatever', must be a bit of a berk, Cordelia. Come on, you know I haven't got any time for him, or that lanky wife of his."

"Fine, I get the message. It's just that Frank tells me that Morganstein is going to be there."

"Oh Jesus-bloody-Christ! In that case I'd love to. Are you going too?"

"Yes, Frank and I are both going. We're meeting at the gallery at eight. Can you pick us up?"

"Okay. I'll see you at eight."

Buchanan put the phone down and looked around him at the room. With the addition of the bloodstains to the floor, it now resembled the aftermath of a bomb-blast. He telephoned Mrs Higgins, his daily.

"Hello Mrs Higgins. It's Charles Buchanan here."

"Oh, Hello Mr B.," she said. She instantly went on the defensive, "I was going to do the bathroom, but I was short of time, so I just did the kitchen and bedroom like usual. What's the matter?"

"Nothing, nothing at all, I was just wondering if there was any chance you could pop round today?"

"On a Saturday...whatever for? I'm just settling down to watch the wrestling, and then I'll have to get my Paddy his supper."

"I had a bit of a disagreement last night and the place needs sorting out. You know I'm no good at this sort of thing; I really don't know where to start."

"I've just put my feet up."

"There's an extra twenty pounds if you do come, Mrs Higgins, it needs your magic touch. You can always put the wrestling on round here and watch it as you go."

"Oh all right Mr B. I'll be round in half an hour."

Irritated that he'd had to go cap in hand to the damn woman, but relieved that she was coming, Buchanan switched on the answerphone back on to assure himself of some peace and hobbled away to get dressed.

In the kitchen he waited blankly for the expresso machine to gurgle into life. A thick creamy cappuccino would help to settle his rumbling stomach. He watched the fresh coffee bubbling out of the nozzle and then began to rummage in the fridge for some milk: he knew there were two unopened bottles left from yesterday. The discovery of both bottles empty on the table where Nikki had left them after drinking the contents was almost the final straw. He went to the lift, picking up his keys from where they lay on the floor on the way, and punched the down button. Thankfully the milkman had already been.

In the downstairs lobby he stood with the cold bottle tucked under one arm while he sorted through the pile of post. There were just three items for him: a letter from his bank, his telephone bill and a reminder from his insurance company to renew the cover on the car. He saved the letter from the bank to read with his coffee.

It was brief and to the point,

*Dear Mr Buchanan,*

*I feel you should be advised that following your withdrawal today of two hundred pounds the balance in your current account is now £22,178.85 overdrawn. This exceeds the present overdraft limit on your current account of £20,000.*

*There is now only £13.00 remaining in your deposit account, and so we are unable to transfer sufficient funds to clear the end of month deficit as agreed.*

*May we also take this opportunity to remind you that we have still not received August or September's payment on your mortgage as there were insufficient funds to make the standing order debits.*

*Whilst we are aware that Romulus Fine Art has £44,035.84 at present in its trading account, and that you are the sole director, we are unable to cover your other debts to the bank from this account without your authorization. Would you please call my clerk, Mr Batchelor, as soon as possible to arrange a meeting to discuss your present financial position.*

*Yours faithfully,*

*J.Dempsey. Manager.*

Buchanan was furious with himself that his cavalier attitude to Morganstein had resulted in this unpleasant reminder of his shortage of cash. All in all, with a final demand from the Inland Revenue for £8000, a rates bill of nearly £2000, and the outstanding mortgage payments on the flat...

The truth was this: he badly needed the money. And even though he might be able to stall the bank for a while, he needed it soon.

If only he had accepted the offer when it was on the table yesterday. It didn't look like he had any option: it looked like he was going to have to accompany Cordelia and Frank to the Carver's house. Maybe the 'chance' meeting with Morganstein would do the trick?

# CHAPTER ELEVEN

HALF AN HOUR AFTER THE LONDON CAB DRIVER pocketed his tip and left, Megan stood at the window of her studio gazing blankly out over the conservatory roof to the recently-harvested wheatfields beyond. The distant blast of a shotgun startled a rabbit that was quietly grazing in the long grass at the base of the adjoining hedgerow, and a nearby flock of crows beat their way into the sky. The sudden flurry of activity broke Megan's unfocused stare.

She looked down at the rings on her hand, the engagement ring and the plain gold wedding band, and twisted them on her finger with her thumb. Another wave of anger rose inside her. It caused pain, real physical pain, in her chest. She leaned forward and let her forehead rest on the glass until it had passed.

After a couple of minutes, she turned to face the room, resting against the window-sill. Spread out on the floor were the contents of the bag she had collected from London: the two canvasses, the letters, photographs and the file bearing her name.

She picked up one of the canvasses and held it in her hands.

"It was all to do with this?" she asked the empty room. "Was there nothing else?"

Even though the room stayed silent, she heard the answer ring out clearly.

She put the painting down again and said quietly, "Well, do you know what I'm going to do? Charles Buchanan, wherever you are, I'm going to crush you like a cockroach. It's what I'm going to do. Thanks to you, I now know how much I hate being on my own...and how much I hate getting old....and it's all your fault. I'm going to bring you crashing down."

Megan pushed herself away from the wall with her hands as if launching a boat, and glided across the room. At the door, she turned and tried to see the studio dispassionately. It was impossible. There was no way to see the paint spattered easels, the battered furniture which had made the final journey to the studio as a reprieve from being burned by the gardener, without seeing her husband struggling alone up the stairs with the chaise longue - red faced, eyes bulging and loudly insisting he could manage. If she caught the smell of raw turpentine anywhere she was instantly transported back to this room.

These illusions and memories were as real to her as the walls themselves. A reality that was uniquely hers, because no matter how well she explained it, it could never be as complete as her memory.

She trailed her fingertips along the wall, through the door frame and began descending the stairs. There were memories in everything. On the half landing she stopped by a pair of paintings bought on a trip to London. A small Nash landscape and a Wyndham-Lewis watercolor of the First World War. With her finger she traced the line of the hills and the copse of trees that sat on the crest. It wasn't like a photograph of a view of a valley, it was far more. It was more because there was life and there was Art. And there were the impossibly-complex interconnections between them.

During his illness, Major Copeland-Watts had often sat holding the painting: trapped in his body and his room - and yet, at the same time, he was in the Oxfordshire countryside as certainly as a hiker ten miles out of Chipping Norton.

Megan turned away from the picture and thought about his illness as she descended the stairs - the degeneration of his brain that somehow happened three decades before it should have - the quirk of biology that stole the man she married, and left in his place a shadow that dribbled, swore and urinated in the bed.

And, above all, she thought about the long slow wait for his body to reach the point of death - a body she had known for seven years before he became ill. Even to the empty house she didn't speak the thought she was hiding at the back of her mind. Peter's lovemaking was...well, genuine enough, but it was boring. God help her for thinking it, but the truth was that it was boring. With Charles she felt sensations and desires that frightened her they felt so good.

She was glad she had lived through the empty years of her husband's illness with only the memory of his uncomplicated lovemaking, and without the confusion of emotions generated by Buchanan's. Armed with that knowledge, she suspected she would not have managed to stay faithful.

How was she to deal with the rest of her life now that she knew what she was missing? Now that she knew the truth about Buchanan? And now that she knew why he had courted her?

With the paintings, the photographs and the forged letters she had enough evidence to take to the Police, or even to Morganstein. Either way would finish Buchanan for ever in the Art World. It would be impossible for a Dealer or Collector to be seen even talking to him.

But...

It was easy: one phone call leading to one meeting, and that would be the end of it.

No...it was too easy. It would be over too quickly.

An idea began to form: the beginnings of a plan to make

him regret the day he lost the paintings - as much as she was going to regret the day he walked away from her. If she had her way, he would regret it for the rest of his life. She picked up the telephone.

Less than an hour later she watched Bill Montague, the Copeland-Watts family solicitor, lever himself out of his battered Alvis and struggle towards the front door. He was a small man, barely five feet nine tall, and the hand that grasped the cane he used to help him walk was so thin and weather-beaten that it seemed like a twisted root growing from the wood of the cane itself. She knew his healthy color was the result of a division of the time since his retirement between the stands of one race course or another and his office. Arthritis caused him pain in all his joints, and he moved slowly and deliberately. In contrast to his body, his mind was unimpaired by age and, in fact, he frequently displayed a mental agility that left younger men floundering. He was the great-grandson of Hamish Montague, who had established the business.

Peter Copeland-Watts, used to dealing with the elder Montague - and despite being less than ten years older - had always referred to Bill as 'the Montague boy'. However, as Megan opened the door to the white-haired old man helping himself with his walking stick up the couple of steps to the threshold, it was difficult for her to think of him as a child.

Montague paused for a moment, leaned on his cane and said,

"I think if I'd been able to see myself gasping for breath while you stood and watched, you know, back when Peter first introduced me to his heavenly young bride, I'd have borrowed his shotgun and taken the top off my head. The indignity of age, Megan. The damnable indignity of it all." He finally got his breath back and continued, "Well, young lady, are you going to keep me hanging about out here all day, or are you going to invite me in?"

Five minutes later Montague was seated in the library with

a heavy tumbler containing a club measure of barely diluted Whisky in his hand. After taking a couple of swallows from the glass, and exchanging the customary polite remarks about health and the weather, he sat back in the leather arm-chair and asked,

"Why all the secrecy and panic, Megan? What is so important that I've had to drag myself all the way out here on a Saturday? Not that it isn't a delight to see you, of course."

Since her phone call she had been planning what she was going to say to him, but she didn't expect to have an easy time explaining herself. She had been unable to think of a delicate way of phrasing what she had in mind so she launched straight into it. "What would you say if I said I wanted to blackmail someone?"

Apart from an extra large gulp of Scotch, Montague showed no more surprise than he would have done if she had told him that Thursday was the day that followed Wednesday. He stared deep into his glass and asked calmly,

"Anyone I know?"

"No."

"Well, I suppose that's something in these hard times. Listen, before you tell me any more and make things complicated, you do know, of course, that blackmail is illegal?"

"Of course."

"Fine. It was just a thought. Fire away then. Why do you want me?"

"Because the kind of blackmail I have in mind is slightly different from the usual sort. Normally, if I was to blackmail you for instance, I would know something about you, that you didn't want anyone else to know. That's the first step?" She paused for reassurance before continuing, "Then I would ask you for a large amount of money not to tell anybody else what I know. That's how it works, isn't it?"

"Normally, yes."

"Well, what if you knew that somebody had found out your

guilty secret but you didn't know who it was?"

"I'd know when they asked me for the money, wouldn't I?"

"Not if they didn't ask you for money either."

"Megan, I pride myself on being fairly sharp - even in my dotage, but you aren't making an awful lot of sense."

"Let me show you something. It will make things clearer. If you stay here I'll bring everything in."

While she was out of the room Montague drained his glass and refilled it from the decanter Megan had thoughtfully left on the table next to him. He held the cut glass tumbler up to the light and squinted through it as if searching for a clue in the reflections.

Within half an hour he was well on his way to grasping the thrust of Megan's scheme. His brain, which had been more or less idle since his retirement, now flared back into life. Before long, as the two of them pored over the paintings, photographs and letters spread out on the floor, he had begun to refine her clumsy plan for revenge into a viable and intricate operation. He would have to do a lot of research very rapidly, both in the Art World and the Legal, but he was looking forward to it.

Two hours later, acting on her lawyer's advice, and shortly after she had watched him steer the old Alvis up the drive, Megan lifted the telephone from the cradle and dialed 192 for the directory inquiry service.

The operator finally answered and asked, "Which town do your require? And what name?"

"London, please. Morganstein, Oscar Morganstein picture restorer."

After a brief pause, the operator gave her the number, and she dialed it. It rang several times before being answered in a mid-European accent.

Megan asked cautiously, "Mr Morganstein?"

"I don't work week-ends. You'll have to call back on Monday."

"Please don't hang up. I just want some information about

two paintings you appraised."

"Which paintings?"

"Two studies by Egon Schiele. You gave them both the provisional title *'Liegender Weiblicher Akt mit Gespreitzen Beinen'*."

"Who is this calling?"

"You don't know me. I'm calling on behalf of the present owner."

"How do you know about these paintings?"

"I have them here. My client wants to know where they should be sold."

"What about Charles Buchanan, if I may ask? Does he still have control of the pictures?"

"No, I have total control."

"Charles Buchanan has nothing to do with them at all?"

"Believe me, Mr Morganstein. Mr Buchanan is no longer involved."

"Well......depending on the price, I could possibly arrange a sale for you."

"Would there be much publicity?"

"No, none at all. It would be a matter solely between ourselves."

"That's no good. My client wants the maximum of publicity."

"I don't understand you. One minute you want to be anonymous and the next you want T.V. coverage. Is this some kind of joke. How do you know about these paintings?"

"Mr Morganstein, this is no joke, believe me. We have the paintings and want to sell them as publicly as possible, but we want to keep our client's identity a secret. Can you arrange it? I'll be happy to pay you a percentage of the final sale price."

"What percentage?"

"I don't know. Maybe ten percent."

"Wait a moment, I want to get this clear. You will pay me ten percent of the final price just to protect your client's identity?"

"...and to ensure that everyone from Mexico City to Milan knows when the sale is going to take place."

"If you sell at auction you will have to pay a seller's commission. You will have to pay this as well as my fee. Are you aware of this?"

"Of course. I will pay your ten percent and the auction house's commission."

"But why?"

"What do you mean?"

"Why do you need me? All the major auction houses will help you to sell anonymously."

"Mr Morganstein, you are in a position to affect the value these paintings fetch enormously. I want it to be in your best interests that they sell for as much as possible. I don't want you to appear on the eve of the sale with doubts about their authenticity."

"I'm curious how much you gave Mr Buchanan for them. He wouldn't sell to me for a hundred thousand. Even with my strongest representation these two paintings may not fetch as much as that at auction. Privately they could fetch much more if the sale is presented in the right way to the right client. I think I can arrange it. At auction you only need one powerful voice to start casting doubts about their authenticity and the price will tumble. You might very well be selling at a loss on what you have paid Mr Buchanan already."

"With two paintings of this quality I doubt it."

"Pouf! In the Art World anything is possible."

"Look, I'm prepared to take a chance. What I want to know from you is can you arrange it for us. and would it possible to talk to you in person tomorrow?"

There was the briefest pause and then the accented voice said, "Of course."

"Thank you Mr Morganstein. My lawyer will be in touch with you later to arrange the details."

Megan hung up, and for the first time since she opened the sack and saw the paintings she felt relaxed.

She selected a tall tumbler from the glass cabinet in the drawing room, carried it into the kitchen, filled it with ice from the freezer, poured a generous amount of gin over the top, enjoyed the splintering and cracking of the ice, dropped in a sliver of lemon and topped it up with tonic water. Carrying the glass carefully in one hand, she opened the door to the conservatory with the other and went in. Amongst the rakes, hoes, and lawn mowers were a pair of wicker chairs.

Megan lifted a box of daffodil bulbs from one and brushed the seat clean of cobwebs. She settled herself in the chair, with her feet on the chest containing the croquet hoops and mallets, and her gin and tonic on a cast-iron table at her side. Taking a deep swallow she said out loud,

"You know," she paused for a moment. "Your bad luck, Charles Buchanan, you smooth talking little spiv, is that, contrary to what you might have expected, I'm not just going to lie down and die. I'm going to make you pay for the empty years I've had, and all the empty years ahead."

# CHAPTER TWELVE

BUCHANAN ARRIVED OUTSIDE THE GALLERY five minutes before eight. Frank and Cordelia were sitting on one side of the secretary's desk with glasses of wine in front of them. Frank was wearing a trilby hat and sitting in a pool of light cast by the downlighters concealed in the ceiling. From the car outside they looked like the couple sitting at the counter of the diner in Edward Hopper's painting 'Nighthawks': isolated, almost in a separate universe from the street outside, cut off by the sheet of glass in the gallery window.

After watching them for a couple of moments Buchanan hobbled over to knock on the door. Both Cordelia and Frank were startled into action by the noise. They finished their drinks and joined him in the street.

Cordelia noticed his lined face and his labored walk back to the car, and as they drove away she asked,

"Charles, I'm dying to know. What *did* you get up to last night?"

"If I told you I had a quiet evening at home, you probably wouldn't believe me, would you?"

"No. You look terrible. Doesn't he look terrible, Frank?"

"I wouldn't know," answered Frank noncommittally.

"As a matter of fact, I feel terrible," he snapped irritably.

"There, does that make you feel better, Cordelia?"

"You don't have to come, you know. I don't want you being miserable all night. Now's the time to bail out if you want to."

"What, bail out and miss my chance of meeting Morganstein? You must be joking. He is definitely going to be there, isn't he?"

"He never misses free booze, and I overheard him telling Nares all about it. They'll be there all right," answered Frank firmly.

Buchanan drove through to Piccadilly, across the Circus and down the Haymarket. The early evening rush of theater-going traffic had finished by now and they were soon cruising along Whitehall towards the river.

As they drove over Westminster Bridge, Buchanan turned in his seat and spoke to Frank, "Cordelia tells me you don't share Morganstein's and Nares's enthusiasm for the Schiele's."

"I guess. I'm just not quite so carried away as they are."

"Why's that?"

"Oh, several reasons."

"Like what for instance?"

"Well, for one thing I don't know of any other examples of Schiele making studies in oil on canvas at that point in his career. He was so short of materials that most of his preparatory work was done in watercolor or drawings. For another, the treatment of the bedclothes is out of period. I know that later on he used to make fabric look almost alive by the way he built up swirls of color, but I don't think that was until about 1914. I may be wrong, but they just don't have the proper feel. I can't put it into words."

"What about all the paperwork that supports them? Doesn't that weaken your argument?"

"No. I think it's just a smokescreen."

"What do you mean?" said Buchanan nervously.

"It's too neat, too tidy. Nowhere does it come out and say, these paintings are the work of Egon Schiele. It's all left to you to read it into what it does say. That's why I think it's so clever. Anyone who knows about painting will make the connections for themselves. Look," he leaned over the back of the passenger's seat, "First, there's the hint about the exhibition in 1911. Everybody knows how important the show at Klammer's gallery was to Schiele: his first successful show outside Vienna. Secondly the guff about them being a present from the artist: that doesn't make sense. Schiele had already been selling work for a couple of years; he wasn't about to start giving away canvasses - not when he was so short of money he couldn't afford to buy new ones. It's true everything changed at the end of the year, and I accept it's possible that they date from the autumn or winter. I don't know, the whole thing is too perfect. I think that the guy that left them with his landlady was interrupted by the Nazis in the middle of a scam. I reckon it could have been someone doing a Han van Meegeren. You know, that guy that got arrested for selling Vermeer's to the occupying Germans? The one who had really been ripping them off by painting them himself? Just because Schiele's work was banned it doesn't mean to say it wasn't collected by the Nazi's. You've got to admit it's possible, even though you've got a lot to lose. What do you REALLY think, Mr Buchanan?"

"Well, what you say makes sense, but I can't believe anyone could forge his style so convincingly. As soon as I saw them, I thought they were genuine Schiele's."

"Yeah, well...there isn't much point in a forgery unless you do. Personally, I think you've accidentally stumbled on a forty-year-old plan to fool the Nazi's into buying fake pictures. The guy that set it all up must have been stuck into one of those camps before he completed the sale. What is amazing is your hunch about the pictures in the first place. That, plus the fact that you didn't give up when you saw that they were dull old landscapes. Most people would never have taken them to someone like Morganstein. But you did, and suddenly - Hey Presto! He finds two paintings underneath. You WANTED them to be something special, so you believe in them. For your sake I hope I'm wrong, but I still don't think I am."

"Well, time will..."

The car hiccuped and juddered.

"Damn, we're out of petrol," said Buchanan. "Don't worry, there's enough in the spare can to get us to a garage."

He climbed out, took the red metal container from the boot, and emptied it into the car's fuel tank. For several minutes he turned the engine over.

The huge twelve-cylinder engine spluttered, back-fired, and finally ground to a halt. It resisted all his efforts to coax it back into life. With every turn on the starter the engine sounded worse and worse. Finally he gave up and turned to Cordelia and Frank.

"Cordelia, if you sit behind the wheel and steer, Frank and I can try and push it off the main road into a sidestreet. I'm afraid it looks as if we'll have to go on by taxi."

"Charles, I hope this isn't an omen for the success of the evening. What's wrong with the damn thing anyway?"

"I haven't got a clue. I'll try and get Wesley to come and sort it out. He'll possibly still be in the garage. Let's try and get it off the main road, and I'll find a phone."

The two men struggled to heave the heavy car up a slight incline and around the first corner into a narrow side street.

As Cordelia pulled on the handbrake, they exchanged glances. The two parked cars nearest to the Jaguar were propped up on bricks where the wheels had been stolen. Further down the street a cluster of youngsters were busy hurling rocks at the remaining fragments of glass in the windows of a derelict house. Frank shrugged his shoulders as if to say, what option do we have? Buchanan kicked at a can in the road and said angrily,

"That's just what I need. I could have broken down five minutes ago and left the sodding car outside number ten sodding Downing Street. But, is that what happens to me? No -

I break down in what the bloody Prime Minister refers to as a sodding deprived-inner-city-sodding-area. It's a fucking car graveyard! You two stay here, I'll see if I can find a phone."

While Frank rejoined Cordelia inside the Jaguar, Buchanan went into the nearest pub to call his mechanic. Wesley listened in horror as Buchanan described where the broken down car was parked. He offered to come and collect it straight away; Buchanan happily agreed.

From the crowd of Saturday night drinkers in the bar, the landlord pointed out a cabby. The man was finally persuaded to leave his group of friends to make the journey to Crystal Palace, and it was with a considerable feeling of relief that the three party-goers climbed into the cabby's beaten-up Cortina.

By the time they arrived at the Carver's detached Victorian house, Buchanan was miserable. The breakdown had added to the gloom he was already feeling. In the exertion of pushing the car, he had worked up enough of a sweat to make his shirt stick clammily to his back, and it was smeared with dirt where he had inadvertently rubbed against the London grime on the boot of the Jaguar. His hands were grubby, and he felt a long way from his best. Cordelia was dabbing at Frank with a dampened handkerchief and muttering about people who drove old and unreliable cars.

Buchanan made excuses for his appearance to Max Carver at the front door and went off in search of the bathroom...and Morganstein.

On every floor the three storey house sprawled outwards from a massive central staircase. It had enough corridors and rooms to stage a complicated farce. Throughout the building were signs of 'tasteful' do-it-yourself renovation: the broad pine floorboards were clumsily sanded and varnished, antique porcelain knobs were badly fitted on the stripped pine doors, and the decorative plaster cornices were painted in an effort to recreate the effects of soot from oil-lamps and candles: the end result, in fact, looked as if the decorator had never got further than undercoating.

The marbled paintwork of the walls was covered with huge daubed abstract expressionistic paintings: they were mid-Atlantic versions of the school of painting that had shaken America in the fifties and sixties. Buchanan was certain they were Max Carver's own work. He stood staring at one of them as he waited to get into the bathroom. To his amusement he noticed pencil lines under the paintwork where the areas of color had been roughed in before the paint was applied. Far from being a spontaneous explosion of emotions captured in paint, it was simply rather messy coloring in.

After he had washed his hands and sponged the worst of the stain from the front of his shirt, he collected a drink from a table in the hall and began mingling with the other guests. As he searched amongst the groups of smartly dressed people for Morganstein he caught snippets of their conversations. What he overheard did little to cheer him up.

It was like walking around in one of George Grosz's scathing line drawings. With the addition of the occasional monocle the party-goers would have made perfect subjects for his scornful pictures. In common with most gatherings peopled almost exclusively by the Art World the topics of conversation were fairly predictable: who had seen David Hockney where, doing what with whom, the protagonists of various illicit affairs, and the latest 'new discoveries' at the various galleries.

As far as Buchanan could see the subjects under discussion were part of the same overall picture. Talent appeared to have little to do with the measure of success an upcoming Artist achieved. It was far more important to have influential friends, or to be sleeping with someone involved in a gallery.

With no sign of Morganstein, and his depression growing, Buchanan began making frequent stops at the drinks table on his circuits of the party.

The alcohol combined with his lack of sleep and his throbbing foot to lure him into an armchair. The instant he sat down, his head began nodding, and he soon collapsed into sleep.

He was woken by Morganstein shaking his shoulder and asking him loudly, "Who is your new partner, Charles? Is it anyone I know?"

"Good evening, Mr Morganstein," he said, blinking rapidly and climbing a little unsteadily to his feet. "Well, what a surprise meeting you here! What partner are you talking about?"

"Don't play games with me, Charles. I don't mind being beaten, but I don't need you to lie to me. I was going to call you this evening and repeat my offer; I thought you would at least give us the chance to match our competitor's price."

"Match what price? I'm sorry Mr Morganstein, but I don't understand what you're saying. I haven't even shown anybody the paintings apart from you," said Buchanan.

"Charles, really. You annoy me with this 'little boy' innocence. How stupid do you think I am?"

"What makes you think I don't want you to have the paintings?" asked Buchanan in genuine puzzlement.

"I'm sorry you choose to take this attitude with me; I can be the wrong person to cross in this small world of ours. Goodnight!" He turned away angrily.

Buchanan took a couple of paces after him, protesting his ignorance loudly. "Mr Morganstein, Oscar, I've thought it over, I want you to have them. You must be confused."

"Confused?" shouted Morganstein at the top of his voice, "I think it is you who are confused. How can you sell me paintings you don't own! I can understand you selling them to someone else, but what have you to gain by this charade that the sale has not taken place. Once again I wish you goodnight!" The little man strode away through the crowd of people who had gathered at the sound of the raised voices and were staring at them.

Buchanan stood blankly for several moments while the

circle of onlookers nudged each other and murmured. He was rescued by the appearance of Frank Price at his elbow.

"What was all that about? Cordelia wanted to know," asked the young man.

"She's not the only one...I want to know as well. He kept saying I hadn't got the paintings anymore. I have no idea what he is talking about. Can you see if you can find out what's going on, Frank? Please?"

"I can try. Wait for me here."

While Frank was gone, Buchanan limped out to the hall to refill his glass. He returned with it to the place he had arranged to meet Frank, and was cradling it quietly in his hands, when Max Carver came blustering up to him,

"What's going on, Buchanan?"

"Nothing, why?"

"Somebody told me you were trying to start a fight."

"I don't start fights; it's not my style of doing business. They were wrong."

"Well, they said you were arguing with Oscar Morganstein. Is that true?"

"It was a misunderstanding, nothing more. I'm sorry you were bothered."

"I don't want any trouble. That's all. If you can't hold your drink, you should go. I'm warning you, Buchanan, if there's any fighting, it'll be with me outside. Do you understand?"

"Max, I said I was sorry about raising my voice. I have no reason to fight with anybody, least of all you. I'm just standing here quietly waiting for some news on a sale."

"I lift weights you know. I can handle myself."

Buchanan's self control snapped as he saw Frank returning with an unhappy expression on his face.

"Excuse me, Max, I have to talk. Why don't you run along and bite a few chunks out of a tree-trunk. I promise you this, if I decide that I'd like to have a fight with a moron - I'll come and find you." He stepped away from the stocky figure towards

Frank. "What's the story?"

"One wrong move, Buchanan, and I'll be waiting," warned Carver, wagging a stubby finger. Buchanan ignored him and listened intently to the news from Morganstein.

"He thinks you double-crossed him. Apparently some woman telephoned him this afternoon and said she had the paintings. She wanted to know where she could sell them at auction. He tried to buy them from her, but she turned him down."

"Who was it?"

"He doesn't know. She refused to give a name. She just said she'd read his report on the paintings and wanted to know where they would fetch the most money. He didn't want anything to do with her at first, but she offered him ten percent of whatever they fetch. He's hopping mad with you, Charles. I can't say I blame him. I can't think why you wanted to come to the party, if you'd already sold the damn things. Why didn't you tell Cordelia and me?"

"I haven't sold them. They're sitting in my studio. It must be someone playing a joke. Go and tell him."

"You better be telling the truth."

"Frank, I give you my word - they're in my studio and not a soul has seen them. I don't know who this woman was, but I suspect it's someone Morganstein blabbed to, having a joke. Tell Morganstein he can have them if he wants to remake his offer. Tell him I'm sorry for messing him around yesterday," pleaded Buchanan.

"If you promise it's true, I'll tell him you haven't sold them, but you can do your own negotiating."

"Honestly, Frank, I haven't."

While the young man disappeared to see Morganstein again, Buchanan wondered who on earth had made the phone call. Nobody had seen the report apart from him. Baffled, he hoped Frank's reassurance would do the trick and reopen the way for a sale.

The effect of the alcohol receded as he racked his brains for an answer.

His thoughts were interrupted by a voice from behind him.

"Charles? Charles Buchanan?"

He turned to see a smiling figure holding out his hand in greeting. The man was fiftyish, good-looking, with just enough gray at his temples to complete an image of paternal wisdom. It was Robin Malcolm, the psychotherapist whose invoice had so irritated Buchanan the other day. He was a frequent guest at these gatherings of dealers, artists and buyers.

After a brief check to see if he could see Frank returning Buchanan shook the outstretched hand.

"Hello, Robin. How are you?"

"I'm fine, thank you. And how are things with you? I didn't think that these shindigs were your cup of tea?"

"They're not. And things are a bit hectic at the moment. I'm here because I'm trying to close a deal."

"You never came back for your second visit."

"No," admitted Buchanan, "I've been very busy."

"You should never be too busy to look after your health. I was looking forward to seeing you again."

"Why?"

"After you'd gone, I listened to the tape I made of the session, and I think you'd find another visit very helpful."

"I doubt it. I only came the first time to shut Cordelia Babbington up. She's a great fan of yours, although, to be blunt, I suspect her high opinion of you owes rather more to your skills on the bed than it does to your skills on the couch. Personally I have a hunch that you're a bit of a con-merchant. I wonder whether you don't just feed off a group of people who have more money than sense: who enjoy a self-indulgent chat with their 'therapist'."

Malcolm chuckled, "You don't mince your words, do you, Mr Buchanan?"

"I can see when the Emperor's new clothes aren't all they're cracked up to be."

"As a matter of fact, there's a lot of truth in what you say. Many of my clients have no reason to be seeing me other than a desire to keep up with the Jones's. That's why I enjoyed having you come along."

"I scarcely know whether to be flattered or outraged. Are you trying to tell me that I'M interesting? Or that I'm an interesting CASE? Or is this just your standard sales patter?"

"None of those things...and all of them, I suppose. It's just that I wouldn't be surprised if one day you didn't benefit from another session."

"What does that mean?"

"Exactly what I said...and, actually, I'm not touting for custom. As a matter of fact, I'm turning prospective clients away. I just think you could be storing up trouble for yourself."

Buchanan could feel his irritation mounting.  He said, "Good grief. Do you often conduct these impromptu sessions at cocktail parties?"

"No." Malcolm grinned for an instant, and then he said, "But for you I'm making an exception. I think you are in many ways a remarkable man. I've watched you over the last few years at these sort of gatherings and admired the way you seem able to cut through most of the pretentious chit-chat that goes on. From what Cordelia tells me, you seem to have a sixth sense for the way the Art market moves - you always seem to be ahead of the crowd."

"Flattery, Mr Malcolm, is exactly what I expect from someone like you."

"Oh, it's not flattery. It's the sweetener," he paused and looked around. Their conversation was drowned in the general hubbub; nobody was paying any attention to them. He continued, "If you like I can add a whole lot more..."

"Go ahead. I'm fascinated," said Buchanan sarcastically.

"Oh, I don't know...I wonder about your inability to separate fact from fiction; about your tendency to retreat into a private world where you are able to make people behave as you want them to; about your resistance to letting people get close to you....I think you should be careful, Charles; contrary to your belief, you are not an unacknowledged God. You may find that, under pressure, your fantasies about yourself become confused with reality. So, remember, if you want to give me a ring anytime, I'll be only too happy to talk. Someone like you makes a refreshing change from menopausal women whining about their inability to reach multiple climaxes."

"Is there any charge for this advice?"

"No. It's on the house. Good-bye."

Buchanan watched him vanish in the crowd and craned his neck to see if he could see Frank and Morganstein. There was no sign of either, so he set off to look for them.

His conversation with Malcolm played on his mind. He tried to remember what he had talked about when he had visited the Psychotherapist. He clearly recalled telling him about the woman that figured in his dreams - how he found it unsettling that he could never see her face properly.

He even remembered how he tried to explain it. He wondered whether the man had understood the analogy he had used: that she was like the Plaeides. Should he have explained what they were? - a group of stars visible in the northern hemisphere. The seven sisters - a constellation that you could only really see if you didn't look directly at it: stars that, as long as they were out of the center of your vision, were a bright cluster, but which, if you concentrated on them, disappeared into the blackness of the night sky.

It was a perfect description of the way his dream woman kept her face hidden from him. What was so unusual about her constant presence? After all, most people had recurring dreams, didn't they? It surely wasn't unusual to have somebody that kept figuring in them.

Malcolm was not only a con artist, he was probably ignorant, concluded Buchanan as he spotted Cordelia hovering a short distance away from where Morganstein and Frank Price were talking. He managed to catch her attention and she came over to join him.

"I take it you're not having a wonderful time?" she asked. "Listen, I know you hate these affairs, Charles, but do try and at least look as if you're enjoying yourself."

"Enjoying myself?" echoed Buchanan, "So far tonight my car has broken down; I've passed out with boredom and the effects of alcohol; been called a liar by Oscar Morganstein; and then subjected to a free psychoanalysis by one of your cronies. Oh yes, and I've also been invited to have a brawl with the host. Actually, Cordelia, this evening has lived up to all my worst expectations."

"I knew you were in a foul mood when you came to pick us up. You set out to have a bad time. It's been like a self-fulfilling prophesy. I don't have any sympathy for you at all. You could have had a good time talking to Robin Malcolm. He's perfectly charming and thinks very highly of you. He told me he wished he had a son with half your intellect."

"Oh terrific! Now I hear that some home-spun psychiatrist has been discussing my mental state with his other patients, and trying to claim me as kin. Did you compare notes?"

"Charles, you're behaving like a spoilt child. Calm down. Will it make you feel any better if I tell you that I think Frank has smoothed Morganstein's ruffled feathers? I was ear-wigging on their conversation, and I'm sure it's all sorted out."

"Thank God for that. If that's settled, I just want to go to bed and have a good night's sleep. How long do you think Frank will be?"

"I don't know. Look, if you go and telephone for a cab, I'll go and rescue him."

"You two are leaving with me?"

"Oh no, not yet. I want to parade my toy-boy about a bit. Thanks to you I've hardly had him to myself at all this evening. And I don't want anybody thinking I'm here on my own."

"Thanks Cordelia. I appreciate what you're doing for me. I'm sorry I've been so bad tempered."

"Don't apologize, Charles. I think I prefer you angry to hang-dog and contrite. I'll see you by the front door in ten minutes."

When they rendezvoused, Buchanan discovered that Cordelia was right: Frank had sorted things out with Morganstein. He was to take the paintings to the restorer's workshops first thing on Monday morning to resume negotiations.

At last, he could go home.

Buchanan stood in the street waiting for the arrival of his taxi. Now that the Schiele's seemed to be sold, he could devote his mind to his next project. What would the dealers buy? For a long time he had been working on the paperwork to support an Otto Dix or Max Beckman; something lampooning the very people he was going to be selling to. He could even slip in a caricature or two of faces from the London scene. With their eyes clouded by money the 'Arty' punters would never notice. Hell, why not?

Above him an aeroplane droned. The navigation lights spun a beam of light that spiraled through the thick cloud like slow lightning. A police siren wailed a long way away; the pitch of the noise curled up and down as the unseen car altered its direction.

From out of the bushes less than four feet away from where he was standing, stepped a fat, black, cat. It walked up to him, circled his legs a couple of times and then rolled over onto its back in front of him. Buchanan bent down and stroked it, scratching it gently under the chin. The cat began purring loudly.

The noise of inconsequential conversation drifted from the house. Buchanan longed to go inside and whisper to just one person, *'I am a forger!'*, then step back and watch the news spread. That would really give them something to talk about.

But  no-one could be allowed to share his secret, or he would be finished.

It was a joke at their expense, and it was just a little frustrating that he was forced to laugh on his own. He returned his attention to the cat and whispered gently to it,

"I'm going to tell you something, puss. I'm a forger. And not another living soul knows that."

When he thought about it later, he convinced himself that he must have accidentally touched a hidden wound, for the cat suddenly bared its teeth and lashed out with its claws. They ripped through the skin of his hand. And as the animal backed away snarling he swore it was saying,

*"Liaaar. Liaaar"*

# CHAPTER THIRTEEN

BUCHANAN SET OFF FOR HIS STUDIO early on Monday morning feeling optimistic.  Even the rain which was washing the first major autumn fall of leaves from the trees, and which had made finding a taxi difficult, couldn't dampen his spirits. The only thing that had spoiled an otherwise restful Sunday had been the nagging irritation of Morganstein's strange story about the mystery woman caller.  He was certain it wasn't Cordelia playing a joke on him, but he couldn't think who else it could have been. For a while he had wondered whether Frank and Morganstein had concocted the whole scenario between them to get him to move on the price, but he had dismissed the idea as being too involved and circuitous. Eventually he had decided that it might have a been a ploy of Morganstein's to force his hand on the sale; and he had to admit it had worked.  Coupled with Frank's doubts about the pictures, it had been enough to make up his mind to go for a quick and painless sale.

As the taxi pulled into the narrow cobbled mews, Buchanan was pleased and relieved to see his Jaguar parked amongst the cars outside Wesley's garage.  Externally at least it seemed to have survived its time alone in South London. He was sure it wouldn't take the black mechanic long to sort out the mechanical problem which had spoiled Saturday evening. Maybe it would even be repaired in time for him to run the paintings over to Morganstein's later in the morning.

He paid the cab-driver and sheltered from the rain as much as possible in the doorway whilst he switched off the alarm and undid the heavy Banham mortise-locks on the studio door. Once inside, he hung up his dripping cavalry officer's mac downstairs and went up to the first floor.

The first wave of panic hit him the instant he reached the top of the stairs and glanced over at his desk. He was sure he had left the Schiele's on top.

Trying to keep calm, Buchanan began looking for the bubble-wrapped parcel. He checked under and behind the desk before moving to the racks above the plan chests along the end of the studio. A cursory glance satisfied him that the sizable package was nowhere amongst the stored canvasses. A wild notion, that he might have forgotten unwrapping them and putting them away, made him decide to check properly.

As he moved along the racks of canvasses pulling each one out in turn, even the ones that he knew were too large to be the Schiele's, he began taking less and less care about putting them back. By the time he reached the end of the line he was simply tossing them onto the floor. In response to another wild suggestion from the increasingly less confident voice in his head that he might have taken the paintings off their stretchers and forgotten about it, he pulled out all the rolled-up, stripped but unworked canvasses and unfurled each one before discarding them on the floor.

The immaculate order of the plan chests was destroyed as the drawers (labeled either with Artists and dates - Picasso 1930's, Macke watercolors 1914 Kairouan, Tunisia; or with details of papers - Cotman hand-made early-20th-C, Arches 1930-50) were all rifled with mounting desperation.

[ 152 ]

By the time Buchanan began emptying the plastic sacks of rubbish onto the floor there were voices in his head screaming,

*"I told you they'd been stolen!"*

*"IF THEY'VE BEEN STOLEN WHY DIDN'T THEY TAKE ANYTHING ELSE?"*

*"They knew what they wanted!"*

*"'THEY'?"*

*"Yes, 'they'"*

*"WHO ARE 'THEY'?"*

*"I don't know, I don't know!"*

He collapsed into the chair in front of his desk and pressed his face into his hands. When he looked up, he noticed for the first time that the photographs of all his past forgery successes were missing from the wall in front of him.

*And he was hit by the second, more devastating, wave of panic.*

He felt himself tumbling backwards, spinning and disoriented. A horrible heavy churning sensation filled his guts as he flicked through the files in the cabinet, hoping against hope to find the marbled one bearing Megan Copeland-Watts' name. It wasn't there.

Buchanan's confusion was interrupted by a loud banging at the street door. He waited, hoping whoever it was would go away. After a couple of minutes there was more knocking, and he made his way reluctantly downstairs. He opened the door a crack and was relieved to see Wesley's grinning face.

"Mr Buchanan, sorry to bother you, man, but Andreas from the rag factory said he saw you go in," the mechanic paused as he looked at Buchanan. The smile vanished from his face and was replaced by a look of concern, "Hey, man, are you okay? You look terrible."

"Yes, I'm fine. I'm fine. I've just had a bit of a shock."

"Wow, you look like death, man. D'you want to come over to the garage and have a cup of tea?"

"No, I'll be all right in a minute."

"I don't know if you're going to like my news too much. Your car's fucked up pretty good."

"What d'you mean?" asked Buchanan uncomprehendingly.

"Listen, I'll come back when you're feeling better. I hate to hit a man when he's down." Wesley turned to leave.

"Hold on, Wesley. What's the big deal? I only ran out of petrol."

"Yeah, but you filled up with fucking diesel, man."

"Diesel?"

"Yup. I'll have to strip her right down and clean all that shit out. How come you did such a dumb thing?"

"It's impossible. I just used the spare can."

"That's right Mr B., only the spare can didn't have petrol in it. If you don't believe me, come over and have a look. I may not be a fucking genius, but I know the difference between my arse and a hole in the ground, and I'm telling you that you filled up with diesel."

"Can you fix it?"

"Can I fix it? - do I get dirty at work? - of course I can fix it, it's just that it's going to cost you a bob or two. Even if I do it myself it's going to run damn close to a monkey."

"For a can of diesel? Five hundred pounds?"

"And the rest. I've got to flush out the tank, have the head off and clean all the valves, adjust the..."

"Okay, Wesley. Spare me the details, just do it. I've got more important things on my mind at the moment."

"As you say Mr B. Are you sure you don't want a cuppa?"

"Thanks, but no thanks. I'll come and see you when the car's finished."

"Catch you later."

Buchanan began to close the door, but he suddenly paused and called out,

"Hey, Wesley you didn't see anyone come in here over the week-end did you?"

"No. Why? You been turned over?"

"Turned over?" echoed Buchanan.

"Robbed."

"Yes...I think so."

"You think so? Don't you know?"

"I'm not sure. There's something missing, but the alarm hasn't been tripped."

A look of concern flashed over the mechanic's face,

"Hey, are you going to call the Old Bill? Only if you are...well, there's a couple of Andreas' mates that should come and pick up their cars, if you know what I mean."

"Don't worry. I shan't be calling the Police. If you hear anything will you let me know?"

"Sure. See you later."

Before he shut the door Buchanan looked for any signs that the door had been forced. It was in pristine condition. Whoever had been inside must have keys for the door and the alarm. It was a thoroughly professional job.

As this concept of professional thieves breaking into his studio tumbled against the memory of Morganstein's account of the strange phone call about the pictures from the mystery woman, a third wave of panic hit him.

*This theft was not simply about a one-off sale.*

This was about extortion - he hadn't just been robbed; he had been set up. He could hardly go to the Police and ask for protection.

Could he?

The bastards were going to squeeze him dry, and there would be nothing he could do about it. There was no doubt about it: he was in BIG, FAT, TROUBLE. He would have to go to ground for a few days.

He would have to miss his meeting with Morganstein, but keeping him happy was now the least of his problems.

This was no longer just about two paintings - it was about his life. He wondered how long it would be before the thieves got in contact.

# CHAPTER FOURTEEN.

AS HE STOOD AT THE END OF THE BURLINGTON ARCADE for a brief second, Bill Montague realized he hadn't felt as relaxed and cheerful as this since he had successfully invested 50 at 33-1 on 'Legal Billy' in the 3.15 at Weatherby - purely on the basis of a wild hunch and two bottles of excellent claret shared with an old friend from chambers in the hospitality tent. Despite the rainy weather, he was definitely enjoying his Monday morning in town. During the drive up from Oxfordshire, Megan and he had finished their discussions about the scheme and fixed a timetable for the day.

Montague's program involved visiting all the galleries named by Buchanan in his notes. He was curious to find out how worried the gallery owners were about fakes, and he wondered how they would react if he confronted them with proof that they had been duped. At each stop on his route the elderly lawyer introduced himself as a Legal Expert researching a paper on forgery, and at every single one he received a similar, abrupt, rebuff. By the time he arrived at the last of the galleries on the list, he was beginning to have a grudging admiration for the forger who had hoodwinked them all. And this admiration was despite the sorry story Montague had dragged from Megan about Buchanan's duplicity and callousness.

He wondered whether 'Babbington's' would be any more forthcoming as he introduced himself to the receptionist,

"My name is Deakins, and I would like to talk to Mr Babbington if it is at all possible. Is he available?"

"I'll check, sir. Will you take a seat? Can I have some idea what it is about?"

"I'm representing the Weatherby Foundation of Dallas; we're an organization who act as advisors to major collectors in the United States." Bill Montague, alias Joshua Deakins, was enjoying himself immensely. He was a trifle surprised how easily he slipped into the role of 'menteur'.

Shortly afterwards, Terry Maguire, the receptionist, helped him to a chair in Jeremy's Babbington's office.

"I'm sorry Mr Dealings.." began the man at the desk in front of Montague.

"DeaKINS." he corrected him.

"I'm sorry Mr Deakins. I don't quite understand how I can help you. You're a major collector from Texas; is that right?"

"No it isn't." This interview was getting off to no more of an auspicious start than any of the others. "I am the British representative of the Weatherby Foundation. We provide a confidential advice service to art collectors in the United States. You may not have heard of us because the sort of clients we represent - people of the ilk of Mr Malcolm Forbes, Dr. Armand Hammer, Mr Wendell Cherry, et al. - they like us to respect a fair degree of confidentiality. However, I imagine that someone in your position may well know of our work." Montague beamed at Jeremy Babbington.

"The Weatherby Foundation? Oh yes, of course, I'm sure I've heard of your organization."

Montague smiled again at the beautifully attired man across the desk. This time because, in common with all the other gallery owners, Jeremy Babbington had lied rather than show himself to be ignorant. The Weatherby Foundation had only come into existence during the car journey between Oxford and London - and then only in Bill Montague's imagination.

"In the light of the fuss at Sotheby's over the allegedly forged Piranesi drawings, some of our clients have become nervous about the possibility of the value of their investments being undermined. And we were wondering whether you, as a gallery owner, have had any contact with fakes over the last few years?" Montague braced himself for the reply. If the events of the previous couple of hours were anything to go by it would run something like: We haven't had any in our gallery, but occasionally we've been offered them and subsequently seen them in other galleries. He was not disappointed.

"We haven't had any in our gallery - that I know for a fact - not in the twenty years I've been here," began Babbington, "However, I did get offered some Modigliani drawings a few months ago, which any idiot could have spotted as fakes, and I refused to touch them. I can't answer for other galleries, though, because I saw the same drawings on sale a week later on my way for lunch - not a million miles from here. So the best advice I can give you is to tell your clients to buy only from reputable dealers who insist on faultless provenance - like Babbington's. Is that any help?"

"More than you can imagine, Mr Billingsgate. Thank you for your time." Montague struggled to his feet.

"Babbington," interjected Jeremy, "Billingsgate is the fish market; the name's Babbington."

"No, it's Deakins - Joshua Deakins. Good Morning. I'll certainly be in touch if I have clients in London."

It was the same story everywhere. A smug, self-satisfied, wholly misplaced faith in their own, individual, ability to spot an Art Fraud. And every gallery he had visited was already the victim of one of Charles Buchanan's schemes: the man deserved admiration for the way he was taking these idiots to the cleaners. But with Megan it was a different story; she had dealt naively and in good faith with him. The man had no need to sting suckers when the professionals were ripe for exploitation. Montague hurried creakily away to his meeting with Morganstein.

The crippling pain of his arthritis had been pushed away from the front of his mind, where it normally interfered with every waking movement. The excitement of the last two days when he had been busy on Megan's scheme, had rekindled a long forgotten pleasure in working. His enthusiasm had even been heightened by the questionable legality of the whole scheme. In many ways it reminded him of his early days in the family firm when he had been despatched to the Metropole Hotel in Brighton to work on seedy divorce cases.

Like any good lawyer he attached a great deal of importance to research. As a consequence he had been into his office on a Sunday for the first time since his father died and worked through his collection of legal records late into the night without a trace of fatigue. Even the trudging round London hadn't been too painful, mainly due to the amusement value of the fictitious persona he had adopted, and he was looking forward to meeting Morganstein and laying out the plan for the sale of the paintings.

In line with the cloak and dagger ambiance that he was enjoying so much, he had arranged to meet the picture restorer at a neutral venue - in the 'Polo' bar of the Westbury Hotel in New Bond Street. It was a stone's throw from Sotheby's; where he had left the wrapped paintings and provenance; along with instructions that they were to be collected only by Morganstein or himself. The bar was a popular rendez-vous for foreign businessmen and tourists, and any meeting would pass unnoticed. In the reception area he paused to ask the gray-suited young man at the desk to send Oscar Morganstein to his table in the bar when he arrived, and then he settled himself at a corner table under one of the mock-Indian mural panels.

It had been nearly twenty years since he last visited the Westbury, and even though the hotel was now part of a chain, it had managed to maintain some of the qualities of excellence. The tables were well spaced and the two men would be able to talk normally with little risk of being overheard. He ordered a very dry martini and arranged his legs as comfortably as possible on either side of the brass, clawed-feet that supported the reproduction mahogany table.

His initial reaction, when he saw the bell-boy bringing an elderly man towards his table, was one of surprise. The picture restorer was even shorter than the tiny uniformed adolescent leading him across the bar - shorter, and so round shouldered he resembled a tweed-clad beetle. As the odd couple came closer Montague rose to his feet and palmed a pound coin, which he pressed into bell-boy's hand. In a hotel as popular with Americans as this, not tipping would be the more remarkable event, and he was trying to be as inconspicuous as possible. He motioned for Morganstein to sit down and made a sign to the waiter for drinks.

Montague waited until they were alone again before saying, "Mr Morganstein, as I believe has been outlined to you over the telephone by my secretary, we would like you to perform a service for us. A service in confidence. You have no need to know the identity of my client, and in many ways the next few weeks will be easier for you if you do not know. However, as a respected member of the Art World, I feel it is only right to give you a broad background.

"My client has a Schiele painting coming onto the market shortly. It is a fine painting of great historical importance in the artist's catalogue - a well known and documented work which will command a figure comparable with that paid by Ronald Lauder in 1983 for the portrait of *'Karl Zavoscek,'* and possibly as much as that paid by Wendell Cherry, in '84, for *'Liebespaar'.*" This information about past sales of Schiele's Montague had gleaned from Sotheby's a couple of hours earlier and committed to memory as accurately as he did when he was due to conduct a legal argument. "My client feels that the publicity generated by a find of this magnitude can only help push the price upwards. Obviously if it became known that we were using the sale to this effect, the gesture would fail. So you see, absolute secrecy is paramount on the one hand; and maximum publicity on the other. Do you follow me?"

"Certainly," replied Morganstein gravely.

"I'm sure I have no need to point out to a man of your impeccable credentials how damaging a breach of confidence could be to everyone involved, do I?"

"No. I understand perfectly."

"In return for this my client will pay you fifteen percent of the final sale price."

"Fifteen percent, at auction?" the restorer's eyes blazed with interest.

"Yes. We want you to be well rewarded for generating the maximum amount of publicity."

"How do you wish to describe them in the sale? It is most unlikely that the auction house will allow them to be described as by Schiele."

"Could we describe them as attributed to Schiele, or possibly by Schiele?"

"Yes, I think they will be options. You do realize that at auction the paintings will be subjected to the fiercest scrutiny. It is inevitable that doubts will be expressed as to their authenticity. If we were to take some time and seek the opinion of Dr. Rudolph Leopold in Vienna they would be more likely to be accepted as genuine. Solely on the basis of my opinion it is possible their value will be destroyed." Morganstein was obviously concerned that he might be getting fifteen percent of nothing.

Montague continued, "We want people to know that the paintings are to be sold without a reserve. That way we are hopeful that bidding will be brisk, even in the early stages. As for an air of controversy, it can only help my client, whose own Schiele is beyond reproach. If we lose all the money we have already paid it will be a small price to pay for the advertising. However, it is obviously in your best interests to see they sell for as much as possible. This is the strategy of our plan, and if you are still interested I will fill in the details."

"I am still interested," replied Morganstein with almost blatant haste.

"Do you have any idea if and when we can get the paintings into an auction soon? It must be with one of the major houses."

"Sotheby's and Christie's don't have anything coming up until the end of the season, not in London in any case. There's a major sale in New York, but I don't think that is viable," he paused and rubbed his chin, "But in Paris, Sabatier's have a big sale in less than a month. There might be a problem with export licenses but with a little effort I'm certain I could use my contacts and arrange for them to be sold there. Would that meet with your client's approval."

"Yes, Sabatier's is perfect. When exactly is the sale?"

"October second."

"Excellent. After this meeting you can collect the paintings from the main desk at Sotheby's. They also have an envelope containing all the receipts and letters relating to the pictures. You will obtain quotes for insuring them and shipping them safely to Sabatier's Paris office. I will call you in a couple of days and find out how much money you need. This is a contract I have drawn up defining the terms on which the paintings are released into your custody, your share of the sale price and the terms of payment. Will seven days be agreeable?"

Morganstein nodded and produced a fountain pen from his jacket pocket. He signed both copies of the paper Montague produced and could scarcely contain his impatience as he waited for the lawyer to sign. The moment the ink was dry Morganstein shuffled the document away and rose to his feet,

"Good-bye. I will obtain those quotes and wait for your call. Thank you, Mr Deakins."

The two men shook hands without warmth, and

Morganstein bustled out of the room. Montague had no doubt that the man was good at his job, but he found his keenness to get his hands on the fifteen percent most unwholesome.

He ordered a second dry martini and asked for it to be sent through to the restaurant where he anticipated finding Megan waiting.

She was sitting alone at a table watching the ice slowly melt in her gin and tonic. Normally she avoided spirits in the daylight hours, but, with her nerves on edge, she had allowed herself just one - and been content to cradle it until Montague arrived. She took a hearty swallow as he lowered himself into his seat across the table from her.

"Well, it's all set. Morganstein is going to put them into Sabatier's Paris auction next month."

"So is that all there is to it?"

"Provided Buchanan hears about the sale AND takes the bait."

"And what if he doesn't?"

"Then you pull the rug and release all the information from the files and photos. The only thing about that is the colossal quantity of egg there is going to be on the faces of the galleries named in his lists of forgeries. Frankly it doesn't bother me that much, and I don't think it should worry you. The gallery owners I spoke to this morning were so damned smug."

"If we have to do that, will it ruin him?"

"Totally."

"What makes you so sure?" asked Megan finishing her gin and tonic and taking two menus from a hovering waiter.

"The whole business seems to me to be nothing more than a house of cards. All the gallery owners live on the confidence of their clients. Once that confidence is gone there is nothing left to justify the high prices art is fetching at the moment. I can scarcely believe how fragile the entire empire is. Buchanan will be finished as a dealer, but ironically he may be the only one to emerge with any credit. You may unwittingly turn him into an anti-hero."

"What do you mean?"

"Well, look at it logically. Buchanan is the joker who has been exposing the greed and gullibility of the gallery owners. Who knows, he may even end up with his own TV. show like that Keating fellow! Hardly the effect you were aiming for."

"It'll be a while before he's finished with the Police, though."

"Don't count on it, Megan. As I suspected, Art forgery is still not a crime, and most forgers get away with it."

"What?" said Megan in amazement.

"I'm afraid so. I meant to tell you about it in the car this morning. It seems the Institute of Criminology were so worried about it a few years ago that in 1962 they held a special conference at Leiden, Germany to debate the issue. I've managed to track down the history of most of the top Art forgery cases this century, and I'm more or less certain the only thing the Police will be able to charge him with is deception. And that is dependent on someone being willing to admit that they were mug enough to buy a fake and ready to go into the witness box to testify against him. If not, he could get off scot-free."

"I don't believe it!"

"Unfortunately it's true. But looking positively at our plan, I think it most likely that he will try and buy them back and destroy the evidence. So, if you're happy, I'm happy. It all seems to be settled. We wait until we hear from Morganstein that they have been entered in the sale, and then tip off the Fourth Estate."

"Fourth Estate?"

"The press, Megan, the press."

"What if he doesn't see it in the newspapers?"

"I think an indignant hurt phone-call from you about being swindled would be in order. That should do the trick. It might also divert any suspicion away. Shall we eat? All this excitement has given me an appetite. My stomach is sending out inquiries as to whether my throat's been cut."

# CHAPTER FIFTEEN

FOR NINE DAYS BUCHANAN WAS UNDER THE KOSH. Time passed slowly. With every passing day his confusion and depression grew. Why the hell didn't they get in contact? How much did they want? Anything would be better than just waiting for the phone to ring, or a letter to drop through the door. And yet, even then, when the phone did ring he was loathe to answer it in case it was the blackmailers. How much would they want to return everything? Would that be an end to it? He doubted it.

He was unshaven and bedraggled. The flat was in chaos; his daily woman no longer came. He couldn't bear her bustling presence, and he couldn't bring himself to go out while she was there. He had told her not to come again until he called her. For over a week he had been living on sandwiches and bottles of cheap red wine from a corner shop two streets away. He no longer went to the delicatessen, preferring to stay away from anyone that knew him.

When he did manage to sleep his dreams were structured around the plots of kidnapping stories and blackmail cases. He woke sweating and wondering how he would end up paying the money. Visions of late night meetings in underground car-parks or being led from one public phone box to another flashed through his mind.

So, when the ransom demand came he was taken totally by surprise. There was no phantom telephone caller or message cut laboriously from old typescript.

Nothing at all like that.

Instead there was a smallish article on page 14 of his morning newspaper:

---

# A GAMBLE ON THE ART MARKET?

PARIS (SPF) - Sabatier's showroom here in the fourth arrondisement, today confirmed that there were a couple of unusual late additions to their forthcoming Modern Masters sale. Two figure paintings, reputed to be the work of the early twentieth-century Austrian expressionist Egon Schiele, were until recently hanging AS LANDSCAPES on the walls of an English country house. They had been there since the end of the Second World War.

Two months ago the owner sent them to be cleaned and restored at the London workshops of Oscar Morganstein.

Morganstein said that during the course of the restoration, he discovered that the landscapes were painted over a pair of "exquisite nudes" underneath. Morganstein added that the over-painting had been done with such care that he had no doubt that it had been done deliberately.

There is considerable conjecture in the art world as to why the paintings may have been over-painted. Morganstein suggested that, assuming they are genuinely the work of Egon Schiele, they were covered in an attempt to keep them out of the hands of the Nazis some time prior to the start of the Second World War.

If this is so, the sale at Sabatier's marks the final, bizarre twist in the story. If the Art World accepts the paintings as genuine, and they fetch the estimated £75,000 each, the present owner stands to nearly double his money over a period of a few weeks, if not it will prove to have been a costly gamble.

The foremost authority on the works of Egon Schiele, Dr Rudolph Leopold of Vienna, has not had the opportunity to examine the paintings themselves, but, on the basis of photographs we showed him, he had no hesitation in saying he thought it 'highly possible' they were authentic.

The present owner, who is remaining anonymous, paid an undisclosed sum for the works from the woman who sent them to be restored.

The sale takes place on October 2nd

---

Charles threw back his head and laughed. The biter bit. He laughed until he was gasping for breath, tears rolled down his cheeks, and his hands hurt from being banged together in applause. It was beautiful. If he wanted the evidence back he would have to pay for it. Only with the paintings in his possession would the rest of the material be deniable. It was possible that one or two gallery owners if shown the photographs would stop dealing with him, but he was certain no-one would risk being shown as a dupe by taking him to court. There was to be no simple demand for money, he would just have to pay the going rate!

He knew from past experience of selling at auction that the seller's identity would be protected come Hell or high water. Nothing short of an Interpol investigation would prise the name from Sabatier's, and even that would have difficulties. The thieves would have to pay a commission on their proceeds, but there would be no backstreet meetings or covert communications.

An hour, and several telephone calls, later he was considerably more subdued. As he suspected, the newspaper did not know the identity of the seller and Sabatier's would not reveal it. The auction house had a guide figure on the paintings of between £50,000 and £70,000. Getting them back was going

[ 169 ]

to cost him around £170,000 including commissions and taxes.

He was in deep trouble. There were eight days until the auction. Eight days in which to raise more money than he had ever had in his life. Just to stand still. He might be able to sell them privately afterwards, but that would always be a risk. He would never know whether the prospective buyer was in contact with the thieves who stole the paintings.

# CHAPTER SIXTEEN

LONDON AIRPORT, BUCHANAN THOUGHT, was not a good place to be depressed. He was surrounded by acres and acres of inhospitable surfaces: concrete, black studded-rubber flooring, and chewing-gum-spattered carpets. He sat in one of the cafeterias and prodded at the tea-bag floating in the earthenware mug that was so thick-walled that it was practically blast-proof. Finally, he scooped the tea-bag out and took a drink.

He was still waiting for his flight to be called. While he stared at the hypnotic rolling display of information on the monitor, he made and smoked two of the cigarettes on which he was becoming increasingly dependent. They left a foul taste in his mouth that he dispelled by chewing on a piece of gum.

A portly Asian woman in a dirt-spotted apron appeared alongside the table with a trolley. She clattered his cup away, and wiped the table with a rag that trailed lines of grease in its wake. Charles watched her work her way vacantly along the line of tables.

He checked, for the fortieth time in the last hour, the contents of his brown hide briefcase, and cradled it protectively on his lap. Inside were three bank drafts and the two most valuable works of art he owned: a pair of genuine Picasso pen and ink drawings that he had been unable to sell for a realistic figure in London. He was hoping that the subject matter, a man and a woman involved in athletic sexual intercourse, would appeal to either Charigot or Daubigny, two French collectors who specialized in erotica, and who had bought from him in the past. It was in order to leave himself time to negotiate a sale of the Picasso's that he was traveling to Paris three days before the Sabatier's auction.

He had his entire life in his hands. The bank drafts in his case were for a hundred and fifty thousand pounds. They represented the cash equivalent of everything that Charles owned in the world: the proceeds of the hurried sale of his small collection of drawings and his Bokhara rugs, combined with a second mortgage very reluctantly arranged by the bank, and a twenty thousand pound loan begged from a mystified Cordelia Babbington. Everything that he had earned in the last ten years, and everything that he was likely to earn for several years to come, was reduced to these three pieces of paper.

With his two mortgages, and Cordelia's loan - a total of over a hundred and ninety thousand pounds - he was in debt beyond any hope of repayment. He was doing little more than treading water and hoping that...somehow...everything would work out.

His scramble for money had been painful and costly. As if sensing that he was not in a position to wait for a sale, the dealers that he offered his drawings to had paid rock-bottom prices. And to sweeten his request for the loan, he had even sold Cordelia Babbington a pair of Hans Bellmer's drawings for *less* than he had paid for them.

His pulse rate never seemed to have dropped below a hundred and fifty from the moment he finished reading the article in the newspaper. The adrenaline released into his system by the fear of discovery had caused his appetite to drop to nothing, and he spent the hours of darkness lying - without a hope of sleep - on his bed: his mind racing as he tried to think who could have stolen the Schiele's. One thing he wasn't short of was enemies in the Art world - there were times when he had been trying to negotiate a fair price for a drawing, when he had almost been convinced that the smug-faced dealer in front of him must have been responsible for the scheme.

It was a beautifully conceived plan to destroy him. He wondered if the person that had thought of it realized how much he admired the skill with which he had been tripped up. Whatever the outcome of the sale at Sabatier's he was a loser.

Even if he managed to buy both the Schiele's back, he would be colossally in debt - with no immediate hope of repayment; the proceeds would pass undetected to the thieves. The flat would have to go, there was no question about that. So would Romulus (Fine Art) Ltd, now nothing more than a name with an overdraft. If he could manage to pay back Cordelia, then it was possible he could salvage his reputation and continue to trade in the London market. If not she would see that nobody dealt with him - the old-boy network of dealers would be united against a common upstart.

If he failed to secure the paintings, and his photographs were made public, the floodgates of litigation would open as the same old-boy network realized the full extent of the fraud perpetrated against them. Charles knew that collectively they would feel much happier about going to court. No individual would feel that they alone had been duped.

Forty minutes later he boarded the plane and lowered himself into his seat in the back row of the economy class. As he had calculated, it was the least popular row, and he ended up with the pair of seats to himself. He placed his briefcase on the floor, did up his seat belt and settled himself for the gut-churning thrust of take-off.

During the flight he made a mental list of what he had to do before the sale. Obviously the first priority was to sell the Picasso's. He would try Charigot first; he spoke perfect English. Realistically, that was neither here nor there; his French was perfectly able to cope with selling to Daubigny, but Charles liked the slovenly Charigot far more than Daubigny - who was an elderly weasel with a closet fascination for written and painted pornography. The most important thing was to finalize a sale with one or other of them. After that he would go to Sabatier's and find out any peculiarities in the bidding arrangements. If he had time then he could have a wander around the galleries. At the back of his mind was a scheme to vanish from London and resume his forging in Paris, but that depended on getting back the Schiele's and avoiding a scandal. There were so many 'ifs'.

In an effort to clear his mind of the whirling possibilities of the next few days, he read the French version of the in-flight magazine. At thirteen his father had packed him off to spend a lonely month at a summer school in Paris at the Petit Lycee Condorcet on the Rue d'Amsterdam. The unhappy visit, which he confirmed later was merely to get him out of the way whilst his parents finalized their messy divorce arrangements, had been such a miserable experience that it had jaundiced his view of Paris to the extent that he had never been back to stay. However, as a result of this groundwork, and three successive holidays in Cezanne country in the south, he had achieved an 'A' level pass at grade A in French, and he could carry on a conversation in French almost faultlessly. The writing in the magazine bored him, though. He slipped it back into the seat pocket and closed his eyes.

For the first time in a week he could feel waves of tiredness washing over him and the constant drone of the engines was just lulling him to sleep as the aircraft began its descent.

At Charles de Gaulle airport he made his way along the escalators which climbed inside the transparent Plexiglas tubes to the baggage reclaim area, collected his suitcase, cleared customs and found the free bus shuttle to the station for the forty minute journey to the Gare du Nord. He had booked himself into a hotel recommended by Cordelia on the

Boulevard Saint Michel. Encumbered as he was by his baggage he chose to take a taxi for the journey across the city.

The "Grande Hotel des Mineurs," where he was staying, was a hundred meters or so past the Place Edmond Rostand entrance to the Jardin de Luxembourg; opposite the Ecole des Mines from which it took its name. In many ways it was a typical Parisian hotel: arranged around a central, well-like, courtyard five meters by ten, the flaking, gray painted, stucco walls rose six floors before ending in a pantiled roof pierced by tall, thin, dormer windows. The hundred-year-old building had recently been renovated in an Art Nouveau style, and the entrance doors and mirrors in the lobby were decorated with swirling Acanthus leaves.

Charles's room was on the fifth floor and could be reached either by the spiraling stairway with its original wrought-iron balustrading, or by the tiny elevator which rose in the center of the stairs.

While he was unpacking his suitcase, Charles first began thinking he wasn't alone. Twice he turned around sharply thinking he had caught sight of someone in the room out of the corner of his vision. The first time it was his dressing-gown hanging on the coat stand, and the second time it was his own reflection in the long mirror on the bathroom door. He reassured himself that the pressure wasn't getting to him and that it was just the strange room.

He tried to tell himself that as soon as he felt comfortable these illusions would vanish.

At twenty to four in the afternoon, he left his room to take a walk. He had nothing better to do, and it still wasn't too late to try and sell his drawings. At the front desk of the hotel, he deposited the bank drafts in the safe before checking with the clerk the easiest way to get to Maurice Charigot's apartment. Charigot lived just off the Rue Cortot in Monmartre, and he had bought from Charles before in London. On every occasion the Frenchman had invited Charles to visit his atelier.

Outside the hotel, the weather was the same as he had left behind in London: cold rain drifted on gusts of wind, and heavy banks of cloud hung low over the city. He buttoned his Burberry in the shelter of the hotel lobby and set off walking down the Boulevard Saint Michel towards the Ile de la Cite. On his way towards the twin towers of Notre Dame cathedral he passed between rows of brightly lit shops selling fashionable clothes. They were much like those on the Kings Road in London.

However, from the moment he crossed the bridge over the Seine and walked past the Palais de Justice, he felt the weight of history and foreign culture around him. Black uniformed soldiers stood clutching sub-machine guns outside the massive metal gates of the law courts. Images of an army of occupation flashed through his mind. With a shudder he ducked down into the metro - leaving on the street the notions of martial law.

The Boulevard de Clichy, outside Pigalle station where he finished his train journey, looked especially seedy in the drifting drizzle. Around the peepshow theaters and blue-movie cinemas single men hovered nervously in raincoats. Charles walked past an Arab gazing at a sex-shop window-display consisting of about fifty different styles of crotchless underwear, and turned into the Rue Steinkerque. The air on the narrow bustling street was thick with the smell of cooking kebabs.

Above him the domed towers of Sacre Coeur stood like a cut-out against the dense cover of cloud. He stopped and relieved himself in a pissoir before taking the funicular railway up the steep side of the hill. Ten minutes later, after walking through the heavily touristed streets near the Place du Tertre, he stopped outside Charigot's house and rang the bell.

# CHAPTER SEVENTEEN

THE RECEDING-HAIRED CHARIGOT OPENED THE DOOR and stared blankly for a second before he recognized Buchanan. Charigot was fortyish, five feet eight tall, powerfully built, and dressed in an old and crumpled cream linen suit. From the state of his clothes it was impossible to guess that the collector received a private income of more than twice what Charles had made in his best year: there was a red wine stain below one of the jacket pockets, and another just visible on the thigh of his trousers. After he recognized Buchanan, he grabbed his hand and pumped it enthusiastically.

"Charlie Bookanan! Well, I never! What a surprise. What the hell are you doing in Paris? Come in. Come in."

He ushered Buchanan up a narrow flight of stone stairs to the first floor.

Charigot worked in a dilettante fashion as an interior designer. As Charles surveyed the room he wondered why it was that, in common with barbers who always seemed to have unkempt hair, designers lived in chaos. Charigot's flat was a hodge-podge combination of modern high-tech furniture in an ancient Parisian building. The main room was a combined living and sleeping space. In one corner an unmade bed was partially screened by a line of parlor palms growing from a trench set into the floorboards. Next to that was the seating area: armchairs and a sofa arranged around a low glass table.

Charigot helped Buchanan out of his coat at the end of the room next to the kitchen and another glass table surrounded by tall dining chairs each pressed from a single sheet of aluminum. On the table were the remains of at least two meals, and six bottles of red wine - all more or less empty. Charigot hung Buchanan's coat on a coat-rack consisting of nails pounded into the wall at the top of the stairs, and ushered him to a seat at the dining table. He scavenged two glasses of wine from the dregs of the bottles, cleared the table by transferring all the debris to the kitchen sink, and then sat down alongside Charles. He raised his glass.

"Salut, Charlie. It is good to see you. Why didn't you telephone me? How's business?"

"Cheers, Maurice. I left London in a hurry. I'm sorry to drop in like this. I've come for the 'Modern Masters' sale at Sabatier's."

"Yes, I know of it. The day after tomorrow, no?"

Charles nodded.

"Are you buying or selling?" Charigot asked.

"Buying; I hope," Charles took a large swallow from his glass and continued, "That's why I'm here to see you. I may need more money, and I have something in my briefcase you might be interested in."

Charigot looked on keenly as Charles opened the case and took out the two cardboard folders. Charles placed them on the table, untied the ribbons holding them closed and lifted the Picasso's out of the tissue paper they were wrapped in. He laid them carefully on the glass in front of Charigot.

"What do you think?" asked Charles.

Charigot sucked air through his teeth. "Beaux, tres beaux." He finished his glass of wine and opened a fresh bottle. He refilled Buchanan's glass. "How much?"

"A hundred and eighty thousand francs each. Or if you want them both I'll take a little less."

"Eh bien. Et la provenance?"

Buchanan had been expecting this; he pulled a book from his briefcase. It was Christian Zervos's *'Pablo Picasso Oeuvres de 1967 et 1968'* He opened the book at the pages he had previously marked and showed Charigot the illustrations of the drawings. Tucked into the book was a bill of sale for them.

"Are you interested?" Charles asked as casually as he could. He tried desperately to disguise any sign which might indicate how important the sale was to him.

At this moment he felt like a man standing up in a canoe. The slightest disruptive movement could send him crashing into the water.

Selling was all about recognizing the moment to back off: to give the buyer a feeling of being in control. That moment was here. He waited, still and silent, while Charigot pondered the deal. If he sold the Picasso's he would really be in with a chance of making it back to dry land from the auction. If not...

Charigot pursed his lips, traced the line of the woman's breast thoughtfully with his finger, and finally responded, "Yes, I am interested, but the price we must talk about. Listen, I have an idea. It is now six o'clock. Why don't we go and have a few drinks at a bar, then later go to eat? Did you ever eat chez 'Flo'?"

"No. Why?" said Charles.

He was sure the man was hooked. The only remaining problem was how far he was going to end up being pushed on the price. He hoped he had allowed himself a big enough margin for negotiation.

"I like to do my business over food, and in a beautiful atmosphere. For Art there is no better place than 'Flo'." Charigot stood up and put his hand on Buchanan's shoulder, "Come, we'll play at being Modigliani and Utrillo - we'll get very, very, drunk, talk Art, and then do business."

Trapped in the unstable moment, not wanting to reimpose himself on the situation, Charles agreed. His next move would have to wait until after Charigot made an offer for the drawings - however long that took.

The two men moved from one bar to another around the tiny sidestreets of Montmartre; dodging tourists every step of the way along the pavements - and yet...thanks to a skill of Charigot's...somehow they managed to drink in bars undisturbed by foreign voices. Charigot was obviously a dedicated drinker and womanizer. At every stop he was recognized and welcomed by barmen; and occasionally women would detach themselves from their escorts to come and speak quietly in his ear.

Charles said little, kept his fears and worries about the sale to himself, and drank at the same pace as his host. By the time they were dropped by a taxi next to the shellfish stalls in the Cour des Petites Ecuries outside the 'Brasserie Flo,' he was having difficulty keeping his vision focused.

Inside the restaurant Charles understood exactly what Charigot meant about the ambiance. Conversation and laughter were ringing noisily around a room which looked as if it hadn't changed in over a century. A crowd of people waiting for tables were crammed into a space just inside the main door. The head waiter recognized Charigot and broke away briefly to shake his hand before returning to his work. The other waiters were dressed in black waistcoats and white aprons and moved everywhere carrying their trays at a pace only marginally short of a run.

During the ten minutes that they waited for a table, Charles studied the diners, half expecting to see someone from another age: Toulouse Lautrec quietly sketching, or German Generals of the army of occupation. The candle-lit restaurant was timeless.

Against a background of vociferous protests from an American and his wife in the throng, Buchanan and Charigot were the first of the crowd to be shown to a table. They squeezed into seats on either side of a small table, which - with several others - formed a line all along one wall of the restaurant. To one side of them were a dozen laughing guests from a wedding, the bride and groom still with rice in their hair; and on the other side were a group of eight French businessmen arguing and gesticulating extravagantly about something Charles could only guess at. Both groups were conducting their conversations noisily across the tables. In order to see the person they were talking to they were forced to peer around tall, multi-layered, silver trays on stands, topped with crushed ice and covered with shellfish.

Charles listened as Charigot pointed out the different sizes of oysters to him, and then went through the rest of the menu. His drunken brain was incapable of a choice and he asked Charigot to order a specialty of the house for him. A bottle of Champagne appeared as if from nowhere on the table and moments later the waiter arrived with a stand containing a dozen of the biggest oysters he had ever seen. Charigot offered him one; he tipped the ice-cold shellfish down his throat and took a sip at his champagne.

It should have been delicious, but he tasted nothing. His mind was so filled with the uncompleted sale he might just as well have tipped the ash-tray into his mouth. Charles was vaguely aware of Charigot speaking between mouthfuls,

"Huitres, Charlie. How do you say....Hoysters?"

"Oysters."

"Yes, of course, Oysters. A food of love. After oysters and champagne you cannot sleep without sex. Believe me, it is true. It is science. Did you ever have them before? "

"Once before."

"Were they as good as these?"

"No, they were not," answered Charles. He wasn't going to spoil Charigot's good humor by disagreeing with him.

As Charigot seemed determined to avoid talking about the Picasso's until he was good and ready, Charles wished he would shut up and let him absorb every detail of the crowded restaurant.

Six feet away from him was a woman sitting with her back to him.

Her hair was cut high on her neck, and he felt a strange compulsion to walk over and stroke her skin from the line of her hair to the limit of her bare shoulders. Even from the back he was sure he recognized her from somewhere. With her were three other women whom he knew he did not know, but there was something about that neck that he recognized and wanted.

He resolved to get up in a minute and walk to the toilet in such a way that he could look at the woman's face. Staring past Charigot's right shoulder he finished the last oyster.

Charigot continued talking, oblivious to the fact that his guest was no longer really listening, "...alors, Amadeo Modigliani, now there was a man. But, like me, a slave to women. He was killed by a woman..."

"No he wasn't; he died of drink," cut in Charles, returning suddenly to reality.

"Mais oui, bien sur. But why did he drink? I'll tell you why. After the death of his lover he said, 'I'm going to drink myself dead,' and he did. Just like that."

"Stupid bugger," said Buchanan, "Women are like busses, there'll be another one along in a minute." He returned his gaze to the beautiful nape of the unknown neck.

"No, no, no, there is only ever one woman; everything else is an illusion," said Charigot.

"That's just a load of romantic shit," countered Buchanan, unable to keep up his cheerful pretense any longer, "On the basis of our drinking session tonight, I reckon you must have had more women than I've had hot dinners. You don't seriously believe that crap, do you Maurice?"

"Of course!"

"Well, who is she then? And why isn't she with you tonight?" asked Buchanan sarcastically.

"I didn't find her yet!" laughed Charigot with a twinkle in his eyes, "But, until I do, I will keep on looking. That's the problem - so many women and so little time." He laughed again as the waiter appeared with their main courses: a huge plate of sauerkraut topped with pig's trotters for Charigot, and a piece of lamb covered in chopped garlic which bled profusely when Buchanan cut into it.

The champagne was finished as magically as it had appeared, and in its place the waiter brought a bottle of Margaux '73. The wine complemented his gigot of lamb perfectly, but again Buchanan was unable to really enjoy it. If he drank too much he was liable to let the paintings go too cheaply in a fit of drunken generosity. He ordered a mineral water. For several minutes Buchanan ate his way quietly through the meat and the little garden of watercress which accompanied it - his private love-affair with the unknown woman momentarily forgotten as he worried about selling his Picasso's.

When he next looked up from his plate, he was shocked and horrified to see that her chair was empty.

The waiter was flapping breadcrumbs from the tablecloth onto the floor with a napkin in readiness for the next group of diners. Buchanan half-stood to see if he could see her on her way out. She had gone.

Charigot followed his stare, "What is it, Charlie?"

"Oh, nothing. Just some woman I thought I knew."

"Forget it. It's the oysters. Only the oysters, I warned you. Forget it. How did you say, There will be more driving the next bus?"

"Something like that, Maurice."

Try as Buchanan could to put the woman out of his mind, he still retained the image of her shoulders rising out of the blue silk of her dress. It stayed with him whilst he watched Charigot eat a bowl of fresh strawberries washed down with pink champagne, sip at a coffee and drink two large balloons of

Calvados. He was still brooding when Charigot called for the bill.

He watched distantly as the designer pulled out his check book and wrote a check. From a great distance and through a haze of noise he heard him saying,

"Now, while I have money in my hand and food and drink inside me, I feel ready to talk about your drawings."

"Eh?"

"The Picasso's. Will you accept two and a half millions?"

"What?" answered Buchanan in confusion.

"For both. One million and a quarter for each one."

The figures tumbled like acrobats through Buchanan's brain. Nothing made sense at all. Charigot added defensively,

"My friend, you and I both know they are not worth more than this. I am offering a fair price. Do we have a deal?"

"I'm not sure," said Buchanan grimly now that he finally understood. Charigot was referring to the old currency and was, in fact, offering only twenty-five thousand pounds in total - although Buchanan had asked for the equivalent of thirty-six thousand pounds, he had been prepared to accept twenty-eight.

Once again he was faced with the option of a bird in the hand, or a bird in the bush. At least with the Picasso's he was selling the genuine article; he could always try Daubigny. As a last resort he offered Charigot a compromise,

"For three million old francs they're yours, Maurice. If you don't want them I'll try Edouard Daubigny."

The mention of the other collector's name shook Charigot visibly. He tapped his pen on his check-book,

"It's a lot of money, Charlie. But I would hate for that cochon to beat me to it. I will talk tomorrow morning with my family, maybe it is possible."

Buchanan tried to conceal his irritation. Why couldn't the damn man give him an answer there and then and be done with it? Once again he was in limbo.

"I will give you first option, Maurice. If you call me at my hotel before noon then you can have them. If not, I must try elsewhere."

"Allons-y!" said Charigot paying the bill and draining his brandy glass, "Enough of business, now we play. I can tell you are nervous and irritable. You need a woman. Shall we take a little walk along the Rue Saint Denis and see if we can find one to help you sleep?"

Buchanan looked at the man across the table from him and tried to make Charigot's face stay still as it drifted about his field of vision.

*A woman?*

The bloody man must be bloody joking.

What he really needed was a positive decision on the pictures.

# CHAPTER EIGHTEEN.

OUTSIDE THE RESTAURANT, THE COBBLESTONES GLEAMED WET in the streetlights even though the rain had stopped. Charigot and Buchanan turned right out of the courtyard into the Rue du Faubourg Saint Denis. It was almost one o'clock in the morning and yet the streets were still bustling with people. The chill in the night air and the exertion of walking rapidly decreased the effects of the alcohol. After only a hundred yards Charles was feeling sober again.

The two men passed beside a soot stained ancient gateway and continued towards the Seine along the narrow Rue Saint Denis. It was so choked with pedestrians that vehicles could barely pass. Along the side of the road there were prostitutes lounging in the doorways of every building. Many of them were attractive. They were all undressed to a greater or lesser extent.

Charigot began laughing, "Look at the men with their wives, Charlie. All of them are thinking the same thing. Why couldn't I find a woman as beautiful as these putains?"

As his drunkenness faded, Charles could feel the first stirring of desire in his groin. Since the dramatic night with the punkette he had slept alone. The scene with Sally and the theft of his pictures had destroyed all traces of his libido. How could he think about sex when his very freedom was threatened? Tonight all his past fears of discovery and imprisonment seemed distant. He was glad that Charigot was ambling so slowly. Most of the other men in the street were hurrying, casting furtive glances, and ignoring the offers they received.

As they came to each new group of prostitutes the Frenchman stopped and tipped an imaginary cap in greeting to the women. Several of the women knew Charigot personally and greeted him,

"Bonsoir, Monsieur Maurice. Comment ça va?"

He in turn introduced them to Charles and told him that all he had to do if he found a woman to his taste was let him know; he would negotiate the fee.

"I never pay for a woman!" said Buchanan.

Charigot burst out laughing, "Always you must pay, in one way or another. And for a woman as beautiful as this..." He stopped and indicated a statuesque blonde dressed only in black lace underwear and a fur coat, "You will pay less than I've paid to eat dinner with you! Please, no more about paying. Are there no women here you would like to make love to?"

"No," said Charles firmly.

"What a shame. For me, half the pleasure of a meal chez 'Flo' is the company I find on my way home."

Charles's refusal seemed to put a damper on Charigot's good humor and the two men walked on in silence. The pace of their progress increased. Charles was trying to think of something to say when he was stopped in his tracks.

Ahead of them a group of half a dozen women were laughing and joking in a doorway. In the middle was the same backless blue silk dress he had been staring at all night in the restaurant.

The same close-cut hair on the neck.

The same woman.

Charigot had failed to notice that he was walking on his own. Suddenly he realized and turned to see where Buchanan was. He walked slowly back to where Charles was standing.

"What is it?"

"That woman," said Charles, "the one in the blue dress. Can you fix it for me with her?"

"Good God! Asterix was right when he said the English were mad. Two minutes ago you were saying no to the best in the business. Now you want to go with an amateur."

"What do you mean?" asked Charles distantly, his eyes fixed on the woman.

"This is Monique's apartment. I know her, she models for some artist friends in the Butte. The other girls work hotels. They pay her a commission on the business they do from here. When this girl in the blue dress has enough money she will get a place on her own. Why not go with Monique, the blonde one? She is an expert. I will wait for you here."

"I want the one in blue."

"As you wish. Wait here. I'll have a word with her." Charigot walked over to the brightly lit doorway and was noisily welcomed by Monique. The two of them began talking; after a minute all the women turned to look in his direction.

Charles wished he had kept quiet.

Maurice broke away from the group and walked over to Buchanan.

"Five hundred francs, Charlie. And you must pay for her taxi back. If you give her seven hundred it will be enough. You might have to pay the man at the desk of your hotel as well. Give him a hundred francs. He will be more than happy."

"Okay," said Charles distantly.

"Viens, Loulou," called Charigot to the girl.

"What about you?" asked Charles.

"I will stay with Monique. I'm an old customer of hers. See you later, Charlie, and have fun! Tomorrow - I will telephone you."

The prostitute stood beside him as he shook hands with Maurice and watched him disappear with Monique. Then she pushed her arm through his and pulled him forcefully, leading him away down the street.

"You are English?" she asked pleasantly - but matter-of-factly - as they walked.

"Yes."

"I speak a little. You must pay me now. It is the way we work."

"Of course," said Charles hurriedly, fumbling in his pocket for his wallet. He pulled out a five hundred franc note and two hundreds. "For you and the taxi," he explained.

She smiled at him and tucked the money into her handbag. "Your friend said your hotel was on the Boulmiche. We can get a taxi from the Boulevard de Sebastopol. Allons-y."

She led him quickly through a narrow sidestreet to the busy main road and found a taxi. She gave directions to the driver and opened the back door for him; he climbed in and she followed. The driver floored the accelerator and rejoined the late-night traffic with a squeal from the tires. The car was moving north, away from the left bank where his hotel was. It swung into a dark sidestreet and for a second Charles worried about the contents of his briefcase on the floor. However, before long they were back on a brightly lit main road and heading towards the Seine.

The woman was sitting as far away from him as she could, gazing out of the window and clutching her handbag on her lap. Charles stared at her intently, trying to take in every detail. It was hard to tell how old she was. Twenty four or five, at most. In profile the slope of her nose followed the line of her forehead. Beneath it the painted gloss of her lips pushed out before cutting back to her chin. The whole attitude of her face displayed an aggressiveness alien to the feminine line of her jaw and cheekbones. The only concession to 'prettiness' was her hair, which swirled like a sixties Beatle-cut around her head, falling low across her eyes at the front and cut high at the back. Where her neck joined her shoulders a small hollow formed between her collarbone and the muscle which swept into the round curve of her shoulder.

The sleeves of her dress were separate from the main body - like gloves without hands - and came to just below the vaccination scar which gleamed white on her tanned skin. From the top of her dress an inch or so of the deep cut between her breasts gave a sufficient indication of their size to make him uncross his legs in order to get comfortable - from the hemline her calves disappeared into the darkness behind the driver's seat.

His inspection came to an abrupt halt as the car skidded to a halt in the darkness outside the Ecole des Mines. He paid the driver and joined her on the pavement. She led him gently by the arm across the road and waited while he searched in his mackintosh for the key to the front door of the hotel.

The lobby was in near darkness, lit by a single dim tablelight. Charles started to speak,

"My room's on the..."

"Taisez-vous! Shut up!" she hissed. Charles followed where she was pointing. In one of the armchairs the Algerian-looking night-porter was snoring as he slept. She stooped to take off her shoes, pressed her finger to her lips and they both crept across the room to the stairs.

In his room she put on the main light just long enough to turn on the two lamps on either side of the bed. Seeing his travel radio and alarm clock on the bedside table, she switched it on and tuned it to a music station. Charles watched all this from the doorway. She turned and beckoned for him to come into the room.

"Do you have anything to drink?" she asked in French.

"Only brandy." Charles walked over and picked up the duty-free bag on the floor by the window. On the shelf in the bathroom he found two Duralex unbreakable tumblers. He put everything on the table and poured two fingers of brandy into each glass. "Is that all right?"

She took the bottle from his hands and doubled the quantity in each glass. After drinking most of it with one swallow she looked at him standing in his raincoat and said, "Parfait. Come here. What is your name?"

"Charles."

She stood facing him about a foot away. During the journey from the lobby to his room she had put her shoes back on and the high heels boosted the top of her head to his eye level. She reached around his shoulders and took off his coat, throwing it over the chair by the table. "Charles," she repeated. To his surprise she pronounced it correctly, "Do you want to talk or shall we begin?"

"Yes, let's start," said Charles quickly, "Your English is good."

"And meine Deutch, Italiano, Espagnol. For work I must speak many languages. Take off your clothes and get into bed."

He did as he was instructed. She poured herself another brandy and drained the glass, standing with her back to him as he undressed. When she sensed he was ready she turned to face him.

With professional expertise she reached behind her back, undid the zip which ran the length of her dress and let it slip to the floor.

Underneath the dress she was completely naked. At the end of the maneuver her arms were folded across her breasts. She shook her hair out of her eyes and, taking off the long blue gauntlets, slowly let her hands fall to her sides.

She enjoyed showing her body and the power it gave her over men. As her breasts came into full view, she was watching Charles intently, waiting. Waiting for the moment when he - like every other man - would pull his knees up towards his chest in a reflex acknowledgment of his mounting excitement. She smiled as he obeyed the unspoken order, and she walked over to the bed. On her way she stopped to take a condom from a packet in her handbag. Pulling back the bedclothes she rolled it slickly into position and climbed in next to him.

She was good at her job, but her performance was that of an actress in a long running play. She did all the right things, moved in the right way at the right time and made all the right noises. What happened to Charles had little to do with her.

As he was being guided mechanically to his climax his brain began filling with images. It was as if a bomb had blasted a hole through the wall that kept his imagination within set limits. He was looking through a kaleidoscope that turned slowly in front of him - watching himself down the wrong end of a telescope - floating in space above the bed. He was watching another woman in another place.

*She was no longer made of flesh and blood, but an animated line drawing. A spiraling Matisse. A fractured Braque.*

Reality could no longer be certainly assumed to be the reports from his senses.

*He was looking through a stone-mullioned window of a belltower in a monastery somewhere high in a mountain range - looking through to insanity - understanding the swirling cornfields and threatening clouds of Van Gogh at Arles. There were scrub pines outside the courtyard: twisted stunted trees like those painted by Cezanne in Aix en Provence. He could feel the cold, thin air of early morning blowing around him. A woman in a hooded cloak was riding a horse through the main gate in the perimeter wall. Then he was falling, falling, spinning through space. His vision clouded over, he could see nothing. Slowly he realized that it was his own breath fogging a window in front of him. With his hand he wiped the cold glass clean and saw there was snow falling outside.*

It was dark.

*A woman's hand took him by the shoulder and pulled him back onto cold sheets. He could hear her asking if it was still snowing. Her hands went to either side of his face and pulled him down. He struggled. He was too close.*

His climax was coming. The face was out of focus. He was awake, this was no dream. It was really happening. He couldn't see clearly. I want to look at you, he tried to shout, but like a dream no sound came. Silently he pleaded, Let me go! Let me go!

Then he shuddered to a standstill.

By the time he had gathered his strength enough to lift his head, the prostitute was squatting on the bidet in his bathroom. He could see her through the open doorway. She stood up, dried herself and retouched her make-up in the bathroom mirror. Charles watched unseeing as she climbed back into her dress. Picking up her handbag she walked to the door.

Charles hardly heard her wishing him goodnight. His reply was little more than a reflex. What was frightening him was that his hand was still cold and wet from where he had wiped the condensation from the glass. That wasn't a hallucination, was it?

Why had this woman caused such chaos in his head? Was he going crazy? - the pressure too much? Had a switch flipped in his brain? He was sure that when you went crazy you were no longer able to tell the difference between your hallucinations and reality. He checked his hand again, this time it felt warm.

He had to pull himself together, just for a few days. After the auction everything would be all right. He would stop forging for a few months, just buy and sell pictures. He was good enough, wasn't he? He could earn a living; he did it before. If he could just get some sleep and relax a little everything would fall into place. All he had to do was get through the next thirty-six hours successfully.

It was as simple as that.

Except, he thought, nothing was ever that simple.

He switched out the lights.

# CHAPTER NINETEEN

BUCHANAN'S HOPE THAT DARKNESS would shut off the images in his head was a forlorn one. Instead it was like a theater with the house lights dimmed; all his attention was focused on them. After what seemed like days he gave up trying to sleep, switched the lights back on and checked his alarm clock. It was only three thirty; the prostitute had been gone less than an hour. He got up and took a steaming hot shower. Slowly, as the hot spray needled at his back he began to feel better. After ten minutes he stepped out of the cubicle and opened the full length windows over the courtyard. Wrapped in his bath-towel he rolled a cigarette, poured another brandy and leaned on the railing across the window.

He didn't notice the cold. He didn't notice the gradual brightening of the gloom as dawn broke. It wasn't until the old concierge clattered into the courtyard with her mop and bucket that he noticed anything. Reluctantly he let go of the nothingness which he had been so happy to let fill his mind.

After remaining almost motionless for hours his ankle joints cracked like uncooked spaghetti when he stepped back into the room. He took another hot shower and was pleased at the irritation he felt when he came to dry himself on the already damp towel. The irritation was a normal reaction, wasn't it?

Comforted, he focused his attention on small tasks - one at a time. He chose what he was going to wear from the wardrobe. His French shirt, the blue and white striped one that he liked so much. A navy pair of woolen loose cut trousers that didn't show any creases from their time in the suitcase. And a tweed sports-jacket to warm away the last of the chill from his time at the window.

He picked up his briefcase and took out the folders with the Picasso's in. He had paid £16,000 for the pair of them five years ago. They represented the profit of an entire year's legitimate trading. Two pieces of paper with drawings that had taken the artist no more than an hour, maybe no more than ten minutes. That was the beauty of forgery. You could short circuit the lifetime's work that instilled the monetary value in a sketch. They were like a pair of £8,000 banknotes drawn on cheap paper with a twenty pence dip-pen: banknotes without watermarks or security codes. It was ridiculously easy. A few hours drawing or painting could replace a year of 'work'. Without thinking he opened the folders to look at the drawings themselves.

Instantly the ink lines shimmered and moved. The woman's eyes seemed to flicker.

He slammed the folders closed again. The telephone rang.

"Good morning, Charlie." It was Charigot. "Did you sleep well?"

"I didn't sleep at all."

"So, she was good. Eh?"

"She made me think. Do you want the paintings?"

"That's why I'm calling; have you had breakfast yet?"

"No."

"Can you meet me in twenty minutes at the Bar Louis Quatorze in the Place Edmond Rostand? It's only a short walk from your hotel."

"I'll find it. See you in twenty minutes."

Buchanan brushed his hair, wondered about having a

[ 196 ]

shave, decided against it and left for the cafe.

Outside a thin sunshine was casting feeble shadows on the street. But it was warm enough, and when he saw that a group of students were monopolizing most of the tables in the bar, he selected a small Formica topped table on the pavement and ordered a coffee and croissant.

From his seat he watched a stream of mothers and children standing in line to buy bread and cakes at a patisserie across the street. It was a normal everyday scene and Charles was grateful for it.

The longer he watched, the more he became aware that even on the street, in daylight, things could slip out of gear.

The brightly colored backpacks that the children were carrying became the fluid flecks of paint on a Raoul Dufy - the sunlight slanting down between the tall buildings organized the street into the planes of color and space of a Feiniger or a Delauney. When he closed his eyes the scene froze on his retina like Seurat's "La Grande Jatte."

Buchanan gritted his teeth and waited.

The arrival of Charigot was a relief. The designer swung breezily from the pavement into one of the heavy cast iron chairs beside Charles, smiling broadly. He was still dressed in the same dog-eared linen suit. He shouted his order for a coffee through the open doors to the barman at the counter, and said to Charles,

"You should have taken Monique." He kissed the tips of his fingers. "She is an artist. A veritable artist. And yours?"

"Okay," said Buchanan without enthusiasm, "What about the Picasso's, Maurice? Do you want them?"

"Doucement, Charlôt, doucement. You are very nervous. I have never seen you like this. Why?"

"Look, it's very simple; if you don't want them I'll try elsewhere."

Charigot reached into his pocket and pulled out an envelope which he passed to Charles. "I spoke to my sister this morning; she has agreed to help with the purchase. Here is a check from the family trust for the drawings. I will call my bank and arrange for you to exchange it for cash. Three hundred thousand nouveau francs we agreed?"

Buchanan ripped open the envelope, read the figures and stuck it into his pocket.

"Thank you, Maurice. Here they are." He reached behind him for the briefcase, opened it and pulled out the folders. After the theft of the Schiele's he wasn't taking any chances. From the moment he arrived in Paris they hadn't left his side. He passed them to Charigot who glanced inside at the drawings before asking,

"What are you going to do before the auction? See the sights?"

"I haven't made any plans. I suppose I'll just kill time - have a bit of a look around."

"I'm sorry, Charlie, I would like to show you the city, but I have a meeting at eleven. And before that I must collect some samples for my client. So I must go. Thank you for bringing the drawings to me. It's what friends in the business are for. Eh? Maybe give me a ring tonight?"

"Sure, Maurice. And I'm glad you got the pictures, not Daubigny."

Charigot, now standing by the side of the table, spat towards the gutter at the mention of Daubigny's name, "So am I. See you soon."

Charles watched him go back to his pristine BMW and looked again at the check in his hands.

He was back in with a realistic chance of securing the Schiele's. It was time for a new list of priorities. Strike off Charigot; and Daubigny. That meant that all that was left of the original list was a visit to Sabatier's to get the bidding sorted out. To add to that was a visit to Charigot's bank to cash the check - it might take some time; he would do it first. Afterwards he could wander over to Sabatier's - it wouldn't

[ 198 ]

hurt to get acquainted with the place - have a leisurely lunch and then a few tension-relieving drinks in a bar.

He finished his coffee and caught the metro to the Tuilleries. A short walk brought him to the Place Vendôme and the head office of Charigot's bank. After presenting the check to the inquiry desk he was passed along a chain of subordinates and their bosses until he finished up in the grand first floor offices of a senior, English-speaking, member of the bank.

True to his word, Charigot had telephoned and warned them that he was coming. However, in the time honored custom of great banking, there was nothing they could do today. The official launched himself into a detailed explanation of the paperwork that was involved in changing Charigot's check into a negotiable form of currency while Charles looked over his shoulder, out of the window to the vast bronze column of the Vendôme. Eventually the man completed his excuses and realized Charles was paying no attention to him. He followed his gaze.

"Ah, the Vendôme Column. It's very beautiful, isn't it? And quite a gesture from a dictator. To make art from twelve hundred cannon that his army captured at the battle of Austerlitz."

"...And they shall beat their swords into ploughshares," said Charles distantly. Before his eyes the column seemed to be melting at the top like a giant candle; dripping great gobs of molten bronze which splashed to the ground. This time he was in control of the hallucination, though. By a slight effort of concentration he could restore the column to normality. He played with the illusion, recalling it and watching it develop. Every drop became a perfectly formed cannon and as the column got shorter and shorter the square slowly filled with row upon row of the ancient weapons.

He became aware of the bank official speaking to him again, "Excuse me, Monsieur Buchanan? Is something the matter?"

"It's nothing. So you can do nothing today, but if I come

tomorrow everything will be all right?"

The bank official nodded, with an air of injured honor. Didn't the Englishman understand that there were some things that couldn't be done hastily however much one wanted to? And removing three hundred thousand francs from the bank was one of them. He shook Buchanan's hand and asked his assistant to lead him back to the street.

It took him twenty minutes to walk from the Place Vendôme to Sabatier's. The famous old sale rooms were in a restored seventeenth-century Hotel at the back of a small courtyard reached from the street by passing through a pair of massive wrought iron gates decorated with masks. These fantastic faces almost seemed to have a life of their own as they leered down from the iron framework which Charles momentarily envisaged as prison bars. With an effort he concentrated his attention on the bland stone frontage of the building until he finally reached the cool of the marble-clad entrance lobby. He joined the short queue of people waiting to have their bags searched at the security desk; the elderly security guard ruffled through the contents of his briefcase and asked,

"Your business, Monsieur?"

"I want to view tomorrow's sale. I also would like to talk to someone about bidding," said Charles in French.

The guard's entire manner changed when this obvious foreigner spoke French and mentioned bidding. A deferential tone replaced the boredom of his first question, "Viewing is in the old stable-block, and the offices are up the main staircase on the left. If you need any help, you know where to find me. Good morning, Monsieur. Et bonne chance."

Charles followed the old man's directions up the gently curved, marble staircase to the first floor. When he stepped through the doorway it was all he could do to restrain himself from gawking like a child in a toyshop. The office was a vast Rococo room: laden with gilt and sumptuous drapery. On the painted ceiling nearly twenty feet above his head a winged Diana pursued a stag. After the cramped, almost Dickensian, cubby holes of Sotheby's in London, the splendor of the room was breathtaking. Seated at the antique reception desk was a young man with shoulder length blonde hair and a thin ascetic face. He looked inquiringly at Charles.

"Do you speak English?" asked Charles. There was no room at this stage in the proceedings for a cock-up caused by a misunderstanding.

"Yes, sir." The clerk smiled thinly, almost as if he was apologizing to his French ancestors for the statement that followed. "In this business it is almost obligatory. I spent three years at Sotheby's. What is it you want to know?"

"My name is Charles Buchanan, I represent Romulus Fine Art of London." He handed him a business card. "I'm interested in buying two paintings in your sale tomorrow."

"Sit down," said the young man, indicating a chair in front of his desk. "Which lots are you interested in?"

"I haven't seen the catalogue, but it is the two pictures by Schiele. They're both titled *'Liegender Weiblicher Akt mit Gespreitzen Beinen'*."

"Ah, yes, lots 144 and 145, the late additions. You do understand these paintings are only attributed to Schiele? You would not be covered by the six year clause if they proved to be by another hand. We would not be under any obligation to accept them back. Of course there is some very convincing provenance which you would be welcome to inspect. I can arrange that for you if you wish."

"Thank you, that would be most helpful. My main concern is that I want to buy anonymously." Charles did not want to have to explain in London why he was buying pictures that a few weeks earlier he had claimed to own. It could start people asking difficult questions. "I do not want to go through a dealer. Is it possible that I can lodge my bid with you in advance?"

"A bid 'on the book' will be no problem. I'll get someone to bring up the provenance." The young man picked up the telephone and spoke rapidly in French. "Can I arrange a drink for you while we're waiting?"

"No, thank you. My problem is that I want both paintings. And it is not as simple as just leaving a 'bid on the book'."

"Monsieur?"

"The guide figures I have heard were for between fifty and seventy thousand pounds sterling, each."

"That is our best estimate, sir."

"I would like to deposit a hundred and sixty thousand pounds with you. This is to be used to purchase lot 144, with the surplus to be used for lot 145. The buyer's premium I will handle separately. Do you understand?"

"Yes, sir. I'm sure it's possible, but I'll have to speak to my superiors. Do you mind, I won't keep you waiting long?"

Buchanan waited while he went through a side exit to consult with some unseen executive. The young man arrived back at the same time as the porter came into the room bearing a file. He laid it down in front of Charles. Inside were all the documents that he had so painstakingly prepared for Morganstein. He flicked through them to see if there were any clues to the identity of the seller. There was no mention of anything after Morganstein's report. He closed the file and looked up as the clerk said,

"If you deposit the money with us in advance there will be no problem, Mr Buchanan. The house will have somebody bidding anonymously on your behalf from the floor. If you can come in a couple of hours before the sale tomorrow we can finalize the arrangements."

"Who is the current owner?" asked Charles innocently.

"I'm afraid that is as confidential as you wish your identity to remain, Mr Buchanan," said the young man with a smile.

"Thank you for your help," said Charles heavily, "Is there unrestricted viewing on the paintings?"

"You haven't even seen them yet?" asked the clerk suspiciously.

"No, but I've heard great things," said Charles quickly.

"That I can understand. The level of interest in them has been quite phenomenal. I'll get someone to take you down."

The porter was summoned back by telephone and he led Charles through a maze of corridors until they reached the oak paneled and vaulted hall of the restored stable-block. Charles paused in the doorway and scanned the walls for the Schiele's. He spotted them almost at once: they were in the far corner of the room. In front of them were a man and a woman, deep in conversation, catalogues in hand.

A shudder ran through Charles as the man turned to speak to his companion and he saw his face. He recognized it instantly, even though he had only seen it once before - in an article about the world's major Art collectors on the pages of *Harpers and Queens*. It was the tanned, wide-mouthed grin of Ronald Lauder. A millionaire member of the family that had made its money in cosmetics. Along with Wendell Cherry he was one of the leading buyers of works from the Vienna School; between them they had spent over five million dollars on acquiring just two Schiele's. Now that he knew that one of the truly big guns was here, Charles didn't even bother to go closer to inspect the paintings. With his brain whirring he turned and hurried out of Sabatier's.

Outside he walked quickly but aimlessly. There was nothing else that he could do. Now it was in the lap of the gods. In a half-hearted way he decided to go back towards the Opera. But he was just killing time; he didn't have any set plan - just twenty-four more hours to while away.

A man in a dark business suit collided with him outside a jewelry shop on the Rue de la Paix. Buchanan watched him walk away and then decided for no good reason to follow him. For ten minutes he tracked him back up to the Opera and then down the Rue du Quatre Septembre. When the man climbed into a parked Citroen and drove away, Charles stood for a second, lost. Another car pulled into the free parking space and an immaculately dressed middle-aged woman got out.

It became a game. Against all the rational protestations of a section of his brain, he followed her through a maze of small streets to the colonnaded walk along the Rue de Rivoli, but he was careful to remain far enough away to escape detection; the last thing he wanted was to become involved with the Police.

When the woman turned off the pavement into a couturier's, he began looking for other people that seemed 'significant', and following them until they vanished into shops or offices. The unwitting guides were showing him the city, taking him down streets he would never have dreamed of visiting. He criss-crossed the second arrondissement, found himself outside the Hôtel de Ville and then turned away from the crowded banks of the Seine.

Suddenly he was in a fairy tale city. Here in the fourth arrondissement the buildings were made from a yellowing stone that was eroded by the weather into soft shapes that almost seemed to be melting gingerbread: gone were the wide streets and tall buildings. In a half-hearted way he was tracking a man and a woman. They were twisting and turning through the narrow streets. At some point he had made the decision that if they turned left he would follow them, and if they went right he would follow the man in front of him with the rolled up umbrella. They had turned left, and so had he. They were easy to follow; they moved slowly and stopped frequently. Charles ambled after them.

With a start he realized they had stopped and that he was only about twenty yards away. As he approached the man looked at him and then pulled the woman into a cafe two doors away from where they were standing. Realizing he had been spotted he decided to bluff it out. He followed them into the bar.

They took a table at the back of the bar and Charles sat

down at a stool by the counter. He ordered a Pernod and water.

Behind the bar was a decorated mirror.

It was an Art Deco masterpiece.

Etched into the glass were art deco figures of athletes and the Olympic insignia of five interlocking rings; without doubt it was a treasure from the Games of 1924. Using the reflections in it he looked around the bar at the other occupants. The man he had been following was using the public telephone in the corner; the woman was nowhere to be seen. Over half of the people in the bar were wearing the dark blue cotton overalls worn by tradesmen in France. The others seemed to be a mixture of typical Art students and office workers taking advantage of the forty franc set menu for their lunch. The air was thick with the smell of black tobacco.

He drained the last of the cloudy yellow drink from the glass and ordered another.

The taste of the aniseed formed part of a pattern in his mind. Not a visual pattern, or an aural one, but one that filled the entire bar-room. It acquired an order, a rightness. He felt totally at home in the bar. If he stayed here and never moved again everything would be all right. It became like a hologram. He was able to move in and around it without upsetting or changing it - it existed independently of him. More than that it seemed to exist independent of past, present, or future. It wasn't confined to three simple dimensions of space, but somehow it had stability in time as well.

It was 1987, but it could equally well have been 1967, or 1947, or even 1927. There was nothing in the room which dated it: the bottles behind the bar were dusty and bore labels which were unfamiliar to Charles; the cigarette packets he could see on the counter were decorated with the familiar art-deco Gitanes design; the barman was wearing the time-honored uniform of black waistcoat, trousers and white apron; even the clothes and faces of the workman on the table nearest him showed no signs of a fashion that would place them in time. Here was a place to rest and recharge; it was an island of safety, of security. He ordered another Pernod and water. The fresh taste of aniseed exploded in his mouth.

After he had drunk and paid for two more drinks, the barman began filling his glass without even being asked. An hour passed and the comfortable solidity of the room softened. People began swimming in and out of the unframed edges of the mirror. The bar was as busy as ever, even in mid-afternoon there seemed to be no sign of a slack period.

It was, he reasoned with himself, a bar to visit again, under less stressed circumstances. He swiveled on his stool and tried to read the name from where it was engraved on the glass of the front window. For a second it was too much of an effort to cope with deciphering the reversed letters, and then, as he turned back to the counter, he caught sight of the words reflected in the vast mirror behind the bar. With a growing feeling of contentment he read 'Bar des Olympians'. He laughed. Thanks to his anonymous guides he had arrived in one of Paris's most famous artistic watering holes. The damn place was almost on a par with the 'Lapin Agile' or the 'Moulin Rouge' - a shrine in the Art World. No wonder he felt so at home.

The pressure of the auction receded another fraction. He almost managed to forget the extent of the trouble he was in.

Almost, but not quite.

That didn't happen until about half an hour later. Half an hour after the blind man sat down on the stool next to his at the bar.

# CHAPTER TWENTY.

Closeted alone in the safety of her uncomfortably-grand Parisian hotel room, Megan sat down on the edge of the bed, closed the airmail letter she now knew almost by heart, and worried how Bill Montague would react to the questions she was steeling herself to ask him.

When she had first received Sally's cheery letter she had felt betrayed. After all, the young woman had been hurt as much as her, hadn't she? She'd constructed the plan so they would BOTH have their revenge. But Sally seemed almost to have forgotten how she felt when she made the first telephone call to Oxford. Well, maybe not forgotten, no...written-off. That was more like it. She had simply written-off Charles Buchanan as an emotional bad debt. She wasn't wasting her time and energy demanding her pound of flesh; she was getting on with her life. That showed not only in the words that described what she was doing, but also in her handwriting which hurtled through the wide open spaces of the beginning of the aerogramme, and then crammed up as she realized she was running out of room on the blue paper.

And every time she re-read the letter she asked herself with increasing self-doubt why her attitude towards Charles had changed since the day she had first telephoned Montague.

How and why? The how was easier, it was simply the passage of time, which had found an ally in Sally's blind optimism. The why was more complicated. After all, she wasn't going to shift her anger by simply running away to the sun, was she? Not at her age, she thought bitterly.

What she couldn't understand was why getting her own back on Charles was making her feel uneasy, instead of giving her a great deal of satisfaction.

She was interrupted by a series of brisk knocks at the door.

"Come in," she said.

Bill Montague's tanned face appeared around the edge of the door, "Everything all right?"

"Yes, it's fine, Bill. Come on in."

He closed the door behind him and walked across the room.

There was something odd about his walk that puzzled her. Then it clicked and she asked, "Have you used your stick at all today?"

"Don't need to," he said gruffly, but with a trace of pride, "Thanks to Charles Buchanan. It's amazing how a good sustained shot of adrenaline can sort out what the damn quacks have been dithering over for years."

"How's your room?"

"I've got my usual," he laughed, "Damn manager wouldn't believe that I hadn't just come over early for the 'Prix de l'Arc de Triomphe' on Saturday. The only time he ever sees me is when there's racing at Longchamp. On top of that, I think your presence has started a few tongues wagging."

"Am I an evil temptress or a poor gullible fool?"

"I don't know, and I don't much care."

"How did your visit to Sabatier's go?"

"Just this second got back. I thought you must have settled in by now, and I thought I'd tell you the news."

"Oh, right," she said quietly.

Montague didn't notice her lack of enthusiasm; he was far too excited himself. "He's going to be up against it Megan.

Back to the bloody wall."

"What do you mean?"

"Old Morganstein has done us proud. From what they told me at Sabatier's I reckon every major collector is in town for the sale. The Schiele's are the star attraction. When I went to view them there was a damn crowd camped in front of them."

"Really?" she said without enthusiasm.

"Yes, really. Look, what's the matter? You've got about as much get up and go as nag in a glue factory."

"I'm sorry, Bill."

"What is it, the hotel? Are you tired after the flight?"

"No, the hotel's fine - more to a wealthy American's taste than mine, but fine. And I'm not tired, at least not because of the flight."

"So, what is it?"

There was a long pause.

"Is it too late to call the whole thing off?"

There was another, longer, pause.

"I think you better explain yourself," said Montague finally. He looked around for a chair; her last words had knocked the stuffing out of his legs.

"I'm sorry, Bill."

"For God's sake don't apologize, woman. Tell me why!"

"Don't get cross."

"I'm not bloody cross!"

"You have every right to be."

"I AM NOT BLOODY CROSS!" shouted Montague. Then he smiled as he realized the truth was in the tone not the content of his words. "Okay, okay, I'm a little bit cross. Who the hell wouldn't be after all the work I've put in? But I'm a reasonable man," he smiled warmly at her, "And you're the boss. I'm just the monkey - you're the organ grinder. What's caused this change of heart?"

"Time. The pure and simple passage of time. When I first called you I was almost incandescent with rage. I can't remember ever being so angry in my life. Hell hath no fury etc. etc. But I'm not angry anymore." She spread her hands and added, "It's as simple as that. And I can't help wondering what right I have to play God with his life."

"The man's a bloody crook, Megan."

"There's crooks and crooks."

"Well, that's true."

"And who's he hurting? The filthy rich, not the little people, not with his forgeries. Sure, he tramples over people. He trampled over me, and he trampled over his fiancée. But that's not a crime, is it?"

"No."

"The forgery is a confidence trick, and, as you told me yourself, the first ingredient in the recipe for any confidence trick is greed. Those were your exact words, weren't they?"

"Yes. But..."

"Let me finish and then tell me what you think. Where was I?"

"Greed," prompted Montague. There was irritation in his voice, but Megan tried her best to ignore it.

"Yes, greed. If there wasn't this 'share certificate hanging on the wall' mentality Charles couldn't function. It's precisely because people worry more about the value of paintings - and I mean monetary value not artistic value - that there's a market to be exploited. I hate to admit it, but I think he's right. The value shouldn't be in the signature, should it?"

"What you're saying is true, but it doesn't change the facts. The man's a shit, Megan. He treated you appallingly and he should not be allowed to get away with it. Besides that, the value is in the signature. That's the way the world is."

"It may be the way the world is, but we don't have to go along with it. You've seen Charles's pictures, what do you think of them?"

"That's irrelevant."

"No, it's not. What do you think of them?"

"Damn good," said Montague reluctantly.

"And that's in spite of the fact that you know they were painted by a...a...'shit'?"

"Okay, okay, you win," said Montague. But Megan knew him well enough to know that he would never give something away that easily. She tried to gather her wits for the argument she was sure would follow. It did, and it began by Montague asking, "So what do you want to do?"

"I don't know," said Megan miserably.

"But you don't want to expose him to the world?"

"No."

"Isn't there a bit of you that would like to spit in his eye or administer a swift kick to his rear-end for the way he treated you?"

It was Megan's turn to answer reluctantly, "....I suppose so."

"Don't equivocate, woman!"

"Oh all right, yes. I bloody well would." Against her will she felt her anger flaring up again.

"Good. I want you to keep that in the front of your mind - you want some revenge for the way that bastard treated you. I also want you to remember that, 'Revenge is a luscious fruit which you must leave to ripen'. The passage of time is no excuse for letting a man get away with bare-faced cruelty. Is it?"

She said nothing.

"IS IT?" he barked.

"No," she spoke very quietly.

"And on the other hand the auction will be the only way we will ever know how good a forger he is. Isn't there a part of you that is curious as to how valuable the Art World thinks his paintings are?"

"Yes." Bloody lawyers. He was so sharp. He'd got her angry, and now he was appealing to her curiosity. Damn the man!

"Good. Because I've invested a lot of my time in this project.

At my age time is a very precious commodity. And don't give that 'come on, you're not as old as all that' look, Megan, I can see through your soft soap. Before I got involved with this case I felt like a fossilized relic. I can understand what you're saying, but I'm in too deep to scrap the whole thing now. I've got my teeth into it and I'll be honest, I'm still enjoying it. I've enjoyed it from day one. I've never been emotionally involved, I'm too much of an old cynic, but I want to see this through. So we're going to let the sale go ahead, watch Buchanan wriggle on his own pin for a while, and then, and only then, talk about calling the whole thing off. All right?"

"It'll be too late then."

"Precisely. I'm so glad you've grasped that. Because, you started all this. It was you, Megan, not me, not Morganstein, not Buchanan's fiancée, YOU. I don't think we could call it all off if we wanted to. Morganstein has got to be paid, if you pull them out of the sale Sabatier's will want to be paid, and to be brutally frank Megan, I would LIKE to cover my costs. You can't afford not to go ahead."

"But we still don't have to release the photographs, do we?" Megan tried one last time to regain control of the scene she had initiated.

"That is the one thing we do have to do. If we don't we'll be as guilty as any forger - we'll be offering for sale something we know to be falsely described. I will bend the law for you, Megan; I will not, without damn good cause, break it for you."

"But what if..."

"If ifs and ands were pots and pans we'd have no need of tinkers. Megan, it's all entering the realms of the hypothetical situation. IF Buchanan manages to buy them both back, and you're content with just making a lot of money at his expense, then I'll consider destroying the photo's. BUT only if he buys them both and you're happy with the cash compensation. I promise you we'll talk about it after the sale. Are you happy with things like that? Do you want to talk about it some more?"

"No. There's no point. You've twisted my own words back on me already. You'll only tie me up in knots with your arguments. Peter used to tell me that arguing with you was like backing the favorite in a three horse race - in the unlikely event of a win, it was rarely worth the effort."

"Does this mean I can change the subject and offer you a spot of lunch?"

"Only if we go somewhere less ostentatious than this hotel. All this opulence makes me nervous."

"Another reason not to abandon the whole enterprise; if Buchanan doesn't pay for all this opulence, you'll have to."

"Shut-up! You said the subject was closed, now shut up about Charles."

"All right, all right, let's go and try and find somewhere humble to eat a cheap lunch."

As Montague rose a little stiffly to his feet, Megan sent out a silent apology to Charles Buchanan. It was going to hurt her as much as it hurt him.

This was no ordinary hunt. This one was prepared in advance by the Master of the Hounds. The fox was running, but before he had been released from captivity his pads had been slashed with a knife. Every step left blood on the ground. However much the Huntmaster wanted to avoid a messy kill, it was too late to call the hounds off; now they had the fresh scent of blood in their nostrils.

Something pretty dramatic would have to happen before Bill Montague stopped believing that his work wasn't finished until he'd handed the photographs to the new owner.

# CHAPTER TWENTY-ONE.

THE LOBBY OF THE 'GRANDE HOTEL DES MINEURS' WAS RINGING to the sound of English conversation. It was ringing because the floor, and the walls to the height of the dado rail, were covered with tiles: and also because the talkers were speaking in the unnaturally raised voices of people speaking in a language foreign to the rest of the population; feeling safe in the tenuous belief that no-one could understand what they were discussing.

There were three raised voices. Cordelia Babbington, Frank Price and Robin Malcolm sat sprawled in the armchairs around a low table covered with back issues of 'Marie Claire' magazine.

Frank Price climbed to his feet. "I've got to go and meet Morganstein now. Give me some time to talk shop and then come along. I'll tell him you're still getting dressed or something. All right, Babes?"

"Sure. Robin and I can reminisce about the good old days before you were born."

"I meant that you should give me about ten minutes, not ten days."

"Just run along," said Cordelia with what endeavored to be mock sternness, "And don't be cheeky to your elders and betters. I'll be there. Hey! Don't I get a kiss?"

Robin Malcolm thought he could hear a faint echo of genuine irritation in her words, as if she really didn't care for being reminded of her age. He watched Frank dutifully comply and saunter away across the lobby. As the street doors swung shut behind the departing figure he asked, "So, have you found out any more?"

"Nothing. Zod. Big fat zero."

"What do you make of it all?" asked Robin.

"From what I know of Charles, I think he just goofed."

"Goofed?"

"Yes, goofed. Slipped up. The old biddy must have got wind of what her paintings were really worth and pulled out of selling them to him."

"So, why is he so desperate to get them back?"

"We don't know that he is."

"Oh, come off it, Cordelia. In what you yourself described as a panic he flogs you back two perfectly good Bellmer's for less than he paid you for them in the first place, sells at least six other drawings - that we know of - begs twenty grand off you, and then disappears to Paris on the eve of the sale. I think we can safely assume he's here to buy them back and not just for a sashay down the Champs Elysee."

"Well then, I put it down to injured pride. He finds his lost masterpieces and then before his very eyes loses them again. I'm sure it's something like that."

"I don't believe it. In the first place I don't believe he would have let the old woman wriggle out of selling them to him. He's gone into liquidation how many times?"

"Three," she replied.

"And every time owing you lots of money. If your darling brother could have found a way of suing him to get the money back, he would have - and you know it. But no, every time Buchanan's made sure that his affairs are closed up tighter than a camel's arse in a sandstorm. The man's just too shrewd an operator."

"So...what's the answer?"

"I don't know. I really don't know," said Robin thoughtfully.

"Anyway, why has it become such an obsession with you?"

"Obsession? I don't think that's quite the right word for my curiosity. An obsession is something that persistently intrudes on a person's consciousness despite his will, and despite the fact that they recognize it to be abnormal. As I said, I hardly think my idle curiosity fits that description."

"I hate it when you do that. I hated it when I was going out with you, and I hate it now. You do it all the time. Somebody uses a word that has a perfectly good, everyday, Anglo-Saxon, meaning and then you go and hijack it for the personal use of psychiatrists. It irritates me almost beyond words. Do you know I used to describe myself as leading a fairly gay nightlife until everybody thought I was a closet dyke? Tell me something, if you're not obsessed...then what the fuck are you doing here in Paris?"

"I'm here because for the last three weeks virtually all of my friends have been talking about two paintings that six weeks ago nobody but Charles Buchanan even knew existed. Apart from you and Frank I've heard the paintings - or clandestine trips to Paris - mentioned in a good half dozen sessions. Morganstein's wife told me in her last visit that she's convinced he's over here to see some floozy because he won't give her a straight answer about who's selling the pictures. Then there's Shirley..."

"Hold on, who's Shirley?"

"The girl that does art stories for the Sunday color supplement. You know? The one I brought to your last opening?"

"Oh, yes. Attractive little bitch. What about her?"

"Well, I used to hear nothing from her but remarkably detailed sexual fantasies involving the surprising, and imaginative, use of different household items, now she only talks about the paintings; and I tell you, it's far less interesting.

[ 217 ]

She's had three reporters sniffing around like bloodhounds on aniseed, chasing their tails and finding out nothing. Even Frank's got a pet theory; something about a scheme devised by a Jew with a grudge to swindle Hitler. And to be quite honest, I'm curious. I'm here because I'm curious. I could ask you what you're doing here."

"No, you couldn't. I'm here because Frank is here; he's here because Morganstein is paying him to be here; and he's here because he's being paid to be here to sell the damn Schiele's."

"Okay, but who's paying Morganstein?"

"Presumably the same woman who telephoned him in the first place."

"Well, I don' t think it was the original owner. She spoke to Shirley's reporters, and if she wasn't telling the truth, she gave a pretty damn convincing impression of someone that was bitter about being tricked by Buchanan. So, unless she's involved too, that scotches your theory about her pulling out of the sale to Charles and keeping them for herself."

"Charles must have sold them to someone else, then, but *I* don't know who it is because *Frank* doesn't know, and *Frank* doesn't know because *Morganstein* doesn't know. On top of that, I really don't fucking care. Now, just shut up about the bloody paintings. You and I are the only two who are having a holiday, so why don't we enjoy it? We could be taking advantage of Frank's absence by slipping up to your bedroom and giving your pocket-rocket a test launch, but no; you suddenly want to be a detective. You're making a mountain out of a molehill."

"No, I'm not. I know there's something funny going on. I've known it since the night of the Carver's party."

"Well, I still think you're obsessed. Anyway I've got to go and meet Frank now. Are you sure you don't want to join us? Morganstein will be there." She dangled the last sentence like a carrot.

"No. I'm going to sit here for an hour or so with my book

and see if Buchanan pitches up."

"What makes you think he's staying here? I suggested three or four other hotels to him as well."

"I know he's staying here. He's got room 503. I gave the desk-clerk fifty francs for a quick look at the register. Told him I was trying to find someone that owes me some money. It's the truth, too. Buchanan still hasn't paid me the thirty-five quid for his session."

"I swear you think you're Philip Marlowe. All you trick-cyclists are the same: mad as hatters. I'll see you tomorrow at the sale if I don't catch you tonight." Cordelia got up, checked herself in the acanthus framed mirror on the lobby wall, rearranged the geometric precision of her hair, and blew him a kiss as she left.

Much as it grieved him to admit it, he *was* obsessed by Charles Buchanan. For over five years, he had been hearing the man's name and seeing him around the Art scene. All that time he had watched him and his seemingly never-ending procession of women; admiring the disdain with which he treated the pretentiousness and *'dahling, how absolootly soopah to see yooo'* hypocrisy of arch enemies; the skill with which he did business; and the charm which he could turn off and on at will.

But now, at last, there was a hint of weakness. A flaw in the previously impregnable armor that shielded him from prying eyes. Robin wanted to probe and work at that chink until he was inside with the real Charles Buchanan.

The key was the Schiele paintings. There was something funny about the whole business, but he couldn't get his head round it. It was like the name to a half-forgotten face across a crowded room. He knew it, dammit, he knew it. The Charles Buchanan he had talked to at the Carver's party was a man under stress - a lot of stress. His behavior since then was hardly normal either, was it? The sudden scramble for cash, Cordelia's loan, and on top of all that, he had done everything in such secrecy.

Secrecy, the word seemed to hang in the air in front of him.

Secrecy. That was the clue to the whole business. That was what had been eluding him. That was what had been evident in Buchanan's time in his consulting room.

The man was a walking mystery; and secrets are funny things. It was impossible to be involved in psychoanalysis and not know that secrets are like dead fish, they start to stink after a while. You can bottle up your secrets, but they come oozing round stoppers and permeate through the stoutest of corks; behavior patterns betray long suppressed memories.

And not only were secrets difficult to keep hidden, but trying to keep them covered up was immensely stressful. That was what he had picked up in that first session - the first traces of a scent that was defeating all the man's efforts to keep it under wraps.

He ran his fingers through his hair and tried to concentrate on his book. A load lifted from his mind. Even if nobody else was interested in Charles Buchanan's involvement in the Schiele's, he still was. More than ever. And what was more he was going to challenge him about it. He was going to sit here, all night if necessary, and wait for him to show up.

# CHAPTER TWENTY-TWO.

WITH A LITTLE UNDER TWENTY HOURS TO GO UNTIL THE AUCTION, and with the alcohol keeping all his worst fears at bay, the first time Charles even noticed the old man on the stool next to his at the bar was when a half-empty wine bottle was pushed in front of him. He looked to see who was doing the pushing as a voice asked,

"Join me for a drink, Monsieur?"

The voice carried frequencies from both ends of the spectrum. At the bottom, a bass resonance formed most of the sound, but there was a trace of a whistle as breath was forced through ill-fitting teeth. It conjured an image of steam breaking from an underground chamber: the quiet murmuring of an almost extinct geyser.

Normally Charles would have ignored the offer, but on this occasion his instinctive reluctance was calmed by the effects of half a dozen Pernod's, and what he saw.

The voice belonged to an old man. The old man was blind, but his eyes weren't shielded by dark glasses. The eye-balls were white and filmy, and each was aimed in a different direction; they didn't blink or flinch in the smoky atmosphere of the bar. Over the fixed and useless eyes a pair of bushy white eyebrows were raised and pushed slightly together in the middle, complementing the old man's inquiry.

"Sure, I'll have a drink. That's what I came in here for," said Buchanan neutrally, playing for time as he continued staring at the old man's face, enjoying the freedom of an unchallenged inspection.

The man was dressed in a black woolen suit that hung on his frame loosely. His crumpled shirt collar was fastened at the neck by a gold stud; it didn't appear to have been ironed, even when it was first put on. He wore no tie. His white hair looked as if it had been driven back from his temples to the crown of his head - where it now clung in a futile last-ditch stand against baldness.

Although his eyes were expressionless, the rest of his face worked overtime to compensate. When he heard Charles's reply he smiled, and everything contributed. The corners of his mouth lifted, and with them the bulk of his mustache. Wrinkles around his eyes, across his forehead and in his cheeks reformed from the positions they had taken up to accompany his question, to new ones to welcome Charles's answer.

"Good. Help yourself. I find it a little difficult because of my eyes, you understand."

"Of course. Thank you. And for you?"

"Please." He slid his glass along the bar and Charles refilled it from the bottle. "You're foreign?"

"English."

"My compliments, you speak French very well. What do you do in Paris. You are on holiday?"

"No, I'm here on business."

"Then if you are here at the 'Bar des Olympians' you must be a writer or a painter - am I right?"

"No," said Charles. Already, he was beginning to regret getting involved. He was drinking in the bar to forget his problems. He could do without the third degree, and the painful recollection of the purpose of his visit to Paris.

The lines on the old man's face registered disappointment at

Charles's negative reply. For some reason Charles didn't want to offend the old man. He stumbled on speaking, "But I am involved in the Art business. I'm here for an auction at Sabatier's."

The lines brightened again. The old man said, "There was a time when everybody who came to Paris for Art or Literature came to this bar - it was famous. I've met them all here, Picasso, Matisse, Hemingway, all the greats. Would you believe I lost my sight over a few scratchy strokes of Matisse's pen."

"You what?"

"I lost my sight over a few scratchy strokes of Matisse's pen."

"How?"

The old man drained his glass before replying. "It's a long story, Monsieur. Is there any more wine?"

Buchanan checked the bottle; it was empty. Even through his drunkenness he realized he had been stung. There was nothing for it but to buy the old bugger another bottle. As he ordered and paid for another liter of the house red, he wondered how many times the old sod had pulled this stunt. Ah well, it was only a few francs and he couldn't help admiring the skill with which the hook had been baited, dangled and swallowed.

The blind man raised his freshly filled glass, rumbled a 'Salut', took a healthy swallow, and launched himself, "It was the war. A result of an interrogation by the Nazi's. The fools mistook my ignorance for stubbornness. Believe me, if I could have told them anything I would have. They thought I was with the Resistance. Unfortunately I was. Like all young men I believed in the 'grand gesture,' without even thinking about what it really meant. But I was just a courier, there was no blowing up of railway yards. I was an idealist, but not a stupid idealist!" He laughed at his own joke and continued, "We used to smuggle things out to Switzerland. I never even knew what I was passing on. It was only later that I found out what the

[ 223 ]

grand documents were that I was nearly caught passing on. At the time I was only too glad to be ignorant, and happy that I wasn't arrested two minutes earlier, with the papers in my hands. Do you know, I was worried about being shot as a spy?"

"What were these papers?"

"They told me later, after the Nazis had blinded me; I think they really thought it would make me feel better. I was smuggling drawings for the wealthy Americans. My superiors tried to impress me by telling me that the 'great Matisse' might even have authorized the sale himself. Maybe it was true - an attempt by an old man to lighten his conscience about the rape of his country - maybe not. Who could blame him for being uninterested in the war until '43? Until then it was only an irritation that kept him from Paris. Then the Nazi's started to threaten his elderly wife and his daughter: she worked for the Resistance too. I don't know where exactly the drawings came from. I never found that out. They could have come from him, or from his wife - who was legally separated from him and about to be imprisoned by the Nazi's, or from a patron of his, or even from the daughter herself. The only thing they told me was that I had played an important part in getting them safely to Switzerland, where they were sold to aid the war effort."

"What happened? What went wrong?"

"Someone must have talked, or been careless, or maybe I was just unlucky. They were passed along our chain from Nice until they arrived here in Paris. I had just given them to the 'owl,' and then *PAF!* I was arrested."

"The 'owl'?"

"It was our code-name for the next courier in the chain, Nicolletta Thibou. Even the code-name shows what amateurs we were. Thibou - Hibou - owl, a childish play on words, you understand?"

"Sure, what happened to the pictures?"

"That's what everyone wanted to know. She got away, and as far as I know the rest of the journey, to the dealer Hans

Purrmann in Switzerland, was no problem. He was an old acquaintance of Matisse." The old man's cheerful tone changed to a whine for a second as he added, "I should have been a hero, but by the time they arrived in Switzerland some of them were missing; we were all suspects. Even me. As if I would be so stupid as to let someone force red hot wires into my eyes for the sake of a few lousy drawings. They were something to do with a book on Baudelaire, I believe."

Buchanan listened in amazement. Fact or fiction, there was contained in the old man's story the framework for a fraud that he would have dearly loved to have thought of himself.

He said, "Maybe this 'owl' set you up and helped herself?"

The old man shrugged. "It's possible, anything is possible, but even if she took some of them it did her little good. She was shot later that year in the mountains near Geneva. Her name is on the Croix de Lorraine memorial by one of the mountain passes. At least I came out of it alive, but ever since then I have had mixed feelings about Germans. And if you want to know the truth, about Matisse too...."

The old man continued telling his story with the ease and confidence of someone who has found a fresh audience for a tale he has told many times before. There was plenty of wine, and he was happy to be talking. He required little prompting to keep going.

Charles was no longer hearing his words, and no longer worrying about the auction; his mind was fleshing out the bare bones of a scheme. It was the first time in over a month that the Schiele's weren't at the forefront of his mind. And as he wondered about Matisse and Baudelaire, he could feel his energy and strength returning.

The auction was something taking place tomorrow, but...

Christ, he was still alive!

...Suddenly he was thinking about the day after tomorrow.

# CHAPTER TWENTY-THREE.

AT NINE P.M., WHEN ROBIN MALCOLM WATCHED Charles come into the hotel lobby, he pushed himself deeper into his seat and raised his book protectively in front of his face. Although he didn't understand what he saw, he knew that this wasn't the time to make his move.

Charles was obviously drunk, and judging by the way he lurched across the lobby and asked for his key from the desk clerk in a voice that slurred and stumbled, probably so drunk that conversation would be impossible.

There was something unnerving about his eyes too. They flashed with the manic sparkle of a man possessed. It was a look he had seen before in the eyes of patients trapped deep inside themselves by their own thoughts.

Well, it would most probably pass after he had slept off his drinking spree. There was no rush. If they were going to talk, after the auction would do just as well as before. Maybe it would even be better, the sale might provide him with another couple of clues.

After he had watched Charles stagger into the lift, Robin waited for a couple more minutes and then went up the stairs to his room.

# CHAPTER TWENTY-FOUR.

BY THE TIME HE WAS NEARING THE END OF HIS CONVERSATION with the clerk at Sabatier's who was going to be bidding on his behalf, Charles had mentally nicknamed him 'Droopy' - after the miserable, dead-pan dog in the children's cartoon series.

"Do you understand everything?" asked Charles for the second time.

The little man looked bored. He was about forty and had been in Sabatier's employ all of his working life. From his manner Charles deduced there was nothing, bar an actual fight on the sale-room floor, that was going to surprise him.

"It's not so complicated, Monsieur," sighed the clerk. "For the lot 144 you will open the bidding and drop out after three raises. I will come into the bidding after the first stand-off, and I will keep on bidding until we've bought the picture. For lot 145, I will wait for the first stand-off and then simply keep bidding until we have bought the painting, or I see you take off your glasses; that means you're at your limit. Okay?"

"Exactly. I'll be in the sale room early, so just make sure you can see me."

"Of course, Monsieur. Is there anything else?"

"No. Only...thank you."

"Don't thank me, Monsieur. I'm only doing my job."

All right, thought Charles, I won't thank you. Just make sure you do your bloody job. Because, if you fuck up, or this all goes wrong, I'm going to be in shit way over my head.

It was ten A.M., the Auction started at eleven. Charles didn't know how quickly the sale-room would fill up, so he went to try and reserve a seat.

The sale-room was in the Hotel's old chapel. Even though it had been totally stripped of pulpit and pews, it looked almost as if it hadn't been touched. The auctioneer's desk, complete with microphone, stood on a raised platform at the end of the chancel. Around it - where the old choir stalls would have been - were the sales clerk's desks and the table where the computer operator sat with her banks of equipment.

The computer was linked to a huge scoreboard hanging from the roof trusses above the auctioneer's head, and on this scoreboard was displayed the current bidding price in six major currencies: French francs, American dollars, pounds Sterling, Swiss francs, German marks and Japanese yen. To the auctioneer's left was a battered mahogany artist's easel where the current lot on offer was displayed. In front of all this, in a nave sixty feet by twenty, were ranged the rows of seats for the prospective purchasers, journalists and curious spectators.

At the back of the room on another slightly elevated platform, were a series of Plexiglas cubicles. These were where the telephones were based. Even at small relatively unimportant sales it wasn't unusual for the choice lots to be bought by telephone bidders too busy to attend in person. In the front of each cubicle was a red 'intention to bid' light which was activated by the person inside to call the auctioneer's attention to the cubicle. After the initial illumination, the bids were made in the usual way: nod of the head, flicker of the eyebrows, or wave of the hand.

Charles was very early; there was nobody else in the room

apart from three old porters arranging the pictures in order of sale. He chose a seat to one side of the room, from where he would be able to see and be seen. He hung his jacket over the back of the chair and sat down. There were still fifty minutes to go.

He searched in his pockets for a handkerchief. Sweat was running from all his pores. The palms of his hands were wet and his shirt was sticking to his back even though he actually felt cold. Worst of all the moisture smelled vividly of aniseed - a legacy of his Pernod binge the previous evening. He would have preferred a hangover to the constant nausea-inducing reek.

Slowly as the minutes ticked by on the electronic clock at the top of the scoreboard the room began filling up. The crowd conformed exactly to the usual pattern. First to arrive were the once-a-year punters eager for a specific picture: usually husbands and wives, mainly Americans. They took the seats at the front as near as they could get to the display easel and the auctioneer, or they selected seats on the edge of the central aisle. After them came the dealers: a motley collection, nearly all men, aged from thirty to seventy and dressed in dark suits. They filled the majority of the front half of the room, or else seated themselves in a part of the room for which they had developed a superstitious preference. With fifteen minutes to go came the spectators and underbidders who filled the bulk of the back of auditorium.

The underbidders were the ones for whom Charles had the least respect. Buying for love of a particular picture was one thing, buying for stock was another, but the underbidders did neither. Their sole motivation was greed. They were there representing the sellers, making their living simply by forcing the price up and collecting their percentage. They were old hands at the 'poker' of bidding; they could gauge exactly when to come in on a slow moving sale; how to operate in pairs to bamboozle unwary bidders upwards. But their greatest skill, and Charles recognized it to be a skill, was knowing the precise moment to drop out, leaving a buyer stranded on the beach of overspending. Although Charles knew next to nothing about the Paris scene he was sure that he could spot them moving to their seats. Easy, confident, giving waves and grins to colleagues from other galleries. It came as no surprise to him to see Morganstein coming in with them. The surprise was the entourage of rubberneckers he had in tow, Frank, Cordelia and Robin Malcolm.

Cordelia was the first to spot him. Charles noticed the flash of recognition in her eyes and the poke in the ribs she gave Frank; Charles actually thought he could hear her whispering, as clearly as if it had come over the auctioneer's tannoy - Don't look now, but Charles is over on the far side, half way back. And after a decent interval, Frank glanced over. It was a sly glance, camouflaged as a yawn and a stretch of the neck, but a glance just the same.

Bugger them. He wondered if they knew the Schiele's were forgeries...if they were all here for the pleasure of watching him brought down. If they did, and they thought he was going to buckle under the pressure they could think again. Now he'd sold the Picasso's he was sure he had enough cash. Sure, he would have to pay it back, but right now that was the least of his problems - especially when it was placed side by side with a sensational trial, exposure, and prison.

Jesus....prison. He shuddered and the sweat started flowing again.

The room was practically full now. Last to arrive were the Journalists. As the numbers on the electronic clock clicked over from 10:56 to 10:57 to 10:58, they slid into the room; standing against the last few patches of empty wall space or climbing unconcerned by the irritation they caused into the two or three remaining vacant chairs.

Charles's attention was distracted from the final dribble of people through the gothic arch of the doorway by the sight of the auctioneer appearing from behind a carved screen, and making the short journey from the chancel to his pulpit. Because of this he missed seeing Megan hurry to the seat a few rows from the front under the seventh station of the cross where Montague had defended a seat for her.

The digits flipped over again. 10:59 became 11:00. The auctioneer leaned forward. He was young, thought Charles. Very young to be handling an auction as big as this, no more than thirty four or five, definitely no Parisian Peter Walker. His tightly curled hair made him look like a Greek god.

"Bonjour Mesdames et Messieurs, et bienvenus a la Maison Sabatier tout le monde." He paused before continuing in flawless English, "Good morning, everybody, and welcome to Sabatier's. For those of you who only speak English I'm afraid these are my last words to you, but as you can see all the prices are clearly displayed on the sign above me in dollars and pounds. I hope you have a successful day. Alors allons-y."

Lot number 1 was a watercolor by Renoir. While the scoreboard clicked rapidly from 50,000 francs to 70,000 in bids that came so fast the digital display almost seemed to be tumbling like the letters on the departure board of an airport, Charles was scanning the crowd for 'Droopy', who was nowhere to be seen. It was early days yet and nothing to be concerned about at this stage.

He still hadn't showed up when the auctioneer announced lot thirty. Charles stared at the Raoul Dufy on the easel and tried to hold down the nervousness he felt rising inside him. Where the hell was the bloody man? He was almost standing as he craned his neck this way and that, scouring the room. At one point the auctioneer double checked to see if he was trying to make a bid before spotting an 'intention to bid' lamp come on at the back of the room.

That telephone bidder became the first of the day to break the magical million mark and, even though it was francs and that only represented, according to the scoreboard £100,371, there was a ripple of applause as the Raoul Dufy was finally sold to the unseen buyer.

By an effort of will Charles calmed himself even though the little man hadn't put in an appearance when the auctioneer brought down his gavel on lot 93, a gouache by Christian Rohlfs, for a hundred thousand francs. There were still fifty lots to go and he was beginning to be slightly heartened; many of the pictures were selling for less than the lower guide figure in the catalogue, and only a Modigliani had exceeded the higher guide figure by more than twenty percent. However, he was still nervous enough to raise himself slightly in his chair to look around the room again.

When a figure study by Tsuguharu Foujita was knocked down for eighty-eight thousand francs and lot 140 was lifted onto the easel in its place Charles was really beginning to panic.

Where was fucking 'Droopy'?

In the brief pause while the Foujita was taken away and the next lot moved into position, Charles stood up and began systematically ticking off in his head each row that he scanned with his eyes. He managed a quarter of the room between lot 140 and 141, another quarter between 141 and 142, another between 142 and 143, and the last between 143 and 144.

The first Schiele was maneuvered onto the easel.

The fucking idiot had blown it! With his - *I'm only doing my job, Monsieur* - nonsense. The asshole didn't deserve a job.

While the auctioneer introduced the painting, talking briefly about its sensational discovery and pointing out that, as yet, the painting had not been officially accepted as part of the artist's oeuvre, he gathered himself; aware that his feet were icy cold and that there was a trickle of moisture working its way from his armpit to his waistline.

His attention focused until he was unaware of the presence of anyone else in the room; there was just him, the auctioneer and the bright colors of the Schiele against the white background.

Time slowed; every word lasted for seconds; the auctioneer's bass tones resonated around Charles's brain.

"Shall we begin at five hundred thousand?"

Five hundred thousand? Thought Charles incredulously. That was the bottom guide figure! Nothing else had been started at such a relatively high price! He couldn't even bring himself to move his arm to bid.

Nor did anyone else. Charles prayed the lot would not be withdrawn. There was a seemingly endless pause.

"Eh bien. As you wish, Messieurs, let's try two hundred. Will anyone offer two hundred?"

That was more like it. He waited for the Auctioneer's eyes to flick his way across the room. And as they did he nodded his head vigorously. Whatever the folk stories told of people inadvertently buying with a sneeze or a scratch was nonsense. The auctioneer wouldn't even consider a bid that wasn't accompanied by positive eye-contact. That was why you had to wait until you were full-square in the center of his vision before making your move.

You waited for his eyes to scan your way...waited, and then...Bingo!

The auctioneer's lips pulled back in a smile that lasted for days, "Thank you, Monsieur. Two hundred thousand I am bid." Then he was off and running.

For all Charles knew he was pulling the answering bids off the chandeliers; there was no way he had time to check around the room.

Unknown to Charles there was another bidder. It was Oscar Morganstein boosting the price, and his commission, with his eyebrows on the far side of the room.

"Two hundred and twenty (Across the room) - two hundred and forty (Back to Charles) - two hundred and sixty (across) - two hundred and eighty (back) - three hundred (across) - three hundred and thirty (back) - three hundred and fifty (across)"

This was where Charles had told 'Droopy' he was going to pull out and let it run without him. He decided to give it one more raise and then back off. If nobody else came in he could always jump back with a rescue bid as the hammer was falling.

He nodded.

"Three hundred and eighty?" The auctioneer looked across the room and saw Morganstein raise his eyebrows again. "Four hundred thousand."

Charles waited for the auctioneer to look back at him, and then waited some more.

The auctioneer looked hard at him and said, "Against you, Monsieur. With the gentleman on my left."

Charles shook his head.

"Well, are we all done at four hundred thousand francs? On my left at four hundred thousand, on my left..."

Charles muttered a silent curse at 'Droopy'. He squeezed the pause as long as he dared, waiting to hear another bidder enter the fray. The first stand-off. He had another fraction of a second to wait before he lost the chance to interrupt the falling hammer. Just another fraction of a second....

"New bidder. Thank you, Mademoiselle. I have four hundred and fifty on the aisle at the back. Against you, Monsieur (directed at Morganstein) Thank you. I have five hundred thousand."

Charles caught the direction of the glance and saw for the first time Morganstein raise his eyebrows. Seeing that it was the dumpy figure bidding he relaxed a little and followed the auctioneer's eyes to the woman. It looked like the woman he had seen with Ronald Lauder, but he couldn't be sure. In

'Droopy's' absence he would wait until she pulled out before getting back in.

"Five-fifty (the woman) - six hundred (Morganstein) - six-fifty (the woman) - seven hundred (Morganstein) - Mademoiselle? .... No?"

There was a pause and Charles noticed with some satisfaction the look of panic on Morganstein's face. He had fallen into the classic underbidder's trap and been caught with the picture.

Charles was enjoying that look so much that he forgot to come back with a bid.

Enjoying it so much he didn't hear the auctioneer saying, "All done at seven hundred thousand? Are there no takers at seven-fifty? No takers at seven-fifty? So we're all done at seven hundred thousand francs?"

Charles remembered too late. The man's hand was raised. Christ, he wasn't even looking in Charles's direction! In slow motion his hand grasping the gavel began its downward path.

Then it stopped.

"New bidder. On the telephone at seven hundred and fifty thousand."

Morganstein gave an audible sigh of relief and Charles spun in his seat with the rest of the crowd. Charles stared at the booth with the red light. Inside a man was holding up his hand.

It was bloody 'Droopy'! Charles could have kissed him. He sent him a prayer of gratitude.

Not only was 'Droopy' bidding, but he was SMILING! Charles allowed himself a chuckle of amusement. He had told the man that he wanted his bid to be anonymous. And what better way to allay suspicion than for him to be seen taking instructions from someone who could be half-way around the world? From someone who could be anywhere in fact, anywhere but in a chair in the same room.

"On the telephone at seven hundred and fifty thousand. Any more? Will nobody offer me more? Are we all done at seven hundred and fifty thousand francs?..... All done?"

*CRACK!*

"Sold to Monsieur Fouquet, telephone bid. Next lot, number 145. Another study by Schiele, same source as the previous lot. Will somebody start me at two hundred thousand?"

While he was speaking Charles tried to pull together his shattered nerves. He was half-way there. One in the bag and one to go. He stared up at the scoreboard which was still registering the price of the first Schiele. He did some rapid mental arithmetic and calculated that as long as the price did not go above eight hundred thousand, or eight hundred and fifty thousand at a pinch, he would be all right. He almost whooped with relief. The woman had shown her ceiling price and no-one else had bid. He was going to bloody do it!

His brief moment of elation was noticed by two other people in the room. Montague and Malcolm.

Montague slid lower in his seat and whispered in Megan's ear, "I think we can assume Charles was the buyer of that one despite all the smokescreen. Well, that's him over Beecher's on the first circuit. He's pleased as punch. Though quite why I can't understand."

"Obviously because he's got the first picture back."

"It cost him over SEVENTY-FIVE thousand pounds! All that money for something that was his in the first place? If it was me I'd be crying not cheering."

"He knows what the alternative result would have meant," hissed Megan.

"Hmmm. He must be pretty damn scared to look that happy about things. I wonder how he'll do on the run-in?"

"Sssh! It's starting again."

As the auctioneer scrutinized the faces in front of him for the opening bid, Robin Malcolm, too, wondered why Charles was looking so happy. Malcolm was pleased that his interpretation of Charles's preparations for the auction had been proved right, but he was also surprised that he had given up so early on in the sale. His attention was distracted by a hushed discussion between Morganstein and Cordelia.

"Do you recognize that woman who was bidding?" asked Morganstein.

"No, not for certain. I'm sure I saw her once in New York, though. She must work for one of the big boys over there."

"See," said Morganstein angrily to Frank, "Those boys aren't stupid. They wouldn't send someone over to bid for rubbish."

"Maybe she was the underbidder, not you, Mr Morganstein," replied Frank evenly, "You don't even know who is selling the damn things, do you?"

"Nonsense!"

"Have it your own way. I still reckon they're a pair of fakes. But I don't care. Go ahead and bid." He sat back in his chair pointedly.

At his moment the auctioneer was conducting the sale between an elderly man in the front row who, although he was only a matter of feet away, was bidding with extravagant flourishes of his pen visible all around the room, and the same woman who had bid for the first picture.

As the price mounted over four hundred thousand francs Charles noticed several dealers who had been waiting hopefully for the bidding to come grinding to a halt, lose interest as the price passed the limits of their budgets.

"Four hundred thousand (wave of the old man's pen) - four fifty (nod from the woman) - five hundred (wave of the old man's pen) - five fifty (nod from the woman)....."

There was a pause.

"Against you, Monsieur. With the mademoiselle on the aisle."

The old man leant forward and said something as he gave his pen a less confident wave. He was bottoming out, thought Charles.

The auctioneer confirmed it, "Five eighty, with the Monsieur."

The raise had gone from ten percent to five. Jump to six fifty and you'll finish him, thought Charles. But the woman took it by another small step to six hundred thousand.

Well, thought Charles with mounting excitement, I don't believe it - you're bottoming out too. We're in with a shout, 'Droopy', we're in with a bloody shout!

There was a final doddery wave of the pen.

"Six thirty...at the front - six fifty on the aisle.....Monsieur?"

The old man pocketed his pen and shook his head. The auctioneer returned his attention to the crowd, "At six hundred and fifty thousand francs. Six hundred and fifty thousand. Are you all done?"

Don't wait too long, 'Droopy', prayed Charles. And when you come, raise her. Jump it. She'll never follow you. Take it to Seven fifty. Jump it!

"Are you all done?....."


DON'T BE TOO BLOODY CLEVER 'DROOPY'! GET IN THERE BEFORE HE BRINGS THE FUCKING HAMMER DOWN. GET IN THERE AND RAISE HER.


"New bidder. On the telephone at seven fifty."


YOU'RE A BLOODY DIAMOND, 'DROOPY'! SHE'LL NEVER FOLLOW.


"On the aisle, Eight hundred."

SHIT! DON'T WORRY! DON'T WORRY! SHE'S GROGGY! HIT HER AGAIN, WE CAN AFFORD ONE MORE! DO IT! DO IT!

"On the telephone, eight fifty. - Against you Mademoiselle.... (no movement)"

OH SWEET JESUS, YOU'VE CRACKED HER! WE'VE GOT IT! WE'VE BLOODY GOT IT!

"At eight hundred and fifty thousand francs. Telephone bid. Against you all in the room...."

NO-ONE'S GOING TO BID NOW. THEY'RE ALL DEAD! BRING YOUR HAMMER DOWN.

"At eight hundred and fifty thousand francs. Against you all in the room..."

YOU'VE ALREADY SAID THAT ONCE! SHUT-UP YOU VULTURE. BRING YOUR HAMMER DOWN! FOR FUCK'S SAKE!


P - L - E - A - S - E !



"New bidder on my left at the front (a response to a pair of lofted eyebrows and a vocal raise). Nine hundred and fifty thousand francs. Against you on the telephone..."

As arranged Charles had taken off his glasses when 'Droopy' had made the bid of eight hundred and fifty thousand. He was at his limit. Over his limit. There was nothing more he could do.

In the split-second that it took for the auctioneer's words to sink in, he involuntarily clenched his hand violently. The flimsy gold frames distorted as the glass splintered.

He didn't feel the pain as his hand continued to tighten convulsively around the razor-sharp fragments. He felt nothing even though several shards were forced deep into the flesh of his palm by his own tightening grip.

He felt nothing.

He saw nothing.

His entire world collapsed inwards on itself. He tumbled inside a rushing, thunderous vortex of blackness and confusion and fear.

*CRACK!*

"Sold. At nine hundred and fifty thousand francs .....Oscar Morganstein."

# CHAPTER TWENTY-FIVE.

THE BARONNE JEAN-LOUIS DE COYSEVOX, a tiny bird-like woman in her late sixties with a sun tanned walnut of a face, wished the Englishman on the seat next to her at Sabatier's would be quiet. Lot 148 was the first of four of her late husband's Picasso's to come under the hammer, and she was desperately keen that they should fetch enough money to help sustain her crumbling chateau. The damn man was muttering and mumbling and twitching in his seat.

She turned to face him, intending to fix him with one of her most withering stares, but what she saw stopped her in her tracks.

She forgot everything.

For a second or two she did nothing but draw in air in a long gasp of horror. Then her lark's lungs could take no more, and her diaphragm began forcing its way back upwards. The rapid exhalation tripped her vocal chords into use, and a scream louder than anyone would have thought her tiny body was capable brought the auction to a bewildered standstill. When her first scream finished, she began working on a second...and then a third.

The sight which filled her with such total horror was Charles Buchanan.

When she had first turned towards him, her initial reaction had been to wonder how drunks managed to get into a high-class establishment like Sabatier's. The man's head wobbled from side to side and his lips mouthed words incomprehensible to the French-speaking Baronne.

His eyes blazed. They were illuminated by the reflections of the old chapel's brightly colored stained glass windows shining in his dilated pupils - in the blackness Christ overturned tables in the temple whilst the moneylenders ran for cover and angels hovered overhead. But it was neither of these two things which the Baronne had found so distressing.

It was the sight of the blood pumping out from between the tightly clenched fingers of his right hand that smashed the last traces of decorum from her consciousness - a pulsed river that swirled around his wrist, across the pages of his catalogue and onto the floor.

The Baronne scrabbled her way to her feet, screamed, and screamed, and then gratefully slid into unconsciousness. With her last lucid thought she contrived to topple backwards; it would have killed her to fall face first into the spreading viscous puddle of crimson at Charles's feet.

The auctioneer paused mid-sentence as the old woman's screams filled the room.

As she collapsed to the floor, a highly cultured version of the Mexican wave spread outwards from where she lay. At first it was a simple outward motion of people standing to see what was happening. Then it gathered momentum as people began backing away, overturning chairs and dropping precious belongings as they went.

If Charles had been in any condition to appreciate it, he would have probably allowed himself a grin - the bedlam in the sale-room left 'Droopy' slumped in his telephone booth, slack-jawed and boneless with amazement. As it was, Charles sat unseeing, twitching and bleeding; to one side of him lay the crumpled figure of the Baronne Jean-Louis de Coysevox;

around them both was a circle of confusion filled with upturned chairs and discarded catalogues: like a mine-field which nobody seemed prepared to cross.

Robin Malcolm was the first to move. He forced his way through the retreating crowd and, to their surprise, made directly for the seated figure, ignoring totally the woman on the floor. He bent over Charles and struggled to understand the stream of words coming from his mouth over the hubbub of noise that was beginning to fill the room behind him.

The fractured sentences finally made sense. Charles was repeating over and over again,

"I don't understand....You didn't want them....I tried to sell you them....Don't buy it, Oscar, DON'T BUY IT, it's a fake....IT'S A FAKE, I KNOW - I PAINTED THEM....DO YOU HEAR ME OSCAR?...IT'S A..."

*CRACK!*

A woman's hand slapped the side of Charles's face.

"SHUT UP, CHARLES! DO YOU HEAR ME? SHUT UP!"

For a brief second, possibly less, a rational look of surprise came into Charles's eyes. He and Robin looked at the woman. The crowd steadied its retreat and then began to inch its way back towards the dramatic tableau.

Charles dreamily asked, "What are you doing here, Megan?" His eyes drifted and then focused on Robin Malcolm. "You could be just in time, Doc, I think I'm going crazy. Listen, someone tell Morganstein not to buy the..."

"SHUT UP, CHARLES!" she snapped.

As the crowd drew closer, his head dropped as he became aware that all was not well with his hand. Slowly he uncurled his fingers. A small geyser of blood began spurting five or six inches into the air with the regularity of a metronome. Charles looked at it distantly as the advancing crowd drew in a collective breath and slowed its advance.

Megan looked at Robin, "This is a hell of a time to be making introductions - are you a friend of his?"

Robin nodded.

"If that's true then forget what he just said and help me get him out of here! God, what a mess!"

Robin concentrated his attention on Charles's hand. It was too small a jet to be an artery, but it would do to clear a way through the throng. He took the silk square from around Megan's shoulders, crumpled it into a ball, and placed it into Charles's hand before curling the bloody fingers back over it. Sliding a hand under his legs and another behind his back, he hoisted the limp figure into the air. Calling on all his reserves of schoolboy French he shouted,

"Depechez-vous. Il a perdu beaucoup de sang. Excusons-nous. Je suis un Medecin. Laissons-nous passer!"

With Megan bringing up the rear Robin carried Charles from the room.

From the seat where Megan had left him, Montague watched them leave. He looked down at the file of photographs on his lap, then he looked behind him at the beaming figure of Oscar Morganstein.

What would the man do when he pressed the photographs proving that the Schiele was a forgery into his pudgy little hands?

One thing was fairly certain.

He probably wouldn't smile much. Would he?

# CHAPTER TWENTY-SIX.

A SCRUNCHING OF GRAVEL on the driveway brought Megan to the drawing room window in time to see Montague's rust-scarred Alvis roll to a standstill.

"He's here! Mrs Williams, will you let him in, please?" she shouted into the corridor.

"Thank Christ for that," replied Robin, "I was beginning to think your trusty family lawyer had done a runner with the money. What the hell can he have been doing for three days?" He joined her beside the massive sash-window.

The two of them stood and watched Bill Montague climb out of his car. Megan was not encouraged by his stony expression.

"I should never have left the photographs at the auction with him," said Megan. "He was determined to give them to the buyer."

"Well, we'll know in a few minutes how much trouble Charles is in. As I told you before, even if Bill gave them to Morganstein he might have been too embarrassed to make a fuss. Anyway, you couldn't have stayed, Megan. It was more important to get Charles safely back here."

"I suppose so," said Megan miserably, "But I know I could

have persuaded him if I'd been there."

They watched as Montague picked up his briefcase, slammed the car door, and walked to the front steps. He was still not using his stick.

Out of their sight, his face cracked into a smile when Mrs Williams answered his ring at the front door,

"She charmed you back then, Gwyneth?"

"She thinks she did, but really she didn't have to, Mr Montague. I'd got the garden so tidy the weeds were scared to grow, and the scullery was so full of jam I was having to keep my groceries on the kitchen window sill; I was bored silly. Here let me take your coat. I expect you'd like me to make you a nice cup of tea?"

"Tosh! No, I would not! All the way from the airport I've been dreaming of that bottle of 'Macallan' that Megan keeps hidden at the back of the drinks cupboard. You could bring me a little water, though."

"I'll be with you in two ticks. Oh, by the way, did you know I've got an invalid staying up in the Major's room?" Her happiness bubbled out - she had on her sideboard at the cottage the biggest box of soft-centered chocolates she had ever seen in her life, her old job back, and, to top it all, her invalid in the back bedroom - Mr Buchanan where she could keep an eye on him.

"I thought that might be the case." Montague managed to restrain himself from smiling. He watched her bustle off towards the kitchen, and made sure no trace of his good humor was showing as he walked into the drawing room.

"Bill! Why didn't you call? How did it go? Where have you been?" asked Megan.

"If you must know, I stayed to watch the 'Arc'. Now, have patience, woman. Let me sit down; pour me a malt; and after I've got my strength back I'll tell you everything."

Megan took the jug of water from Mrs Williams as she came through the door, ushered her back out of the room, undid the bottle of scotch, and watched impatiently as Montague drank his first glass straight down and poured himself another.

Megan glanced at Robin, he nodded and she asked again, "Come on, Bill. I've been waiting three days now, talking Robin stupid I was so worried, without so much as a phone call. How did it go?"

Montague studied his drink hard; he seemed to be steeling himself to break bad news. Finally he said, "It was a complete bloody disaster."

He looked up to see what effect his words had had. The two faces opposite him were pictures of depression.

"What happened?" asked Robin quietly.

"Bloody Eddery won it. I lost two hundred quid on 'Reference Point;' the damn nag was so far behind that the stewards almost thought it was the winner of the next race."

"Forget the bloody 'Arc de Triomphe' for a moment! How did things go at Sabatier's?" said Megan angrily.

"Oh! No trouble at all. Were you worried?" He allowed himself a sly grin.

"That was a mean trick, Bill," said Megan with obvious relief. "Robin and I have been worrying all week-end that someone might have heard what Charles was saying. Did you have any trouble after the sale?"

"Not at all. On the contrary, everyone was most concerned that he was all right."

"What about Morganstein?" asked Robin.

"Stupid little man was as happy as a pig in dung. I have managed to work up a healthy dislike for that man. And I can assure you both, that if I had been able to think of a way of telling him that he'd just spent a small fortune on a fake - without involving anyone under this roof - I would have. He was rubbing his trotters with glee at getting a Schiele for fifteen percent less than the asking price."

"So you didn't tell him?" asked Megan. She felt herself beginning to relax.

"Of course not. I suddenly realized that I hadn't put them up for auction - he had. Nobody could suggest he had been duped when all that had happened was that he'd bought his own property. I'd had my fun - setting the whole thing up. You'd had your fun - reducing Casanova upstairs to a gibbering wreck. It seemed churlish not to let him have his moment of glory."

"I thought you'd say something to him," said Megan.

"Well, I didn't. I couldn't tell Morganstein that Charles forged them, not after the way you started beating your breast with remorse, Megan." He drained his glass again and refilled it. "No, everything ran as smoothly as a 'Suffolk Punch'. When you two disappeared with Charles they took a brief recess, revived and placated the hysterical woman, and then carried on as if nothing had happened. As a matter of fact, I'm quite looking forward to giving the invalid the money. How is he, by the way?"

"He's sleeping," replied Robin, "He's higher than a satellite on about a dozen different kinds of dope. For the next few days it'll be the best way. He needs a lot of rest, he's suffering from acute mental exhaustion. He's totally burned-out."

"Oh dear, he will get better I trust?" asked Montague.

"Sure, with the passage of time and a little help from me."

"I must admit that I'm glad to hear it. Anyone that makes a career out of parting those pretentious, self-important, jumped-up commodity brokers from their wallets can't be all bad."

"How much did he make on the sale?" asked Robin.

"After taxes, commissions, Morganstein's fee, and expenses; a little over one hundred and twenty five thousand pounds."

"Hold on a minute," cut in Megan, "Who says that's how much money he made?"

"Megan, it's simple, I've paid everybody and that's how much is left."

"Please don't use that patronizing 'watch my lips and you'll soon understand' voice, Bill. Just tell me one thing: what makes you think Charles should get the money from the sale?"

"I thought you told me..."

"You thought wrong. He was the villain of the piece to start with and, although I don't want him in prison, I refuse to let him get rich as a direct result of his own careless mistreatment of people. What was the gross figure at the sale?"

"One hundred and ninety thousand pounds."

"And the net figure?

"A hundred and twenty-five thousand."

"That makes a total expenses figure of sixty-five thousand. Is that right?"

"Yes."

"Charles can pay that figure out of his half of the gross figure. I think that means he is due....thirty thousand. Oh, and he can have the picture he bought as well."

"What on earth are you going to do with ninety-five thousand pounds, Megan?" asked Montague.

"Nothing immediately, apart from paying Robin for his work with Charles." She smiled at the therapist and Montague thought he could see more than professional warmth in the look that Robin gave her in return. Megan continued, "As for the rest of the money...well, I'll think about it. Do you have any objections?"

"Heaven forfend that I should deign to differ, Megan. I am but a reed bending in the wind." Montague winked at Robin as he pulled a check from Sabatier's from his briefcase and passed it to Megan.

She put the check on the mantelpiece.

What was she planning on doing with the money? She had a couple of ideas, but she would wait until she had spoken to Charles personally before making a final decision.

# CHAPTER TWENTY-SEVEN.

ROBIN SPENT ALL OF the first and second, and most of the third and fourth, weeks after the auction staying with Megan and working with Charles. At first communication was almost impossible, Charles was drugged so heavily that he was only occasionally conscious. When he was awake, his moods swung precipitously between rage and self-pity. Then gradually, as he began to spend more time awake, Robin helped him to come to terms with his situation. Robin also reconstructed for him the events that led to the crisis at the auction, and, as he grew stronger, Robin began filling in the details that Charles didn't know - who stole the paintings, how Morganstein got hold of them, who put them up for auction and lastly who got the money. Charles, for his part, explained the mechanics of Art fraud. In between talking about the events leading up to auction, the two men also discussed the hallucinations Charles had experienced, what had caused them, and how he could prevent them happening again. At the end of the first month Charles was well on the way to making a total recovery, and Robin knew as much about the workings of his brain as he knew about anybody's.

While the therapeutic talking continued, Megan waited. As she waited, she and Robin grew closer. However, it wasn't until the end of the third week that Robin finally told her she could talk to 'the invalid'. She climbed the stairs, knocked on his door and walked straight in.

"How are you feeling?" she asked.

"Much better, thanks, apart from my bloody hand," replied Charles coolly, "Still, I suppose I was lucky I didn't cut any tendons or nerves. All things considered, I'm pretty happy to be where I am. My only real complaint is the food. Can you politely tell the woman that cooks for you that if I have another stew I will scream. I would like a rare fillet steak - one that a reasonably competent vet could get back on its feet again - with fresh water-cress, and a tomato and onion salad in French dressing. To wash it down, I'd like a claret, a Grand Cru claret. If what Robin tells me is true - that you don't hold a grudge against me anymore - then you'll try and save me from her infernal stews."

Megan smiled. "I'll see what I can do about the food; I can always try and get her to take a day off and cook myself. The wine you'll have to skip. The doctor said no alcohol with the medication you're taking at the moment."

"I'm better, Megan. Robin has told me everything that happened. We've talked solidly for days. I feel much stronger already."

"He told you everything?"

"Yes, everything."

"So you know all about my involvement?"

"All about it."

"And about Robin and me?"

"Yes."

"And you're still talking to me?"

"Megan, you're my knight in shining armor. I appreciate what you've done for me; both in Paris and while I've been staying with you - even if it was a bit like being dragged from the flames by the arsonist herself! I've been looking forward to talking to you about things. And I'm really happy for you that

[ 254 ]

you're enjoying Robin's company so much.

"...Do you realize, I still don't know whether you're telling the truth? Or whether you're just turning on the charm to keep me from dropping you in it again?"

"Does it matter?"

"What do you mean?"

"As far as I know, you've still got the file. Morganstein still has one of the pictures. Robin knows the story and so does Bill Montague. If I step out of line, any one of you three only has to get together with Morganstein and - BINGO - I'm pushing porridge round my plate in Pentonville. I'm telling you that I'm not cross - I admire you for it, you and Sally both - you'll just have to believe me." He flashed his best smile at her, and Megan knew he was right. It was so convincing; it didn't matter whether he was telling the truth or not.

There was a heavy silence.

"Aren't you cross about the way I kept most of the money?" she asked.

He shrugged.

"Do you want to know what I'm going to do with it?"

"No." He said the one word with such finality that Megan knew it was time to change the subject.

"So what are you going to do now?" she asked.

"I've got two ideas. Robin and I have worked a bit on one of them. He thinks it's a winner. The only trouble is I promised him I wouldn't do anything illegal again while I was working on the scheme we've come up with together. So I didn't dare tell him about my other one."

"Illegal? Oh Charles, for God's sake..."

"It's a lou-lou of an idea; it can't miss. I could work it for years."

"It's another forgery, right?"

"Yes, but it's infallible."

"So were the Schiele's, and look what happened to them."

"Don't be a pessimist, Megan. I can make it work. Dammit,

the idea's so good anyone could make it work. Even a Sunday afternoon painter like you could produce drawings close enough to Matisse's economic style to fool an expert; especially if they were on paper of the right vintage. I've got nearly fifty sheets of French hand-made paper from the forties at my studio. I don't see how it can fail. Let me tell you about it and see what you think."

"If I think it's a bad idea will you drop it?"

"Yes, so long as I'm still working with Robin."

"Okay then, what is it?"

Charles adjusted himself in the pillows, "I'll pretend I'm trying to interest you in the deal. You pretend you're a dealer and ask me any questions that occur to you."

"Okay, I'm a dealer."

"I come to you and ask you for advice. My father has just died and amongst his effects I've come across some drawings. I think they're possibly by Matisse and I need the cash desperately so I want to sell them, but there's a problem."

"What's the problem."

"The way they arrived in my father's possession is a little unusual."

"Are they stolen?"

"It's impossible to say. My father used to work for the Special Operations Executive in the war....

"Is this really important to a story about a forged drawing?" interrupted Megan.

"Important? Megan, it's more than important. It's CRUCIAL! It's the silly little details that make an impossible story plausible. I want you to ask questions about the details. That's what makes it so good - I can prove everything." He paused and changed his position in the pillows again. "My father was based in France. One mission he worked on in the mountains near Switzerland was with a woman called Nicolleta Thibou: she was with the Resistance. She was killed during the mission, and in her effects my father found the drawings."

"Surely they should have gone to her family?"

"There was no family."

"How did she come to have the drawings in the first place?"

Robin explained the story.

When he had finished, Megan asked, "Can you prove any of this?"

"All of it. All the information about Matisse is freely available in his biographies. Nicolleta Thibou's name is engraved on a war memorial in the mountains, and there are still surviving members of the Resistance that remember the mission."

"What about your Father?"

"Unfortunately the British Government still consider many Second World War operations to be politically sensitive, and they won't confirm or deny his involvement in France, but he kept notes and I still have those."

"Can I see them?"

"When I've written them you can!" laughed Charles.

"All right," said Megan, "Go on."

"That's it. Do you want to buy them?"

"What are they?"

"They're the original drawings for the etchings Matisse did for Baudelaire's 'Fleurs du Mal'. Like most preparatory drawings they're mirror images of the etchings in the published book - the etching process reverses the design."

"What if someone asks why you don't simply sell them at auction?"

"If I did that, it's possible someone might suggest the proceeds go to the British Government, or the French. I can't risk that - I need the money. I'll say that if you know someone that might buy them for cash, I'd let you have them cheaply."

"I admit that if I was in the business, I might be tempted, but there are so many risks. If it all started coming unraveled you could be in terrible trouble. You know what happened this time; next time you might be unlucky."

"I know that, Megan, but the bloody scheme's too good to waste. And I could pull it off over and over again with different dealers; they're so greedy they'd never risk selling them again publicly."

"You promised me you'd take my advice?"

"Yes."

"If I was you I would do anything to avoid ending up in the state you were in at Sabatier's. Surely you don't want to go through all that anxiety again?"

"I knew you were going to say that. I knew it. The worst thing is I think you're probably right. It just seems such a pity. You've got to admit it's a cracker."

"Yes, as you said: as you said, it's a loulou." She smiled at him, pleased that he had asked her advice. "Do you remember what you said when you left with the letters?"

"No."

"You said that we both got what we wanted out of each other. I've talked about our relationship a lot with Robin, and now I think you were right. And that's the nearest thing to an apology you're going to get from me." She leaned forward, fishing for a kiss.

Charles kissed her antiseptically on her cheek.

As soon as she felt the dry touch of his mouth, Megan knew any hopes she may have entertained of renewing their relationship were pointless. She got up quickly and walked to the door.

"I'll go and try and dislodge Mrs Williams from the kitchen."

"Thank you," said Charles as he sank back down into the bed. She was right, of course. Much as he hated to waste a great idea, of the two, it was definitely the more risky. And there was no denying that it was a great idea, but luckily so was the one that he was working on with Robin. The pain in his hand started up again as he re-arranged the blankets. It was a grim reminder of a grim experience; and that was what made him decide to forget about Nicolletta Thibou.

The plan he and Robin had conceived involved a deception of a different kind, but it was just as intriguing.

# CHAPTER TWENTY-EIGHT.

CHARLES SHIVERED as he worked a little more 'Hooker's Green (Deep)' into the swirl of undergrowth in the background of the painting he was working on: he was pleased to see that it created far more of an illusion of depth than the warmer 'Sap Green' he had used at first. The north light in Megan's conservatory was perfect for painting, but the lack of direct sun made it viciously cold, especially in the depths of winter. A portable gas space-heater roared out enough warmth to enable him to paint for an hour at a time. After that, the condensation running from the roof drove him out.

It was the beginning of March and in the five months since the auction at Sabatier's his life had changed dramatically. It had taken a few weeks for him to recover his strength and to adjust fully to the news of how he had been by outwitted by Sally, Megan and Montague, but his initial anger, confusion, and aggressive resistance to treatment had now given way to a genuine respect for the neatness of the scheme they had concocted between them. Now, thanks to the success of his latest venture, he was making enough money not to care too much about that side of the affair.

At the end of November, Robin had helped him load all his

painting equipment and forgery paraphernalia from the studio in Islington into a rented van. Charles had sold the building, and it was about to be converted into a high-class graphics studio by the new owner. The bonfire in Megan's garden which followed the arrival of the van in Oxfordshire, had reduced all of them to hysterical laughter as one painting after another 'by' a well known artist was tossed into the flames. As a result of Robin's high spirits Megan had successfully begged to be allowed to keep the stocks of carefully dated watercolor paper which he had wanted to add to the fire; since Charles's arrival she had rediscovered her enthusiasm for painting, and she couldn't bear to see the hand-made paper - which took watercolor so beautifully - go up in flames. Burning everything which could have aroused suspicion, or brought Charles into conflict with the law, had been the only condition Robin had imposed when they had discussed their new plan.

At about the same time, Bill Montague had managed to untangle the mess Charles's finances were in and found a tenant for his flat in London - an Italo-American film producer who paid a ridiculously large rent - more than enough to cover the mortgage repayments. So, for the moment, Charles was happy to stay with Megan while he waited for the builders to finish converting the barn he had bought three fields away.

His alarm clock rang loudly in the conservatory, signaling that his hour of painting was over. Charles cleaned his brushes and surveyed the picture he was working on. In order to help him view it dispassionately he didn't look directly at it but used a pair of mirrors. He was pleased by what he saw. He wiped his hands on a rag. The picture was going well, and he hoped Robin would share his opinion. He picked up the canvas and carried it into the house.

When Charles walked into the library Megan looked up and asked, "How are things going, Picasso?"

"Apart from the fact that Picasso was last week's thing, I'm pleased, but you'd better ask the patron." He propped the canvas on top of the mantelpiece and sat down in the vacant chair on one side of the fire.

Robin nodded his head admiringly. "It's good, Charles. Very good. Exactly how we discussed it. I'm sure we'll have no problems."

"That's a relief. I was unsure about the father figure," said Charles.

"It's perfect. Don't worry. I'll bring him down next week - just make sure he can't miss it in the studio. Will it be finished by then?"

"I don't see any reason why not. I just want to repaint the two women on the left."

"Who's this one for? I've forgotten," asked Megan.

"Blakelock - the owner of the 'Victorian' gallery, and a big collector of Richard Dadd's. He saw the article in the Sunday color supplement and telephoned the paper. Shirley put him onto me, and he came round to the consulting rooms to see the ones I've got hanging there."

"Let me guess, sweetheart," said Megan with mock surprise. "You told him all about Charles being so withdrawn that he was only capable of expressing himself by painting - just like Dadd. Then you two had a cozy chat about phobias or obsessions - during the course of which you encouraged him to talk about his own sub-conscious. Is that something like what happened?"

Robin grinned, "Not a million miles away, I admit."

"So now he's coming down to Bedlam - in person - to see the loony in his lair?"

Charles crossed his eyes, grunted, and began howling like a wolf.

"Stop it, Charles." said Megan suppressing a smile.

"He is indeed coming to see Charles in his studio, yes," said Robin, still grinning.

"Whereupon you will reluctantly accept a check towards the loony's upkeep - in return for which he will walk away the proud owner of his first original Buchanan - currently the most collectable living painter in London. A painting which will magically seem to depict a scene from his own sub-conscious?"

"Right in every respect bar one. It won't be his first Buchanan. It's his third, actually; he brought two from the consulting rooms. Gave us twenty thousand pounds each for them."

"I don't believe you two - you're behaving like children. How long can you keep pretending that Charles is mad? How long? He hasn't been the slightest bit ill for weeks. It may have been funny the first few times you did it, but there's a respectable part of me that keeps shouting, 'It's corrupt!'"

"Megan, the one thing it isn't, is corrupt. If these people choose to have a collective delusion that Charles is a brilliant painter - then that is none of our business. And bear in mind that Charles has already proved himself, in the marketplace, to be as technically good as Picasso, Schiele, and a half dozen other greats. It's not corrupt because Charles is doing nothing illegal. Like anything in the Art World, it's just a question of taste. In the early days I admit I may have 'suggested' to one or two of my more influential clients when they were in a receptive state that Charles was a worthwhile cause to support. But now the whole enterprise is self-generating. We're just supplying the market's needs - and at the moment the market needs good quality 'Buchanan's'. If you like, you can think of it as Charles forging his own work. That's not a crime.

"It may not actually be illegal, but I thought you told me that Charles shouldn't get involved in anything that put him under stress?"

"That's true, I did say that." Robin looked serious and asked, "Are you under stress, Charles?"

"Not in the least," Charles laughed, "I'm doing exactly what I wanted to do all along - increasing my bank balance and diminishing theirs. In fact, I don't think I've ever been less stressed in my entire life."

[ 264 ]

And, as Robin put his arm around her waist and the two of them looked at Charles, Megan knew she was hearing the truth.

# CHAPTER TWENTY NINE

BILL MONTAGUE LOOKED DISTINCTLY NERVOUS - even sitting motionless on the back of the racehorse - but there was also a flash of real excitement in his eyes as he allowed Megan to help him down from the saddle.

"One word from you, Megan - just one word about me being too old - and I promise that next time I shall take him out of the yard and onto the gallops."

"My lips are sealed. I swear."

"Good. He looks in great shape, doesn't he?"

She stoked the horse's neck. "He looks wonderful. What are his chances next week?"

"It's always difficult to say with a first outing, but Julian reckons he's got a fighting chance."

"How much of that is trainer's optimism, and how much is a true assessment?"

"You're the owner, why don't you ask him?"

"I may be the owner, but he's morally your horse. Your expertise turned my saga with Charles into hard cash; you chose him at the sales. I'll listen to your advice."

"Well, do what I'm doing - have a flutter, but don't put your house on it. Do you want me to put the bet on for you?"

"No, I ought to be able to put a bet on my own horse. When

I go to the bookmakers what do I ask for?"

"Simple, you say, 'I'd like to place some money - let's say fifty pounds for example - on 'Charlie's Gift' to win the three-thirty at York next Thursday."

"Simple as that?"

"Simple as that." Montague handed the horse over to one of the stable lads and took Megan by the arm. They walked slowly towards the yard gates. "Let me take my boots off, and I'll give you a lift. Where are you going? Home or the station?"

"The station, but Robin's waiting out front. I saw your car here and asked him to stop."

"Why don't you come over for a bite to eat when you get back? I'm sure I can rustle up something."

"Thanks, but I'm already spoken for this evening. Robin is taking me out to eat."

"Too bad...I guess that means it's another steak pie down at the "Pig and Whistle" for me. What are you doing in London?"

"I've got a meeting with someone Jeremy Babbington introduced me to at Charles's opening last week."

"How's his show doing?"

"Wonderfully. All sold bar two. Charles and Robin are ecstatic."

"Have you seen Charles since the opening?"

"Yes, he brought some woman journalist over on Wednesday - the one that wrote that article about him in the Sunday color supplement. He seemed to be having a good time. And, I have to say, so did she. It's the third time she's been down to visit in the last month. She seems to be good for him."

Montague could hear the faintest hint of forced enthusiasm in her voice. He put his arm on her shoulder and said, "Look, if you don't want to go to London, we could scoot over to Ascot now and still make the first race?"

"No, thanks. I've got something I want to do." The firmness came back into her voice, and her features set into an expression of determination. Except it wasn't quite determination. It was more than that; it was somehow...almost menacing. By the time Montague took a second look, the expression had gone, and she was her normal self again. "I'll see you later, Bill. Bye."

She kissed him affectionately and went back to join Robin in the car.

Two hours later she lifted down from the luggage rack of the train the small portfolio containing the drawings she had done, picked up her hand bag, and stepped down onto the concourse of Paddington Station. She walked the quarter of a mile to Hyde Park Square and arrived, as she had arranged, at Richard Wright's flat shortly before one o'clock. She pressed the answerphone.

A man's voice boomed out of the speaker, "To whom am I speaking?"

"Gwyneth Williams, Mr Wright," answered Megan.

"How thrilling. Come on up. It's the first floor."

A buzzer sounded, she pushed open the door, and climbed the broad flight of stairs. At the second landing stood a tall thin man in his late seventies.

He smiled broadly and said, "Come in, come in. I scarcely dared hope you would come. Let me take your things."

She slipped off her coat in the hallway and handed it to him. The folio she tucked firmly under her arm. "It's good of you to spare the time to see me, Mr Wright."

"Dicky, my dear. Everybody calls me Dicky. Let's have a sherry while the lunch finishes defrosting. What would you like, a sweet one or an amontillado?"

Megan sat down at one end of a vast curved sofa. The curtains were closed, and the room was very dark even at that time of day. What little light there was came from the table lamps on his desk and at either end of the sofa. Even though the room was so gloomy, it was possible to see that every flat surface in the room was covered with books - and an unbroken layer of dust which clearly indicated how frequently they were opened.

He appeared alongside her with two schooners brimming with sherry, sat down beside her, and said, "You mentioned on the telephone that you saw me at the Buchanan show. Now that I've met you again, I remember you clearly. I hoped it was you; one knows so many dull people. The funny thing was I thought you were avoiding me at the exhibition. Wasn't it a wonderful show?"

"It seemed to be very successful," said Megan.

"Oh, it was. I was reviewing it. You know, something for the glossies to run in the gossip column, who was there, who bought what, that sort of thing."

"I was told you were a poet, "said Megan.

"I am. I am. I do the reviewing in my spare time. It is my poetry that is my life."

"You must be very successful to be able to afford to live here."

"Fairly successful. I've had the odd tome published. Mostly in the vanity press, I admit. But as I always say, I'm a poet because I'm wealthy - I'm not wealthy because I'm a poet." He laughed and moved closer on the sofa. "What made you decide to track me down?"

"Your reputation."

"Oh dear," he laughed, "has somebody been talking out of school?"

"I was told that you were something of an expert on poetry."

"Oh dear again. How disappointing. I thought maybe it was another kind of reputation."

Megan smiled. "I'm afraid not. I wanted to ask your advice about something."

"Fire ahead. Try me."

*

He looked at her and was hit - full-square - by the comforting, disarming, smile of one about to enter into a deceit.

*

She gave the smile a little time to work on him before she spoke.

"You see, Dicky, I have a friend who's in trouble; she's asked me if I can help her. We were both army brides. Her husband was in the same regiment as mine. He died recently, and she's housebound and desperately short of money - the Inland Revenue. You know how *they* are when someone dies? Well, in her husband's effects she found some drawings and asked me if I could find a buyer. She thinks they might be by Matisse, but I don't know enough to venture an opinion. She says the paperwork she found with them indicated that they could be the original designs for the etchings that illustrated the 1940's edition of Baudelaire's 'Les Fleurs du Mal.' I'm sure they must be worth thousands and thousands, but she'll take ten thousand for all of them. And when I heard you were not only an expert on poetry, but also an expert on Art....Well, I was sure you might be just the person to recognize a bargain."

"How exciting. Do you have them here?" Wright leaned forwards on the sofa.

*

She told me later that night, over supper, that at this point she gave him another blast of her warmest smile, and then she untied the strings on the portfolio containing her drawings.

BIOGRAPHY

G. H. Norton was born just outside London in 1955 and attended two Quaker schools. In 1978, he was granted an Upper Second Class Honors degree by the Council for National Academic Awards for the work he did at the Newport School of Art in South Wales. In 1977, and again in 1978, he was nominated for the Conceptual Art Award at the New Contemporaries in Art exhibition at the Institute for Contemporary Arts in London for his pieces entitled "Fire Precautions," and "I Will be Really Happy When...," respectively. His short story, Lunch, was a prizewinner in the Steve Grady short fiction competition in 1994.

He came to visit Maine in the USA for a month in 1989 - as a respite from the social chaos in the United Kingdom caused by over a decade of Conservative Government policies that promoted greed and self-interest over compassion and collective responsibility - he has been here ever since. He has spent most of his working life as a carpenter on construction sites; although he also worked for a couple of years as a mail carrier - as well as spending some time as a factory worker, a clothes salesman, a journalist, and one memorable night as a chicken catcher.

Made in the USA
Middletown, DE
19 August 2020